ELIZABETH'S CAMPAIGN
BY
Mrs. Humphry Ward

ELIZABETH'S CAMPAIGN

Published by Silver Scroll Publishing

New York City, NY

First published circa 1920

Copyright © Silver Scroll Publishing, 2015

All rights reserved

ABOUT SILVER SCROLL PUBLISHING

Silver Scroll Publishing is a digital publisher that brings the best historical fiction ever written to modern readers. Our comprehensive catalogue contains everything from historical novels about Rome to works about World War I.

FRONTISPIECE IN COLOR BY: C. ALLAN GILBERT

TO THE DEAR AND GALLANT
MEMORY
OF
T. S. A.
PASSCHENDAELE, OCTOBER 11, 1917

FOREWORD

This book was finished in April 1918, and represents the mood of a supremely critical moment in the war.

M. A. W.

CHAPTERS: , , , , , , , , , , , , , , , , ,

CHAPTER I

'Remember, Slater, if I am detained, that I am expecting the two gentlemen from the War Agricultural Committee at six, and Captain Mills of the Red Cross is coming to dine and sleep. Ask Lady Chicksands to look after him in case I am late—and put those Tribunal papers in order for me, by the way. I really must go properly into that Quaker man's case—horrid nuisance! I hope to be back in a couple of hours, but I can't be sure. Hullo, Beryl! I thought you were out.'

The speaker, Sir Henry Chicksands, already mounted on his cob outside his own front door, turned from his secretary, to whom he had been giving these directions, to see his only daughter hurrying through the inner hall with the evident intention of catching her father before he rode off.

She ran down the steps, but instead of speaking at once she began to stroke and pat his horse's neck, as though doubtful how to put what she had to say.

'Well, Beryl, what's the matter?' said her father impatiently. The girl, who was slender and delicate in build, raised her face to his.

'Are you—are you really going to Mannering, father?'

'I am—worse luck!'

'You'll handle him gently, won't you?' There was anxiety in the girl's voice. 'But of course you will—I know you will.'

Chicksands shrugged his shoulders.

'I shall do my best. But you know as well as I do that he's a queer customer when it comes to anything connected with the war.'

The girl looked behind her to make sure that the old butler of the house had retired discreetly out of earshot.

'But he can't quarrel with you, father!'

'I hope not—for your sake.'

'Must you really tackle him?'

'Well, I thought I was the person to do it. It's quite certain nobody else could make anything of it.'

Privately Beryl disagreed, but she made no comment.

'Aubrey seems to be pretty worried,' she said, in a depressed tone, as she turned away.

'I don't wonder. He should have brought up his father better. Well, good-bye, dear. Don't bother too much.'

She waved her hand to him as he made off, and stood watching him from the steps—a gentle, attaching figure, her fair hair and the pale oval of her face standing out against the panelled hall behind her.

Her father went his way down a long winding hill beyond his own grounds, along a country road lined with magnificent oaks, through a village where his practised eye noted several bad cottages with disapproval, till presently he slackened his horse's pace, as he passed an ill-looking farm about half a mile beyond the village.

'Not a decent gate in the whole place!' he said to himself with disgust. 'And the farm buildings only fit for a bonfire. High time indeed that we made Mannering sit up!'

He paused also to look over the neighbouring hedge at some fields literally choked with weeds.

'And as for Gregson—lazy, drunken fellow! Why didn't he set some village women on? Just see what they've done on my place! Hullo, here he is! Now I'm in for it!' For he saw a slouching man coming rapidly towards him from the farmyard, with the evident intention of waylaying him. The man's shabby, untidy dress and blotched complexion did not escape Sir Henry's quick eye. 'Seems to have been making a night of it,' was his inward comment.

'Good-day, Sir Henry,' said the farmer, laying a hand on Chicksands' bridle, 'I wanted a word with you, sir. I give you fair warning, you and your Committee, you'll not turn me out without a fight! I was never given no proper notice—and there are plenty as 'll stand by me.'

The voice was thick and angry, and the hand shook. Sir Henry drew his horse away, and the man's hold dropped.

'Of course you had every notice,' said Sir Henry drily.

'I hadn't,' the man persisted. 'If the letters as they talk of were sent, I never saw 'em. And when the Committee came I was out—on business. Can't a man be out on his lawful business, Sir Henry, instead of dancin' attendance on men as know no better than he? The way this Government is doing things—you might as well live under the Czar of Russia as in this country. It's no country this for free men now, Sir Henry.'

'The Czar of Russia has come to grief, my man, for the same reason that you have,' said Sir Henry, gathering up the reins, 'for shirking his duty. All very well before the war, but now we can't afford this kind of thing.'

'And so you've told the Squire to turn me out?' said the man fiercely, his hands on his sides.

'You've had no notice from Mr. Mannering yet?'

'Not a word.'

'But you've heard from the Inspection Committee?'

The man nodded.

'But it's not they as can turn me out, if the Squire don't agree.'

There was a note of surly defiance in his voice.

'I don't know about that,' said Sir Henry, whose horse was getting restive. 'My advice to you, Gregson, is to take it quietly, pull yourself together, and get some other work. There's plenty going nowadays.'

'Thank you for nothing, Sir Henry. I've got plenty to advise me—people as I set more store by. I've got a wife and children, sir, and I shan't give in without a fuss—you may be sure of that. Good-day to you.'

Sir Henry nodded to him and rode off.

'He'll go, of course,' reflected the rider. 'Our powers are quite enough. But if I can't get Mannering to send the notice, it'll be a deal more trouble. Hullo, here's some one else! This is another pair of boots!'

He had scarcely turned the corner beyond the farm when another man came running down the sloping field, calling to him. Sir Henry pulled up his horse again. But his aspect had changed, and his voice took another note.

'Did you want to speak to me, Adam? A nice day, isn't it?'

'I saw you, Sir Henry, from the top of the field, talking to Gregson in the road, and I thought perhaps you'd let me have a few words with you. You know, sir, this is awfully hard lines.'

Sir Henry looked impatient, but the man who had spoken to him was a fine specimen of young manhood—broad-shouldered, clear-eyed, with a natural dignity of manner, not at all a person to be brushed aside.

'I'm sure you can't defend Gregson, Adam,' said Sir Henry, 'you—one of the best farmers in the district! I wish they had put you on the Inspection Committee.'

'Well, they didn't,' said the other, perhaps with a slight emphasis. 'And there's many of us feel, I can assure you, as I do. Gregson's a poor creature, but he hasn't had quite fair play, Sir Henry— that's what we feel. And he's been fifteen years on his place.' The man spoke hesitatingly, but strongly. There was a queer, suppressed hostility in his pleasant blue eyes.

'Fifteen years too long,' interrupted Sir Henry. 'I tell you, Adam, we can't afford now to let men like Gregson spoil good land while the country's likely to go hungry! The old happy-go-lucky days are done with. I wonder whether even you recognize that we're fighting for our lives?'

'I know we are, Sir Henry. But if the war makes slaves of us what good will it do if we do win it?'

Sir Henry laughed. 'Well, Adam, you were always a Radical and I was always a Conservative. And I don't like being managed any more than you do. But look at the way I'm managed in my business!—harried up and down by a parcel of young fellows from the Ministry that often seem to me fools! But we've all got to come in. And this country's worth it!'

'You know I'm with you there, sir. But why don't you get at the Squire himself? What good have he or his agent ever been to anybody? You're a landlord worth living under; but—'

'Ah! don't be in too great a hurry, Adam, and you'll see what you will see!' And with a pleasant salute, his handsome face twitching between frowns and smiles, Sir Henry rode on. 'What trade unionists we all are—high and low! That man's as good a farmer as Gregson's a vile one. But he stands by his like, as I stand by mine.'

Then his thoughts took a different turn. He was entering a park, evidently of wide extent, and finely wooded. The road through it had long fallen out of repair, and was largely grass-grown. A few sheep were pasturing on it, and a few estate cottages showed here and there. Sir Henry looked about him with quick eyes. He understood that the Inspection Sub-Committee, constituted under the Corn Production Act, and on the look-out for grass-land to put under the plough, had recommended the ploughing up of all this further end of Mannering Park. It carried very few sheep under its present management; and the herd of Jersey cattle that used to graze it had long since died out. As for the game, it had almost gone—before the war. No use, either for business or play!

Then—on this early autumn day of 1917—Sir Henry fell to musing on the vast changes coming over England in consequence of the war. 'Who would ever have believed that we—we should put ourselves to school as we have done? Military service, rations, food-prices, all our businesses "controlled," and now our land looked after! How much of it has come to stay? Well, it won't affect me much! Ah! is that the Rector?'

For a hundred yards ahead of him he perceived a clerical figure, spare and tall, in a wideawake hat, swinging towards him. The September sun was westering, and behind the approaching man lay broad stretches of wood, just showing here and there the first bronze and purple signs of autumn.

The Rector, recognizing the solitary rider, waved his hand in welcome, and Sir Henry pulled up. The two men, who were evidently personal friends, exchanged greetings.

'You're going to the Hall, Sir Henry?' said the Rector.

Sir Henry described his business.

The Rector shook his head reflectively.

'You haven't announced yourself, I hope?'

'No, I took that simple precaution. I suppose he's already pretty savage?'

'With whom? The Committee? Yes, you won't find him easy to deal with. But just at present there's a distraction. His new secretary arrived some weeks ago, and he now spends his whole time, from morning till night, dictating to her and showing her his things.'

'Secretary? A woman? Good heavens! Who is she?'

'A great swell, I understand. Oxford First Class in Mods, Second in Greats. I've only just seen her. A striking-looking person.'

'Why isn't she in France, or doing munition work?' growled Sir Henry.

'I don't know. I suppose she has her reasons. She seems patriotic enough. But I've only exchanged a few words with her, at a very hurried luncheon, at which, by the way, there was a great deal too much to eat. She and Pamela disappeared directly afterwards.'

'Oh, so Pamela's at home? What's the name of the new woman? I suppose she's to chaperon Pamela?'

'I shouldn't wonder. Her name is Miss Bremerton.'

'Beryl declares that Pamela is going to be a beauty—and clever besides. She used to be a jolly child. But then they go to school and grow up quite different. I've hardly seen her for a year and a half.'

'Well, you'll judge for yourself. Good luck to you! I don't envy you your job.'

'Good Lord, no! But you see I'm Chairman of this blessed show, and they all fixed on me to bell the cat. We want a hundred acres of the Park, a new agent, notices for three farmers, etcetera!'

The Rector whistled. 'I shall wait, on tiptoe, to see what happens! What are your powers?'

'Oh, tremendous!'

'So you have him? Well, good-day.'

And the Rector was passing on. But Sir Henry stooped over his horse's neck—'As you know, perhaps, it would be very inconvenient to my poor little Beryl if Mannering were to make a quarrel of it with me.'

'Ah, I gathered that she and Aubrey were engaged,' said the Rector cordially. 'Best congratulations! Has the Squire behaved well?'

'Moderately. He declares he has no money to give them.'

'And yet he spent eighteen hundred pounds last week at that Christie sale!' said the Rector with a laugh. 'And now I suppose the new secretary will add fuel to the flame. I saw Pamela for a minute alone, and she said Miss Bremerton was "just as much gone on Greek things as father," and they were like a pair of lunatics when the new vases came down.'

'Oh, blow the secretary!' said Sir Henry with exasperation. 'And meanwhile his daughters can't get a penny out of him for any war purpose whatever! Well, I must go on.'

They parted, and Sir Henry put his cob into a sharp trot which soon brought him in sight of a distant building—low and irregular—surrounded by trees, and by the wide undulating slopes of the park.

'Dreadfully ugly place,' he said to himself, as the house grew plainer; 'rebuilt at the worst time, by a man with no more taste than a broomstick. Still, he was the sixteenth owner, from father to son. That's something.'

And he fell to thinking, with that half-ironic depreciation which he allowed to himself, and would have stood from no one else, of his own brand-new Georgian house, built from the plans of a famous American architect, ten years before the war, out of the profits of an abnormally successful year, and furnished in what he believed to be faultless taste by the best professional decorator he could find.

'Yet compared to a Mannering, what do I mean to the people here? You scarcely begin to take root in this blessed country under half a century. Mannering is exceedingly unpopular; the people think him a selfish idler; but if he chose he could whistle them back with a hundredth part of the trouble it would take me! And if Aubrey wanted to go into Parliament, he'd probably have his pick of the county divisions. Curious fellow, Aubrey! I wonder exactly what Beryl sees in him?'

His daughter's prospects were not indeed very clear to a mind that liked everything cut and dried. Aubrey Mannering was the Squire's eldest son; but the Squire was not rich, and had been for years past wasting his money on Greek antiquities, which seemed to his neighbours, including Sir Henry Chicksands, a very dubious investment. If Aubrey should want to sell, who was going to buy such things at high prices after the war? No doubt prices at Christie's—for good stuff—had been keeping up very well. That was because of war profits. People were throwing money about now. But when the war industries came to an end? and the national bills had to be paid?

'The only thing that can't go down is land,' thought Sir Henry, with the cheerful consciousness of a man who had steadily year by year increased what had originally been a very modest property to something like a large estate.

Mannering had plenty of that commodity. But how far had he dipped the estate? It must be heavily mortgaged. By decent management anybody, no doubt, might still bring it round. 'But Aubrey's not the man. And since he joined up at the beginning of the war the Squire won't let him have a voice in anything. And now Desmond—by George, the twins are nineteen this month!—Desmond'll be off directly. And then his father will be madder than ever.'

By this time the ugly house was near at hand, and the thick woods which surrounded it had closed about the horse and rider.

'Splendid timber,' thought Sir Henry, as he rode through it, measuring it with a commercial eye, 'but all past its prime, and abominably neglected.... Hullo! that looks like Pamela, and the new woman—the secretary!'

For two ladies were coming down the drive towards him, with a big white and tan collie jumping round them. One of them, very tall and erect, was dressed in a dark coat and skirt, reasonably short, a small black toque, and brown boots and leggings. The close-fitting coat showed a shapely but quite substantial figure. She carried a stick, and walked with a peculiarly rapid and certain step. The young girl beside her seemed by comparison a child. She wore a white dress, in keeping with the warm September day, and with it a dark blue sports coat, and a shady hat. Her dress only just passed her knees, and beneath it the slender legs and high heels drew Sir Henry's disapproving eye. He hated extravagance in anything. Beryl managed to look fashionable, without looking outré, as Pamela did. But he reined up to greet her with ready smiles.

'Well, Pamela, jolly to see you at home again! My word, you've grown! Shall I find your father in?'

'Yes, we left him in the library. May I introduce Miss Bremerton—Sir Henry Chicksands.' The girl spoke with hurried shyness, the quick colour in her cheeks. The lady beside her bowed, and Sir Henry took off his hat. Each surveyed the other. 'A strong-minded female!' thought Sir Henry, who was by no means advanced in his views of the other sex.

'The strong-minded female,' however, was not, it seemed, of the talkative kind. She remained quite silent while Pamela and Sir Henry exchanged some family gossip, with her ungloved hand caressing the nose of the collie, who was pressing against her with intrusive friendliness. But her easy self-possession as contrasted with Pamela's nervousness was all the time making an impression on Sir Henry, as was also the fact of her general good looks. Not a beauty—not at all; but, as the Rector had said, 'striking.'

As for Pamela, what was the matter with the child? Until Beryl's name was mentioned, there was not a smile to be got out of her. And it was a very fleeting one when it came. Desmond's name fared a little better. At that the girl did at last raise her beautiful eyes, which till then she had hardly allowed to be seen, and there was a ray in them.

'He's here on leave,' she said; 'a few days. He's just got his Commission and been accepted for the artillery. He goes into camp next week. He thinks he'll be out by January.'

'We must certainly manage to see him before he goes,' said Sir Henry heartily. Then turning to Miss Bremerton with the slightly over-emphatic civility of a man who prides himself on his manners in all contingencies, he asked her if she was already acquainted with the Mannering neighbourhood.

Miss Bremerton replied that it was quite unknown to her. 'You'll admire our trees,' said Sir Henry. 'They're very fine.'

'Are they?' said the lady rather absently, giving a perfunctory glance to the woods sloping away on her right towards a little stream winding in the hollow. Sir Henry felt a slight annoyance. He was a good fellow, and no more touchy as to personal dignity than the majority of men of his age and class. But he was accustomed to be treated with a certain deference, and in Miss Bremerton's manner there was none whatever.

'Well, good-bye, Pamela. I mustn't miss your father. When are you coming over to see Beryl?'

'How am I to get there?' said the girl with a sudden laugh.

'Oh, I see, you've got no petrol allowance?'

'How should we? Nobody's doing any war work here.'

There was an odd note in the speaker's voice.

'Why don't you join Beryl in her canteen work?' said Sir Henry abruptly.

'I don't know.'

'She wants help badly. She passes your gate on her way to Fallerton. She could pick you up, and bring you back.'

'Yes,' said Pamela. There was a pause.

'Well, good-bye, dear,' said Sir Henry again, and with a ceremonious bow to Pamela's companion, he rode on—meditating on many things.

'The Squire's in, Sir Henry, but—well, he's very busy.'

'Never mind, Forest. I must see him. Can you find some one to take my horse round?'

The grey-haired butler looked perplexed.

'I've only got my own small boy, Sir Henry. There's two more of our men gone this morning. I don't know if you'll trust him. He's a good boy.'

'Send him along, Forest. My beast's a lamb—you know him. But look here, Forest'—Sir Henry dismounted, bridle in hand. 'Don't give the Squire notice that I'm here, if you can help it, till you announce me.'

The butler, who, in spite of his grey hair, was a square-set, vigorous-looking fellow, might be said, in reply, to have given the Squire's visitor a wink. At any rate a look of understanding passed between the two. The butler went quickly back into the house, and re-emerged with a boy, who was the small image of his father, to whom Sir Henry cheerfully gave up his cob. But as Forest led the way through the outer hall he stopped to say:

'The Squire's not alone, sir. There was a gentleman arrived just as Miss Pamela went out. But I don't think he'll stay long.'

'Who is he?'

'Can't say, sir. He's lodging in the village, and comes to see the Squire's collections sometimes.'

They were now in a long passage running along the eastern front of the house to a large room which had been added to its southern end, in order to hold the Squire's library and collections. Midway the butler turned.

'You've heard, Sir Henry, about Mr. Desmond?'

'Yes, Miss Pamela told me.'

'Mr. Desmond says he'll be in France by January. He's as pleased as possible, but it's a deal sooner than Mr. Mannering hoped.'

'Well, we've all got to take our chance in this war,' said Sir Henry gravely. 'And the artillery is a bit safer than the infantry. You know my son Arthur's a gunner.'

'I hope he's all right, sir?'

'Well, he's still on light work. He comes home this week for a bit. He was gassed at Ypres a year and a half ago, and had a bullet taken out of his chest about two months since. But he is nearly fit again.'

The butler expressed his sympathy with a complete absence of shyness or servility, then threw open a door at the end of the passage, announcing, 'Sir Henry Chicksands, sir.'

'D-mn!' said a voice loudly within.

Sir Henry gave an involuntary start. Another look passed between him and Forest, amused or interrogative on the visitor's part, non-committal on the butler's.

The library of Mannering Hall as Sir Henry Chicksands entered it presented a curious spectacle. It was a long, barn-like room, partly lined with books, and partly with glass cases, in which Greek vases, Tanagra figures, and other Greek and Etruscan antiquities, all carefully marked and labelled, were displayed. A few large tables stood at intervals on the shabby carpet, also laden with books and specimens. They conveyed an impression of dust and disorder, as though no housemaid had been allowed to touch them for weeks—with one exception. A table, smaller than the rest, but arranged with scrupulous neatness, stood at one side of the room, with a typewriter upon it, certain books, and a rack for stationery. A folded duster lay at one corner. Pens, pencils, a box of clips, and a gum-pot stood where a careful hand had placed them. And at a corner corresponding to the duster was a small vase of flowers—autumnal roses—the only flowers in the room.

But the various untidy accumulations, most of which seemed to be of old standing, had been evidently just added to by some recent arrivals. Four large packing-cases, newly opened, took up much of what free space was left on the floor. The straw, paper, and cottonwool, in which their contents had been packed, had been tossed out with a careless or impatient hand, and littered the carpet. Among the litter stood here and there some Greek vases of different sizes; in particular, a superb pair, covered with figures; beside which stood the owner of Mannering, talking to an apparently young man with an eye-glass, who was sitting on the floor closely examining the vases. The Squire turned a furrowed brow towards his approaching visitor, and putting down a small bronze he had been holding raised a warning hand.

'How do you do, Chicksands? Very sorry, but I'm much too filthy to touch. And I'm horribly busy! These things arrived last night, and Mr. Levasseur has kindly come over to help me unpack them. Don't know if you've met him. Mr. Levasseur—Sir Henry Chicksands.'

The man on the floor looked up carelessly, just acknowledging Sir Henry's slight inclination. Sir Henry's inner mind decided against him—at once—instinctively. What was a stout fellow, who at any rate looked as though he were still of military age, doing with nonsense of this sort, at four o'clock in the day, when England wanted every able-bodied man she possessed, either to fight for her or to work for her? At the same time the reflection passed rapidly through his mind that neither the man nor the name had come up—so far as he could remember—before the County Tribunal of which he was Chairman.

'Well, Chicksands, what do you want with me?' said the Squire abruptly. 'Will you take a chair?' And he pointed to one from which he hastily removed a coat.

'I have some confidential business to talk to you about,' said Sir Henry, with a look at the dusty gentleman among the straw.

'Something you want me to do that I'll be bound I shan't want to do! Is that it?' said Mannering with vivacity.

He stood with his hands on a table behind him, his long spare frame in a nervous fidget, his eyes bright and hostile, and a spot of red on either thin cheek. Beside Chicksands, who was of middle height, solidly built, and moderately stout, with mental and physical competence written all over him, the Squire of Mannering seemed but the snippet of a man. He was singularly thin, with a slender neck, and a small head covered with thick hair, prematurely white, which tumbled over his forehead and eyes. He had the complexion of a girl, disproportionately large nose, very sharply and delicately cut as to bridge and nostril, and a mouth and chin which seemed to be in perpetual movement. He looked older than Sir Henry, who was verging on sixty, but he was in fact just over fifty.

Sir Henry smiled a little at the tone of the Squire's question, but he answered good-humouredly.

'I believe, when we've talked it over, you won't think it unreasonable. But I've come to explain.'

'I know, you want me to give Gregson notice. But I warn you I'm not the least inclined to do anything of the kind.' And the speaker crossed his arms, which were very long and thin, over a narrow chest, while his eyes restlessly countered those of Sir Henry.

Chicksands paused a moment before replying.

'I have a good many papers here to show you,' he said at last, mildly, drawing a large envelope half-way from the inner pocket of his coat to illustrate his words, and then putting it back again. 'But I really can't discuss them except with yourself.'

The Squire's eyes shot battle.

'It's the war, of course,' he said with emphasis; 'it's all the war. I'm told to do things I don't want to do, which affect my personal freedom, and other people's, because of a war I don't believe in, never asked for, and don't approve of. Here's Levasseur now, a clever fellow, cleverer than either you or me, Chicksands, and he's no more patriotic than I am. You talk to him!'

'Thank you, I'm too busy,' said Sir Henry sharply, his face stiffening. 'Where can you see me, Mannering? I'm rather pressed for time. Is the smoking-room free?' And with a marked avoidance of any concern with the gentleman on the floor, who had by now risen to his feet, Sir Henry made an impatient movement towards a door at the further end of the library which stood ajar.

Levasseur looked amused. He was a strongly-built, smooth-shaven fellow, with rather long hair, and the sallow look of the cigarette-smoker. His eyes were sleepy, his expression indolent or good-natured.

'Oh, I'll make myself scarce with the greatest pleasure,' he said civilly. 'I can stroll about the park till you're ready for me again,' he added, turning to the Squire. 'Lovely day—I'll take a book and some cigarettes.' And diving into an open box which stood near he filled his cigarette-case from it, and then looked round him for a book. 'Where's that copy of the Anthology? That'll do nicely.'

The Squire burst into a laugh, observing Sir Henry.

'He's over military age, Chicksands.'

'I suppose so,' said Sir Henry stiffly.

'But only by six months, when the Act passed. So he's just escaped you.'

'I've really no concern whatever with Mr. Levasseur's affairs.' Sir Henry had flushed angrily. 'Is it to be here, or the smoking-room?'

'Ta-ta! See you again presently,' said Levasseur. 'Ah, there's the book!' And diving to the floor for a hat and a book lying beside it, he made off, lighting a cigarette, with a laughing backward glance towards the Squire and his companion.

'Well, now, what is it?' said Mannering, throwing himself with an air of resignation into a low arm-chair, and taking out a pipe. 'Won't you smoke, Chicksands?'

'Thank you, I've had my morning's allowance. Hullo! Who did that? What an awfully fine thing!'

For suddenly, behind the Squire's head, Chicksands had become aware of an easel, and on it a charcoal sketch, life-size, of a boy, who seemed about eighteen or nineteen, in cricketing dress.

The Squire looked round.

'What, that sketch of Desmond? Haven't you seen it? Yes, it's jolly good. I got Orpen to do it in July.'

Now that Sir Henry had once perceived the drawing it seemed to him to light up the whole place. The dress was the dress of the Eton Eleven; there was just a suggestion of pale blue in the sash round the waist. But the whole impression was Greek in its manly freedom and beauty; above all in its sacrifice of all useless detail to one broad and simple effect. Youth, eager, strong, self-confident, with its innocent parted lips, and its steadfast eyes looking out over the future— the drawing stood there as the quintessence, the embodiment, of a whole generation. So might the young Odysseus have looked when he left his mother on his first journey to hunt the boar with his kinsfolk on Mount Parnassus. And with such an air had hundreds of thousands of English boys gone out on a deadlier venture since the great war began, with a like intensity of will, a like merry scorn of fate.

Sir Henry was conscious of a lump in his throat. He had lost his youngest son in the retreat from Mons, and two nephews on the Somme.

'It's wonderful,' he said, not very clearly. 'I envy you such a possession.'

The Squire made no reply. He sat with his long body hunched up in the deep chair, a pair of brooding eyes fixed on his visitor.

'Well, what is it?' he said again, in a voice that was barely civil.

CHAPTER II

Sir Henry had been talking some time. The Squire had not interrupted him much, but the papers which Sir Henry had presented to him from time to time—Government communications, Committee reports, and the like—were mostly lying on the floor, where, after a perfunctory glance at them, he had very quickly dropped them.

'Well, that's our case,' said Sir Henry at last, thrusting his hands into his pockets and leaning back in his chair, 'and I assure you we've taken a great deal of trouble about it. We shouldn't ask you or anybody else to do these things if it wasn't vitally necessary for the food-supply of the country. But we're going to have a narrow squeak for it next spring and summer, and we must get more food out of the land.'

Whereupon, in a manner rather provokingly reminiscent of a public meeting, Sir Henry fell into a discourse on submarines, tonnage, the food needs of our Allies, and the absolute necessity for undoing and repairing the havoc of Cobdenism—matters of which the newspapers of the day were commonly full. That the sound of his own voice was agreeable to him might have been suspected.

Mr. Mannering roughly broke in upon him.

'What was that you said about ploughing up the park?'

'We ask you to break up fifty acres of it near the Fallerton end, and perhaps some other bits elsewhere. This first bit is so far from the house you'll never notice it; and the land ought to do very well if it's properly broken and trampled down.'

The Squire sat up and began to tick things off on the fingers of his left hand.

'Let me understand. You want me to give three of my farmers notice to quit—Gregson first of all—for bad farming; you ask me to plough up fifty acres of my park; and you have the goodness to suggest that I should cut some of my woods.'

Sir Henry realized that possibly a strain on his temper was coming, but he felt sure he could stand it.

'That is what we suggest—for your own advantage and the country's.'

'And pray who are "we"? I don't yet understand that clearly.'

'"We,"' said Sir Henry patiently, 'are the County War Agricultural Committee, formed for the express purpose of getting more food out of the land, and so making these islands self-supporting.'

'And if I refuse, what can you do?'

'Well, I'm afraid,' said Sir Henry, smiling uncomfortably, 'we can act without you.'

'You can turn out my farmers, and plough my land, as you please?'

'Our powers are very wide.'

'Under—what do you call the beastly thing?—"Dora"—the Defence of the Realm Act?'

Sir Henry nodded.

The Squire rose and began to pace up and down, his hands under his coat-tails, his long spider legs and small feet picking their way in and out of the piles and boxes on the floor. At last he turned impetuously.

'Look here, Chicksands, I shall not give that man warning!'

Sir Henry surveyed the lanky figure standing opposite to him.

'I should be very sorry, Mannering, to see you take that course,' he said, smiling and amiable as before. 'In some ways, of course, I am no more in love with some of the Government's proceedings than you are. We landlords may have to defend ourselves. I want, if I may say so, to keep your influence intact for the things that really matter. You and I, and all the other Brookshire landlords, may have, at some point, to act together. But we shall resist unreasonable demands much more easily if we accept the reasonable ones.'

The Squire shook his head. The suave tone of the speaker had clearly begun to rasp his nerves.

'No! You and I have really nothing in common. You may take it from me that I shall not give these men notice. What happens then?'

'The Government steps in,' said Sir Henry quietly.

'And turns them out? Very well, let them. And the park?'

'We are, of course, most anxious to consult you.'

'Excuse me, that's nonsense! I refuse—that's flat.'

Sir Henry shrugged his shoulders. His tone became a trifle colder.

'I can't believe that you will refuse. You can't deny—no sensible man could—that we've simply got to grow more food at home. The submarines have settled that for us.'

'Who brought the submarines upon us? The politicians! No politicians, no war! If it hadn't been for a pack of idiots called diplomats making mischief abroad, and a pack of incompetents called politicians unable to keep their heads at home, there'd have been no war. It's Russia's war—France's war! Who asked the country whether it wanted a war? Who asked me?' The Squire, standing opposite to Sir Henry, tapped his chest vehemently.

'The country is behind the war,' said Chicksands firmly.

'How do we know? How do you know? I've as much right to an opinion as you, and I tell you the country is sick and tired of the war. We are all dying of the war! We shall all be paupers because of the war! What is France to me, or Belgium? We shall have lost men, money, security—half the things that make life worth living—for what?'

'Honour!' said Sir Henry sharply, as he got on his feet.

'Honour!' sneered Mannering—'what's honour? It means one thing to me and another to you. Aubrey bangs me over the head with it. But I'm like the Doctor in the Punch and Judy show—he thinks he's knocked me flat. He hasn't. I've a new argument every time he comes. And as for my daughters, they think me a lunatic—a stingy lunatic besides—because I won't give to their Red Cross shows and bazaars. I've nothing to give. The income tax gentlemen have taken care of that.'

'Yet you spend on this kind of thing!' Sir Henry pointed to the vases. He had grown a little white.

'Of course I can. That's permanent. That's something to mend the holes that the soldiers and the politicians are making. When the war's become a nightmare that nobody wants to remember, those little things'—he pointed to a group of Greek bronzes and terra-cottas on a table near—'will still be the treasures of the world!'

In the yeasty deep of Sir Henry's honest mind emotions were rising which he knew now he should not long be able to control. He took up his hat and stick.

'I'm sorry, Mannering, that I have not been able to convince you. I'm sorry for your point of view—and I'm sorry for your sons.'

The words slipped out of his mouth before he knew.

The Squire bounded.

'My sons! The one's a fire-eater, with whom you can't argue. The other's a child—a babe—whom the Government proposes to murder before he has begun to live.'

Sir Henry looked at the speaker, who had been violently flushed a minute earlier, and was now as pale as himself, and then at the sketch of Desmond, just behind the Squire. His eyes dropped; the hurry in his blood subsided.

'Well, good-bye, Mannering. I'll—I'll do what I can to make things easy for you.'

The Squire laughed angrily.

'You'll put on the screws politely? Thank you? But still it will be you who'll be putting the screw on, who'll be turning out my farmers, and ploughing up my land, and cutting down my trees. Doesn't it strike you that—well, that—under the circumstances—it will be rather difficult for Aubrey and Beryl to keep up their engagement?'

The Squire was sitting on the edge of the table, his thin legs crossed, his thumbs in his waistcoat pockets. Sir Henry coloured hotly.

'You gave your consent to their engagement, Mannering.'

'Yes, but I propose to withdraw it,' said the Squire coolly.

Sir Henry's indignation kept him cool also.

'You can't play ducks and drakes with young people's lives like that. Even you can't do that.'

'I can. I can withdraw my consent.'

'Because you mean to fight the County War Committee, of which I am Chairman?'

'Precisely. The situation is too difficult,' said the Squire with sparkling eyes. 'The young people will no doubt see it for themselves.'

'Pshaw! Nonsense!' cried Sir Henry, finally losing his temper. 'Aubrey is long since of age and his own master.'

'Perhaps, but he is an extravagant fellow, who likes money and spends it. And if he is his own master, I am the master of the estate; there is no entail.'

Chicksands laughed aloud.

'So because I come on a mission to try and save you friction and trouble, you are going to avenge yourself on your son and my daughter?'

'I merely point out the properties,' said the Squire provokingly, his legs dangling.

There was a pause. Sir Henry broke it with dignity, as he turned away.

'I think we had better break off this discussion. I cannot—I do not—believe you will carry out what you say. But if you do, I shall stand by the young people.'

'No doubt!' said the Squire, who seemed to bristle from head to foot. 'Well, good-bye, Sir Henry. Sorry your visit has not been more agreeable. Forest will look after you.' And ringing the bell vehemently as he passed the fireplace, the Squire walked rapidly to the door and threw it open.

Chicksands passed through it, speechless with indignation and, if the truth were told, bewilderment.

The Squire shut the door upon his adversary, and then, with his hands on his sides, exploded in a fit of laughter.

'I always knew I must be rude to the old boy some time,' he said, with the glee of a mischievous child. 'But, ye gods, how his feathers drooped! He looked like a plucked cockatoo as he went out.'

He stood thinking a moment, and then with a look of sudden determination he went to his writing-table and sat down to it. Drawing a writing-pad towards him, he wrote as follows:

'MY DEAR AUBREY—Your future father-in-law has just been insulting and harrying me in ways which no civilized State had ever heard of before the war. He is the Chairman of a ridiculous body that calls itself the County War Agricultural Committee, that lays absurd eggs in the shape of sub-Committees to vex landlords. They have been going about among my farmers and want me to turn out three of them. I decline, so I suppose they'll do it for me. And they're going to plough up a lot of the park—without my leave. And Chicksands is the head and front of the whole business. He came here to-day to try and coax me into submission. But I would neither be coaxed nor bullied. I've broken with him; and if my children stand by me properly, they'll break with him too. I really don't see how you're going to marry Beryl after this. At least, I shall certainly not help you to do it, and if you defy me you must take the consequences. The whole world's gone mad. My only consolation is that I have just got some new Greek things, and that Levasseur's helping me unpack them. However, it's no good talking to you about them. You wasted all your time at Cambridge, and I doubt whether you could construe a bit of Euripides to save your life.

'Of course if you want to talk this over, you had better run down. I have got a new secretary— came here six weeks ago—a topping young woman—who reads Greek like a bird. But her quantities are not always what they should be. Good-bye.—Your affectionate father,

'EDMUND MANNERING.'

Having finished the epistle he read it over with a complacent countenance, put it up and stamped it. Then he looked at his watch.

'What a long time that young woman's been away! I told her to take two hours off, but of course I didn't mean it. That was just my excessive politeness. D-mn my politeness. It's always getting in my way. I forget that women are naturally lazy. I daresay she was a bit fagged. But if she's interested in her work, what does that matter? I wonder whether she's looked out all these references?'

And walking over to the one neat table In the room he surveyed it. There were some sheets lying on it mostly covered with an excellent Greek script, which he turned over. Suddenly he swooped on one of them.

'Hullo! That line's wrong. Won't scan. Trusted to her memory, I suppose. Didn't look it up. And yesterday I caught her out in her accents. Women play the devil with accents. But she writes a pretty Greek. Eh? What?' For he had become aware of the re-entry of Levasseur, who was standing at his elbow.

"Fraid I can't stay now,' said that person. 'I've promised to pick up some wounded at the station to-night.'

'You—wounded!—what do you mean?' said the Squire, turning upon him.

Levasseur's large, thin-lipped mouth showed what seemed an habitual grin.

'I'd been getting so unpopular, it was becoming a nuisance. Line of least resistance, you understand. Now everybody's quite civil again. And I like chauffing.'

'A mere bit of weakness!' grumbled the Squire. 'Either you keep out of the war, or you go into it. You'd better go off to a camp now, and get trained—and shot—as quickly as possible—get done with it.'

'Oh no,' laughed the other. 'I'm all for middle courses. If they'll let me go on with my book, I don't mind driving a few poor fellows now and then!'

The Squire looked at him critically.

'The fact is you're too well fed, Levasseur, or you look it. That annoys people. Now I might gorge for a month, and shouldn't put on a pound.'

'I suppose your household is rationed?'

'Not it! We eat what we want. Just like the labourers. I found an old labourer eating his dinner under a hedge yesterday. Half a pound of bread at the very least, and he gets as much for his supper, and nearly as much for his breakfast. "I shall eat it, Squire, as long as I can get it. There's nowt else packs ye like bread." And quite right too. Good word "pack."'

'What'll he do when he can't get it?' laughed Levasseur, taking up his hat.

'Stuff! This food business is all one big blague. Anyway the Government got us into the war; they're jolly well bound to feed us through it. They will, for their own necks' sake. Well, good-night.'

Levasseur nodded in response, with the same silent, aimless grin, and disappeared through the garden door of the library.

'Queer fellow!' thought the Squire. 'But he's useful. I shall get him to help catalogue these things as he did the others. Ah, there you are!'

He turned with a reproachful air as the door opened.

The westerly sun was coming strongly into the library, and shone full on the face and figure of the Squire's new secretary as she stood in the door-way. He expected an apology for an absence just five minutes over the two hours; but she offered none.

'Pamela asked me to tell you, Mr. Mannering, that tea was ready under the verandah.'

'Afternoon tea is an abominable waste of time!' said the Squire discontentedly, facing her with a Greek pot under each arm.

'Do you think so? To me it's always the pleasantest meal in the day.'

The voice was musical and attractive, but its complete self-possession produced a vague irritation in the Squire. With his two former secretaries, a Cambridge man and a spectacled maiden with a London University degree, he had been accustomed to play the tyrant as must as he pleased. Something had told him from the very beginning that he would not be able to tyrannize over this newcomer.

But his quick masterful temper was already trying to devise ways of putting her down. He beckoned her towards the table where she had left her work, and she went obediently.

'You've got that line wrong.' He pointed to a quotation from the Odyssey. 'Read it, please!' She read it. He stopped her triumphantly.

'No, no, you can't make that long!' He pointed to one of the Greek words.

Her fair skin flushed.

'But indeed you can!' she said eagerly. 'Merry quotes three parallel passages. I have them in one of my notebooks.' And she began to search her table. Mannering stopped her ungraciously.

'Of course there's always some learned fool behind every bad reading. Anyway, what do you say to those accents?' He pointed severely to another line of her Greek. This time Miss Bremerton's countenance changed.

'Oh dear, what a blunder!' she said in distress, as she bent over her pages. 'I assure you I don't often do anything as bad as that.'

Mannering was secretly delighted. His manner became at once all politeness.

'Don't worry yourself, please. We all make mistakes.... You have a beautiful Greek handwriting.'

Miss Bremerton took the compliment calmly—did not indeed seem to hear it. She was already scratching out the offending words with a sharp penknife, and daintily rewriting them. Then she looked up.

'Pamela asked me to go back to her. And I was to say, will you come, or shall she send tea here?'

'Oh, I'll come, I'll come. I've got something to say to Pamela,' said the Squire, frowning. And he stalked in front of her along the library passage, his brilliant white hair gleaming in its shadows. It was well perhaps that he did not see the amusement which played round Elizabeth Bremerton's handsome mouth as she pursued him.

Tea was laid on a flagged walk under a glazed pergola running along part of the southern wall of the house. Here Pamela was sitting waiting, with a basket of knitting on her knee which she put out of sight as soon as she heard her father's step. She had taken off her hat, and her plentiful brown hair was drawn in a soft wave across her forehead, and thickly coiled behind a shapely head. She was very young, and very pretty. Perhaps the impression of youth predominated, youth uncertain of itself, conscious rather of its own richness and force than of any definite aims or desires. Her expression was extremely reserved. A veil seemed to lie over her deep, heavy-lidded eyes, and over features that had now delicacy and bloom, but promised much more—something far beyond any mere girlish prettiness. She was tall and finely made, and for the school tableaux in which she had frequently helped she had been generally cast for such parts as 'Nausicaa among her maidens,' 'Athene lighting the way for Odysseus and Telemachus,' 'Dante's Beatrice,' or any other personage requiring dignity, even a touch of majesty. Flowing skirts, indeed, at once made a queen of her. It was evident that she was not at her ease with her father; nor, as yet, with her father's new secretary.

The contrast between this lady and Pamela Mannering was obvious at once. If Pamela suggested romance, Elizabeth Bremerton suggested efficiency, cheerfulness, and the practical life. Her grandmother had been Dutch, and in Elizabeth the fair skin and yellow-gold hair (Rembrandt's 'Saskia' shows the type) of many Dutch forebears had reappeared. She was a trifle plump; her hair curled prettily round her temples; her firm dimpled chin and the fair complexion of her face and neck were set off, evidently with intention, by the plain blouse of black silky stuff, open at the neck, and showing a modest string of small but real pearls. The Squire, who had a wide knowledge of jewels, had noticed these pearls at once. It seemed to him—vaguely— that lady secretaries should not possess real pearls; or if they did possess them, should carefully keep them to themselves.

He accepted a cup of tea from his daughter, and drank it absently before he asked: 'Where's Desmond?'

'He went to lunch at Fallerton—at the camp. Captain Byles asked him. I think afterwards he was going to play in a match.'

The same thought passed through the minds of both father and daughter. 'This day week, Desmond will be gone.' In Pamela it brought back the dull pain of which she was now habitually conscious—the pain of expected parting. In her father it aroused an equally habitual antagonism—the temper, indeed, of ironic exasperation in which all his thinking and doing were at the moment steeped. He looked up suddenly.

'Pamela, I have got something disagreeable to say to you.'

His daughter turned a startled face.

'I have had a quarrel with Sir Henry Chicksands, and I do not wish you, or Desmond, or any of my children, to have any communication henceforth with him, or with any of his family!'

'Father, what do you mean?'

The girl's incredulous dismay only increased the Squire's irritation.

'I mean what I say. Of course your married sisters and Aubrey will do what they please, though I have warned Aubrey how I shall view it if he takes sides against me. But you and Desmond are under my control—you, at any rate. I forbid you to go to Chetworth, and your friendship with Beryl must be given up.'

'Father!' cried his daughter passionately, 'she is my best friend, and she is engaged to Aubrey.'

'If they are wise, they will break it off. Family quarrels are awkward things. And if Aubrey has any feeling for his father, he will be as angry as I am.'

'What has Sir Henry been doing, father?'

'Taking my own property out of my hands, my dear, giving notice to my farmers, and proposing to plough up my park, without my consent. That's all—just a trifle. But it's a trifle I shall fight!'

The Squire struck the arm of his chair with a long and bony hand.

'Why, it's only because they must!' said the girl half scornfully, her breath fluttering. 'Think what other people put up with, father. And what they do! And we do nothing!'

Every word was said with difficulty, torn out of her by the shock of her father's statement. The Squire stared at her threateningly a little, then quieted down. He did not want a wrangle with Pamela, to whom in general he was not unkind, while keeping a strict rule over her.

'Do nothing? What should we do? As if the war did not bleed us at every turn already. I warn you all I shan't be able to pay the income tax next year. Mannering will be sold up.' And thrusting his hands again into his pockets, he looked gloomily before him, over a piece of ill-kept garden, to the sloping park and blue interlacing hills that filled the distance.

Elizabeth Bremerton put down her teacup, glanced at the father and daughter, and went discreetly away, back to the library and her work.

Pamela hesitated a little, but at last moved nearer to him, and put a hand on his arm.

'Father! I dreadfully want you to let me do something!'

'Eh, what?' said Mannering, rousing himself. 'Don't try and coax me, child. It doesn't answer.'

'I don't want to coax you,' said the girl proudly withdrawing her hand. 'It's a very simple thing. Will you let me go and do day work at the new Hospital, just across the park? They want some help in the housework. There are fifty wounded men there.'

'Certainly not,' said Mannering firmly. 'You are too young. You have your education to think of. I told you I engaged Miss Bremerton to give you two hours' classics a day. When we've arranged these pots, she'll be free. You must also keep up your music. You have no time for housemaiding. And I don't approve of housemaiding for my daughter.'

'The nicest girls I know are doing anything—scrubbing, washing up, polishing bath-taps, making swabs, covering splints,' said Pamela in a low voice. 'There are two of the Joyce girls at this hospital, just my age. Of course they don't let you do any nursing—for months.'

'Lord Entwhistle may do what he likes with his girls. I propose to do what I think best with mine,' said Mannering as he rose.

Then the girl's passion broke out.

'It's horrible, father, that you won't do anything for the war, or let me do anything. Oh, I'm glad'—she clenched her hands as she stood opposite him, her beautiful head thrown back—'I'm thankful, that you can't stop Desmond!'

Mannering looked at her, frowned, turned abruptly, and went away whistling.

Pamela was left alone in the September evening. She betook herself to an old grass-grown walk between yew hedges at the bottom of the Dutch garden, and paced it in a tumult of revolt and pain. Not to go to Chetworth again! not to see Beryl, or any of them! How cruel! how monstrously unjust!

'I shan't obey!—why should I? Beryl and I must manage to see each other—of course we shall! Girls aren't the slaves they used to be. If a thing is unjust, we can fight it—we ought to fight it!— somehow. Poor, poor Beryl! Of course Aubrey will stick to her, whatever father does. He would be a cur if he didn't. Desmond and I would never speak to him again!... Beryl'll have Arthur to help her, directly. Oh, I wish I had a brother like Arthur!' Her face softened and quivered as she stood still a moment, sending her ardent look towards the sunset. 'I think I shall ask him to advise me.... I don't suppose he will.... How provoking he used to be! but awfully kind too. He'll think I ought to do what father tells me. How can I! It's wrong—it's abominable! Everybody despises us. And Desmond's dying to be off—to get away from it all—like Aubrey. He hates it so—he almost hates coming home! It's humiliating, and it's not our fault!'

Such cries and thoughts ran through her as she walked impetuously up and down, in rebellion against her father, unhappy for her girl friend, and smarting under the coercion put upon her patriotism and her conscience. For she had only two months before left a school where the influence of a remarkable head-mistress had been directed towards awakening in a group of elder girls, to which Pamela belonged, a vivid consciousness of the perils and sufferings of the war— of the sacredness of the cause for which England was fighting, of the glory of England, and the joy and privilege of English citizenship. In these young creatures the elder woman had kindled a flame of feeling which, when they parted from her and their school life—so she told them—was to take practical effect in work for their country, given with a proud and glad devotion.

But Pamela, leaving school at the end of July for the last time, after a surfeit of examinations, had been pronounced 'tired out' by an old aunt, a certain Lady Cassiobury, who came for long periodical visits to Mannering, and made a show of looking after her motherless niece. Accordingly she had been packed off to Scotland for August to stay with a school friend, one of a large family in a large country house in the Highlands. And there, roaming amid lochs and heather, with a band of young people, the majority of the men, of course, in the Army—young officers on short leave, or temporarily invalided, or boys of eighteen just starting their cadet training—she had spent a month full of emotions, not often expressed. For generally she was shy and rather speechless, though none the less liked by her companions for that. But many things sank deep with her; the beauty of mountain and stream; the character of some of the boys she walked and fished with—unnoticed sub-lieutenants, who had come home to get cured of one wound, and were going out again to the immediate chance of another, or worse; the tales of heroism and death of which the Scotch countryside was full. Her own mood was tuned thereby to an ever higher and more tragic key. Nobody indeed of the party was the least tragic. Everybody walked, fished, flirted, and laughed from morning till night. Yet every newspaper, every post, brought news of some death that affected one or other of the large group; and amid all the sheer physical joy of the long days in the open, bathed in sun and wind, there was a sense in all of them—or almost all of them—that no summer now is as the summers of the past, that behind and around the laughter and the picnicking there lay the Shadow that darkens the world.

One gorgeous evening of gold and purple she was sitting by a highland stream with a lad of twenty, throwing ducks and drakes into the water. She was not at all in love with him; but, immature as she was, she could not help seeing that he was a good deal in love with her. He had been in uproarious spirits all the afternoon, and then somehow he had contrived to find this moment alone with her.

'Well, it'll be good-bye to-morrow, or perhaps to-night,' he had said, as he flung yet another stone into the river, and she clapped her hands as she counted no less than six skips along the smooth water.

'And then no leave for a long time?'

'Well, I'd been ten months without any before.'

'Perhaps we'll meet here again—next year.'

'I don't expect it,' he said quietly.

Her startled eyes met his full.

'It'll be worse fighting this winter than last—it'll go on getting worse till the end. I don't look to coming back.'

His tone was so cheerful and matter-of-fact that it confused her.

'Oh, Basil, don't talk like that!' was all she could find to say.

'Why not? Of course it's better not to talk about it. Nobody does. But just this afternoon—when it's been so jolly—here with you, I thought I'd like to say a word. Perhaps you'll remember—'

He threw another stone, and on the moor beyond the stream she heard the grouse calling.

'Remember what?'

'That I was quite willing,' he said simply. 'That's all. It's worth it.'

She could say nothing, but presently her hand dropped its pebble and found its way into his, and he had held it without saying a word for a little while. Then after dinner, with no good-bye to her, he had disappeared by the night train to the south.

And that had been the spirit of all of them, those jolly, rampagious lads, plain or handsome, clever or slow. Two of them were dead already. But the one who had thrown ducks and drakes was still, so far as she knew, somewhere in the Ypres salient, unscathed.

And after that she had come home to the atmosphere created by her father's life and character, in this old house where she was born, and in the estate round about it. It was as though she had only just realized—begun to realize—her father's strangeness. His eccentricities and unpopularity had meant little to her before. Her own real interests had lain elsewhere; and her mind had been too slow in developing to let her appreciate his fundamental difference from other people.

At any rate her father's unpopularity had been lately acute, and Pamela herself felt it bitterly, and shrank from her neighbours and the cottage people. When Desmond came home with a D.S.O., or a Victoria Cross, as of course he would, she supposed it would be all right. But meanwhile not a single thing done for the war!—not a sou to the Red Cross, or to any war funds! And hundreds spent on antiquities—thousands perhaps—getting them deeper and deeper into debt. For she was quite aware that they were in debt; and her own allowance was of the smallest. Two hundred and fifty a year, too, for Miss Bremerton!—when they could barely afford to keep up the garden decently, or repair the house. She knew it was two hundred and fifty pounds. Her father was never reticent about such things, and had named the figure at once.

'Why wasn't Miss Bremerton doing something for the war? Greek indeed! when there was this fearful thing going on!' And in the evening air, as the girl turned her face towards the moonrise, she seemed to hear the booming of the Flanders guns.

And now Miss Bremerton was to do the housekeeping, and to play tutor and chaperon to her. Pamela resented both. If she was not to be allowed to scrub in a hospital, she might at least have learnt some housekeeping at home, for future use. As for the Greek lessons, it was not easy for her to be positively rude to any one, but she promised herself a good deal of passive resistance on that side. For if nothing else was possible, she could always sew and knit for the soldiers. Pamela was not very good at either, but they did something to lessen the moral thirst in her.

Ah, there was the library door. Miss Bremerton coming out—perhaps to propose a lesson! Pamela took to flight—noiseless and rapid—among the bosky corners and walks of the old garden.

Elizabeth emerged, clearly perceiving a gleam of vanishing white in the far distance. She sighed, but not at all sentimentally. 'It's silly how she dislikes me,' she thought. 'I wonder what I can do!'

Then her eye was caught by the tea-table still standing out in the golden dusk, which had now turned damp and chilly. Careless of Pamela not to have sent it away! Elizabeth examined it. Far too many cakes—too much sugar, too much butter, too much everything! And all because the Squire, who seemed to have as great a need of economy as anybody else, if not more, to judge from what she was beginning to know about his affairs, was determined to flout the Food Controller, and public opinion! What about the servants? she wondered.

Perceiving a little silver bell on the table she rang it and waited. Within a couple of minutes Forest emerged from the house. Elizabeth hesitated, then plunged.

'Take away the tea, please, Forest. And—and I should like to consult you. Do you think anybody wants as much tea and cakes in war-time?' She pointed to the table.

Forest paused as he was lifting the silver tray, and put it down again. He looked at the table; then he looked at the lady opposite.

'We servants, Miss, have never been asked what we think. Mr. Mannering—that's not his way.'

'But I may ask it, mayn't I, Forest?'

Forest's intelligent face flamed.

'Well, if we've really to speak out what we think, Miss—that's Cook and me—why, of course, the feeding here—well, it's a scandal! that's what it is. The Master will have it. No change, he says, from what it used to be. And the waste—well, you ask Cook! She can't help it!'

'Has she been here long, Forest?'

'Fifteen years.'

'And you?'

'Twenty-two, Miss.'

'Well, Forest,' Miss Bremerton approached him confidingly, 'don't you think that you, and Cook, and I—you know Mr. Mannering wishes me to do the housekeeping—well, that between us we could do something?'

Forest considered it.

'I don't see why not, Miss,' he said at last, with caution. 'You can reckon on me, that's certain, and on Cook, that's certain too. As for the young uns, we can get round them! They'll eat what they're given. But you'll have to go careful with the Squire.'

Miss Bremerton smiled and nodded. They stood colloguing in the twilight for ten minutes more.

CHAPTER III

'I say, Pamela, who is this female, and why has she descended on us?'

The speaker was Desmond Mannering. He was sitting on the edge of a much dilapidated arm-chair in the room which had been the twins' "den" from their childhood, in which Pamela's governess even, before the girl's school years, was allowed only on occasional and precarious footing. Here Pamela dabbed in photography, made triumphant piles of the socks and mittens she kept from her father's eye, read history, novels, and poetry, and wrote to her school friends and the boys she had met in Scotland. Ranged along the mantelpiece were numbers of snapshots—groups and single figures—taken by her, with results that showed her no great performer.

At the moment, however, Pamela was engaged in marking Desmond's socks. She was very jealous of her sisterly prerogative in the matter of Desmond's kit, and personal affairs generally. Forest was the only person she would allow to advise her, and one or two innocent suggestions made that morning by her new chaperon had produced a good deal of irritation.

Pamela looked up with a flushed countenance.

'I believe father did it specially that he might be able to tell Alice and Margaret that he hadn't a farthing for their war charities.'

'You mean because she costs so much?'

'Two hundred and fifty,' said Pamela drily.

'My hat!—and her keep! I call that mean of father,' said Desmond indignantly. 'You can't go tick with a secretary. It means cash. There'll never be anything for you, Pam, and nothing for the garden. The two old fellows that were here last week have been turned off, Forest tells me?'

'Father expects me to do the garden,' said Pamela, with rather pinched lips.

'Well, jolly good thing,' laughed her brother. 'Do you a lot of good, Pam. You never get half enough exercise.'

'I wouldn't mind if I were paid wages and could spend the money as I liked.'

'Poor old Pam! It is hard lines. I heard father tell the Rector he'd spent eighteen hundred at that sale.'

'And I'm ashamed to face any of the tradesmen,' said Pamela fiercely. 'Why they go on trusting us I don't know.'

Desmond looked out of the window with a puckered brow—a slim figure in his cadet's uniform. To judge from a picture on the wall behind his head, an enlarged photograph of the late Mrs. Mannering taken a year before the birth of the twins—an event which had cost the mother her life—Desmond resembled her rather than his father. In both faces there was the same smiling youthfulness, combined—as indeed also in Pamela—with something that entirely banished any suggestion of insipidity—something that seemed to say, 'There is a soul here—and a brain.' It had sometimes occurred, in a dreamy way to Pamela, to connect that smile on her mother's face with a line in a poem of Browning's, which she had learnt for recitation at school:

Then all smiles stopped together.

Had her mother been happy? That her children could never know.

Desmond's countenance, however, soon cleared. It was impossible for him to frown for long on any subject. He was very sorry for 'old Pam.' His father's opinions and behaviour were too queer for words. He would be jolly worried if he had to stay long at home, like Pamela. But then he wasn't going to be long at home. He was going off to his artillery camp in two days, and the thought filled him with a restless and impatient delight. At the same time he was more tolerant of his father than Pamela was, though he could not have told why.

'Desmond, give me your foot,' Pamela presently commanded.

The boy bared his foot obediently, and held it out while Pamela tried on a sock she had just finished knitting on a new pattern.

'I'm not very good at it,' sighed Pamela. 'Are you sure you can wear them, Dezzy?'

'Wear them? Ripping!' said the boy, surveying his foot at different angles. 'But you know, Pam, I can't take half the things you want me to take. What on earth did you get me a Gieve waistcoat for?'

'How do you know you won't be going to Mesopotamia?'

'Well, I don't know; but I don't somehow think it's very likely. They get their drafts from Egypt, and there's lots of artillery there.'

Pamela remembered with annoyance that Miss Bremerton had gently hinted the same thing when the Gieve waistcoat had been unpacked in her presence. It was true, of course, that she had a brother fighting under General Maude. That, no doubt, did give her a modest right to speak.

'How old do you think she is?' said Desmond, nodding in the direction of the library.

'Well, she's over thirty.'

'She doesn't look it.'

'Oh, Desmond, she does!'

'Let's call her the New Broom—Broomie for short,' said Desmond. 'Look here, Pam, I wish you'd try and like her. I shall have a dreadful hump when I get to camp if I think she's going to make you miserable.'

'Oh, I'll try,' said the girl with dreary resignation. 'You know I'm not to see Beryl again?' She looked up.

Her brother laughed.

'Don't I see you keeping to that! If Aubrey's any good he'll marry her straight away. And then how can father boycott her after that?'

'He will,' said Pamela decisively.

'And if father thinks I'm going to give up Arthur, he's jolly well mistaken,' said the boy with energy. 'Arthur's the best fellow I know, and he's been just ripping to me.'

The young face softened and glowed as though under the stress of some guarded memory. Pamela, looking up, caught her brother's expression and glowed too.

'Beryl says he isn't a bit strong yet. But he's moving heaven and earth to get back to the front.'

'Well, if they don't give him enough to do he'll be pretty sick. He's no good at loafing.'

There was silence a little. Outside a misty sunshine lay on the garden and the park and in it the changing trees were beginning to assume the individuality and separateness of autumn after the levelling promiscuity of the summer. The scene was very English and peaceful; and between it and the two young creatures looking out upon it there were a thousand links of memory and association. Suddenly Desmond said:

'Do you remember that bother I got into at Eton, Pam?'

Pamela nodded. Didn't she remember it? A long feud with another boy—ending in a highly organized fight—absolute defiance of tutor and housemaster on Desmond's part—and threatened expulsion. The Squire's irritable pride had made him side ostentatiously with his son, and Pamela could only be miserable and expect the worst. Then suddenly the whole convulsion had quieted down, and Desmond's last year at Eton had been a very happy one. Why? What had happened? Pamela had never known.

'Well, Arthur heard of it from "my tutor." He and Arthur were at Trinity together. And Arthur came over from Cambridge and had me out for a walk, and jawed me, jawed "my tutor," jawed the Head, jawed everybody. Oh, well no good going into the rotten thing,' said Desmond, flushing, 'but Arthur was awfully decent anyway.'

Pamela assented mutely. She did not want to talk about Arthur Chicksands. There was in her a queer foreboding sense about him. She did not in the least expect him to fall in love with her; yet there was a dim, intermittent fear in her lest he might become too important to her, together with a sharp shrinking from the news, which of course might come any day, that he was going to be married. She had known him from her childhood, had romped and sparred with him. He was the gayest, most charming companion; yet he carried with him, quite unconsciously, something that made it delightful to be smiled at or praised by him, and a distress when you did not get on with him, and were quite certain that he thought you silly or selfish. There was a rumour which reached Mannering after the second battle of Ypres that he had been killed. The Chicksands' household believed it for twenty-four hours.

Then he was discovered—gassed and stunned—in a shell-hole, and there had been a long illness and convalescence. During the twenty-four hours when he was believed to be dead, Pamela had spent the April daylight in the depths of the Mannering woods, in tangled hiding-places that only she knew. It was in the Easter holidays. She was alone at Mannering with an old governess, while her father was in London. The little wrinkled Frenchwoman watched her in silence, whenever she was allowed to see her. Then when on the second morning there came a telegram from Chetworth, and Pamela tore it open, flying with it before she read it to the secrecy of her own room, the Frenchwoman smiled and sighed. 'Ca, c'est l'amour!' she said to herself, 'assurément c'est l'amour!' And when Pamela came down again, radiant as a young seraph, and ready to kiss the apple-red cheek of the Frenchwoman—the rarest concession!—Madame Guérin did not need to be told that Arthur Chicksands was safe and likely to be sound.

But the Frenchwoman's inference was premature. During the two years she had been at school, Pamela had thought very little of Arthur Chicksands. She was absorbed in one of those devotions to a woman—her schoolmistress—very common among girls of strong character, and sometimes disastrous. In her case it had worked well. And now the period of extravagant devotion was over, and the girl's mind and heart set free. She thought she had forgotten Arthur Chicksands, and was certain he must have forgotten her. As it happened they had never met since his return to the front in the autumn of 1915—Pamela was then seventeen and a schoolgirl—or, as she now put it, a baby. She remembered the child who had hidden herself in the woods as something very far away.

And yet she did not want to talk about 'Arthur,' as she had always called him, and there was a certain tremor and excitement in her mind about him. The idea of being prevented from seeing him was absurd—intolerable. She was already devising ways and means of doing it. It was really not to be expected that filial obedience should reign at Mannering.

The twins had long left the subject of the embargo on Chetworth, and were wrangling and chaffing over the details of Desmond's packing, when there was a knock at the door.

Pamela stiffened at once.

'Come in!'

Miss Bremerton entered.

'Are you very busy?'

'Not at all!' said Desmond politely, scurrying with his best Eton manners to find a chair for the newcomer. 'It's an awful muddle, but that's Pamela!'

Pamela aimed a sponge-bag at him, which he dodged, and Elizabeth Bremerton sat down.

'I want to hold a council with you,' she said, turning a face just touched with laughter from one to the other. 'Do you mind?'

'Certainly not,' said Desmond, sitting on the floor with his hands round his knees. 'What's it about?' And he gave Pamela's right foot a nudge with his left by way of conveying to her that he thought her behaviour ungracious. Pamela hurriedly murmured, 'Delighted.'

'I want to tell you about the servants,' said Elizabeth. 'I can't do anything unless you help me.'

'Help you in what?' said Desmond, wondering.

'Well, you know, it's simply scandalous what you're all eating in this house!' exclaimed Elizabeth, with sudden energy. 'You ought to be fined.' She frowned, and her fair Dutch complexion became a bright pink.

'It's quite true,' said Pamela, startled. 'I told father, and he laughed at me.'

'But now even the servants are on strike,' said Elizabeth. 'It's Forest that's been preaching to them. He and Cook have been drawing up a week's menu, according to the proper scale. But—'

'Father won't have it,' said Pamela decidedly.

'An idea has occurred to me,' was Elizabeth's apologetic reply. 'Your father doesn't come in to lunch?'

'Happy thought!' cried Desmond. 'Send him in a Ritz luncheon, while the rest of you starve. Easy enough for me to say as I'm off—and soldiers aren't rationed! We may be as greedy pigs as we like.'

'What do you say?' Elizabeth looked at Pamela. The girl was flattered by the deference shown her, and gradually threw herself into the little plot. How to set up a meatless day for the household, minus the Squire, and not be found out; how to restrict the bread and porridge allowance, while apparently outrunning it—knotty problems! into which the twins plunged with much laughter and ingenuity. At the end of the discussion, Elizabeth said with hesitation, 'I don't like not telling Mr. Mannering, but—'

'Oh no, you can't tell him' said Pamela, in her most resolute tone. 'Besides, it's for the country!'

'Yes, it's the country!' echoed Elizabeth. 'Oh, I'm so glad you agree with me. Forest's splendid!'

'I say, Broomie's not bad,' thought Desmond. Aloud he said, 'Forest's a regular Turk in the servants' hall—rules them all with a rod of iron.'

Elizabeth laughed. 'He tells me there was a joint of cold beef last night for supper, and he carried it away bodily back into the larder. And they all supped on fried potatoes, cheese, oatcake and jam! So then I asked him whether anybody minded, and he said the little kitchen-maid cried a bit, and said she "was used to her vittles and her mother would be dreadfully put out."

'"Mother!" says I, 'haven't you got a young man!' And then I give her a real talking to about the war. 'You back your young man,' I said, 'and there's only one way as females can do it—barring them as is in munitions. Every bit of bread you don't eat is helping to kill Boches. And what else is your young man doin'? Where do you say he is? Wipers? You ask him. He'll tell you!' So then we were all nice and comfortable—and you needn't bother about us downstairs. We're all right!'"

'Good old Forest!' laughed Desmond, delighted. 'I always knew he was the real boss here. Father thinks he is, but he can't do without Forest, and the old boy knows it.'

'Well, so that's agreed,' said Elizabeth demurely, as she rose. 'I naturally couldn't do anything without you, but so long as your father gets everything that he's accustomed to—'

'I don't see quite what you're going to do about dinner—late dinner, I mean?' said Pamela pensively.

Elizabeth beamed at her.

'Well, I became a vegetarian last week, except for very occasional break-outs. Fish is a vegetable!'

'I see,' reflected Pamela. 'We can break out now and then at dinner, when father's got his eye on us—'

'And be pure patriots at lunch,' laughed Miss Bremerton, as she opened the door. 'Au revoir! I must go back to work.'

She vanished. The brother and sister looked at each other.

Desmond gave his opinion.

'I believe she's a good sort!'

'"Wait and see,"' said Pamela pompously, and returned to her packing.

The preceding conversation took place during a break in Elizabeth's morning occupations. She had been busily occupied in collecting and copying out some references from Pausanias, under the Squire's direction. He meanwhile had been cataloguing and noting his new possessions, which, thanks to the aid of his henchman Levasseur, had been already arranged. And they made indeed a marvellous addition to the Mannering library and its collections. At the end of the room stood now a huge archaic Nikê, with outstretched peplum and soaring wings. To her left was the small figure, archaic also, of a charioteer, from the excavations at Delphi, amazingly full of life in spite of hieratic and traditional execution. But the most conspicuous thing of all was a mutilated Erôs, by a late Rhodian artist—subtle, thievish, lovely, breathing an evil and daemonic charm. It stood opposite the Nikê, 'on tiptoe for a flight.' And there was that in it which seemed at moments to disorganize the room, and lay violent and exclusive hold on the spectator.

Elizabeth on returning to her table found the library empty. The Squire had been called away by his agent and one of the new officials of the county, and had not yet returned. She expected him to return in a bad—possibly an outrageous temper. For she gathered that the summons had something to do with the decree of the County War Agricultural Committee that fifty acres, at least, of Mannering Park were to be given back to the plough, which, indeed, had only ceased to possess them some sixty years before. The Squire had gone out pale with fury, and she looked anxiously at her work, to see what there might be in it to form an excuse for a hurricane.

She could find nothing, however, likely to displease a sane man. And as she was at a standstill till he came back, she slipped an unfinished letter out of her notebook, and went on with it. It was to a person whom she addressed as 'my darling Dick.'

'I have now been rather more than a month here. You can't imagine what a queer place it is, nor what a queer employer I have struck. There might be no war—as far as Mannering is concerned. The Squire is always engaged in mopping it out, like Mrs. Partington. He takes no newspaper, except a rag called the Lanchester Mail, which attacks the Government, the Army—as far as it dare—and "secret diplomacy." It comes out about once a week with a black page, because the Censor has been sitting on it. Desmond Mannering—that's the gunner-son who came on leave a week ago and is just going off to an artillery camp—and I, conspire through the butler—who is a dear, and a patriot—to get the Times; but the Squire never sees it. Desmond reads it in bed in the morning, I read it in bed in the evening, and Pamela Mannering, Mr. Desmond's twin, comes in last thing, in her dressing-gown, and steals it.

'I seem indeed to be living in the heart of a whirlwind, for the Squire is fighting everybody all round, and as he is the least reticent of men, and I have to write his letters, I naturally, even by now, know a good deal about him. Shortly put, he is in a great mess. The estate is riddled with mortgages, which it would be quite easy to reduce. For instance, there are masses of timber, crying to be cut. He consults me often in the naïvest way. You remember that I trained for six months as an accountant. I assure you that it comes in extremely useful now! I can see my way a little where he can't see it at all. He glories in the fact that he was never any good at arithmetic or figures of any kind, and never looked at either after "Smalls." The estate of course used to be looked after in the good old-fashioned way by the family lawyers. But a few years ago the Squire quarrelled with these gentlemen, recovered all his papers, which no doubt went back to King Alfred, and resolved to deal with things himself. There is an office here, and a small attorney from Fallerton comes over twice or three times a week. But the Squire bosses it. And you never saw anything like his accounts! I have been trying to put some of them straight—just those that concern the house and garden—after six weeks' acquaintance! Odd, isn't it? He is like an irritable child with them. And his agent, who is seventy, and bronchitic, is the greatest fool I ever saw. He neglects everything. His accounts too, as far as I have inspected them, are disgraceful. He does nothing for the farmers, and the farmers do exactly as they please with the land.

'Or did! For now comes the rub. Government is interfering, through the County Committee. They are turning out three of Mr. Mannering's farmers by force, because he won't do it himself, and ploughing up the park. I believe the steam tractor comes next week. The Squire has been employing some new lawyers to find out if he can't stop it somehow. And each time he sees them he comes home madder than before.

'Of course it all comes from a passionate antagonism to the war. He is not a pacifist exactly— he is not a conscientious objector. He is just an individualist gone mad—an egotistical, hot-tempered man, with all the ideas of the old régime, who thinks he can fight the world. I am often really sorry for him—he is so preposterous. But the muddle and waste of it all drives me crazy— you know I always was a managing creature.

'But one thing is certain—that he is a most excellent scholar. I knew I had got rusty, but I didn't know how rusty till I came to work for him. He has a wonderful memory—seems to know every Greek author by heart—and a most delicate and unerring taste. I thought I should find a mere dabbler—an amateur. And it takes all I know to do the drudgery work he gives me. And then he is always coming down upon me. It delights him to find me out in a howler—makes him, in fact, quite good-tempered for twenty minutes.

'As to the rest of the family, there is a charming boy and girl—twins of nineteen, the boy just off to an artillery camp after his cadet training; the girl extremely pretty and distinguished, and so far inclined to think me an intruder and a nuisance. How to get round her I don't exactly know, but I daresay I shall manage it somehow. If she would only set up a love-affair I could soon get the whip-hand of her!

'Then there is the priceless butler, with whom I have already made friends. I seem to have a taste for butlers, though I've never lived with one. He is fifty-two and a volunteer, in stark opposition to the Squire, who jeers at him perpetually. Forest takes it calmly, seems even in a queer way to be attached to his queer master. But he never misses a drill for anybody or any weather, and when he's out, the under-housemaid "buttles" for him like a lamb. The fact is, of course, that he's been here for twenty years, and the Squire couldn't get on for a day without him, or thinks he couldn't. So that his position is, as you may say, strongly entrenched, and counter-attacks are useless.

'The married daughters—Mrs. Gaddesden, who, I think, is an Honourable, and Mrs. Strang— are coming to-morrow to see their brother before he goes into camp. The Squire doesn't want them at all. Ah, there he comes! I'll finish later...'

The Squire came in—to use one of the Homeric similes of which he was so fond—'like a lion fresh from a slain bull, bespattered with blood and mire.' He had gone out pale, he returned crimson, rubbing his hands and in great excitement. And it was evident that he had by now formed the habit of talking freely to his secretary. For he went up to her at once.

'Well, now they know what to expect!' he said, his eyes glittering, and all his thick hair on his small peaked head standing up in a high ridge, like the crest of a battle-helmet.

'Who are "they"?' asked Elizabeth, smiling, as she quietly pushed her letter a little further under the blotting-paper.

'The County Council idiots—no, the Inspector fellow they're sending round.'

'And what did you tell him?'

'That I should resist their entry. The gates of the park will be locked. And my lawyers are already preparing a case for the High Court. Well—eh!—what?'—the speaker wound up impatiently, as though waiting for an immediate and applauding response.

Elizabeth was silent. She bent over the Greek book in front of her, as though looking for her place.

'You didn't think I was going to take it lying down!' asked the Squire, in a raised voice. Her silence suggested to him afresh all the odious and tyrannical forces by which he felt himself surrounded.

Elizabeth turned to him with a cheerful countenance.

'I don't quite understand what "it" means,' she said politely.

'Nonsense, you do!' was the angry reply. 'That's so like a woman. They always want to catch you out; they never see things simply and broadly. You'd like to make yourself out a fool—νηπια—and you're not a fool!'

And with his hands in his pockets he made two or three long strides up to the Nikê, at the further end of the room, and back, pulling up beside her again, as though challenging her reply.

'I assure you, sir, I wasn't trying to catch you out,' Elizabeth began in her gentlest voice.

'Don't call me "sir." I won't have it!' cried the Squire, almost stamping.

Then Elizabeth laughed outright.

'I'm sorry, but when I was working in the War Trade Department I always called the head of my room "sir."'

'That's because women like kow-towing—δουλοσυνην ανεχεσθαι!' said the Squire. Then he threw himself into a chair. 'Now let's talk sense a little.'

Elizabeth's attentive look, and lips quivering with amusement which she tried in vain to suppress, and he was determined not to see, showed her more than willing.

'I suppose you think—like that fellow I've just routed—that it's a uestion of food production. It isn't! It's a question of liberty—versus bondage. If we can only survive as slaves, then wipe us out! That's my view.'

'Wasn't there a bishop once who said he would rather have England free than sober?' asked Elizabeth.

'And a very sensible man,' growled the Squire, 'though in general I've no use for bishops. Now you understand, I hope? This is going to be a test case. I'll make England ring.'

'Are you sure they can't settle it at once, under the Defence of the Realm Act?'

'Not they!' said the Squire triumphantly. 'Of course, I'm not putting up a frontal defence. I'm outflanking them. I'm proving that this is the worst land they could possibly choose. I'm offering them something else that they don't want. Meanwhile the gates shall be locked, and if any one or anything breaks them down—my lawyers are ready—we apply for an injunction at once.'

'And you're not—well, nervous?' asked Miss Bremerton, with a charming air of presenting something that might have been overlooked.

'Nervous of what?'

'Isn't the law—the new law—rather dreadfully strong?'

'Oh, you think I shall end in the county gaol?' said the Squire abruptly. 'Well, of course'—he took a reflective turn up and down—'I've no particular wish just now for the county gaol. It would be an infernal nuisance—in the middle of this book. But I mean to give them as much trouble as I can. I'm all right so far.'

He looked up suddenly, and caught an expression on his secretary's face which called him to order at once, though he was not meant to see it. Contempt?—cold contempt? Something like it.

The Squire drew himself up.

'You've made the arrangements, I suppose, for to-morrow?'

He spoke curtly, as the master of the house to a dependent.

Elizabeth meekly replied that she had done everything according to his directions. Mrs. Gaddesden was to have the South rooms.

'I said the East rooms!'

'But I thought—' Elizabeth began, in consternation.

'You thought wrong,' said the Squire cuttingly. 'Do not trouble yourself. I will tell Forest'

Elizabeth coloured crimson, and went on with her work. The Squire rang the bell. But before Forest could answer it, there was a quick step in the passage, and Desmond came bursting in.

'Pater, I say! it's too fine! You can't frowst all day at this nonsense. Come out, and let's shoot those roots of Milsom's. He told me yesterday there were five or six coveys in his big field alone. Of course everybody's been poaching for all they're worth. But there's some left. Forest'll get us some sandwiches. He says he'll come and load for you. His boy and the garden boy'll do for beaters.'

The Squire stood glumly hesitating, but with his eye on his son.

'Look here,' said Desmond, 'I've only got two days!'

Elizabeth could not help watching the boy—his look at his father, the physical beauty and perfection of him. The great Victory at the end of the room with her outstretched wings seemed to be hovering above him.

'Well, I don't mind,' said the Squire slowly.

Desmond gave a laugh of triumph, twined his arm in that of his father, and dragged him away.

'DEAR BELOVED DICK—I must just finish this before dinner. Oh, how I like to think of you at Baghdad, with trees and shade, and civilized quarters again, after all you've gone through. Have you got my letters, and those gauze things I sent you for the hot weather? They tell me here they're right. But how's one to know? Meanwhile, my dear, here are your mother and sister on their knees to you, just to be told what you want. Try and want something!—there's a dear.

'Mother's fairly well—I mean as well as we can expect after such an illness. My salary here enables me to give her a proper trained nurse, and to send Jean to school. As to the rest, don't trouble about me, old man. Sometimes I think it was my pride more than anything else that was hurt a year ago. Anyway I find in myself a tremendous appetite for work. In spite of his oddities, Mr. Mannering is a most stimulating critic and companion. My work is interesting, and I find myself steeped once more in the most fascinating, the most wonderful of all literatures! What remains unsatisfied in me is the passion which you know I have always had for setting things straight—organizing, tidying up! Not to speak of other passions—for work directly connected with the war, for instance—which have had to be scrapped for a time. I can't bear the muddle and waste of this place. It gets on my nerves. Perhaps, if I stay, I may get a chance. I have made a small beginning—with the food. But I won't bother you with it.

'Above all, I must try and make friends with the twins. Desmond would be easy, but he's going. Pamela will be more difficult. However, I shall do my best. As I have already said, if she would only set up a flirtation—a nice one—that I could aid and abet!

'What will the married sisters be like? Desmond and Pamela say very little. All I know is that Alice—that's Mrs. Gaddesden—is to have a fire in her room all day, though the weather now is like July. To judge from her photographs, she is fair, rather pretty, stout and lethargic. Whereas Margaret is as thin almost as her father, and head-over-ears in war charities. She lives, says Pamela, on arrowroot and oatcake, to set an example, and her servants leave her regularly every month.

'Well, we shall see. I run on like this, because you say you like to be gossipped to; and I am just a little lonely here—sometimes. Good-night, and good-bye.—Your devoted sister,

'ELIZABETH.'

CHAPTER IV

'Come in!' said Alice Gaddesden in a languid tone. From the knock, sharp and loud, on her bedroom door, she guessed that it was her sister Margaret who wished to see her. She did not wish, however, to see Margaret at all. Margaret, who was slightly the elder, tired and coerced her. But she had no choice.

Mrs. Strang entered briskly.

'My dear Alice! what a time of day to be in bed! Are you really ill?'

Mrs. Gaddesden grew red with annoyance.

'I thought I had told you, Margaret, that Dr. Crother advised me more than a year ago not to come down till the middle of the morning. It rests my heart.'

Mrs. Strang, who had come up to the bedside, looked down upon her sister with amused eyes. She herself was curiously like the Squire, even as to her hair, which was thick and fair, and already whitening, though she was not yet thirty. Human thinness could hardly have been carried further than she and the Squire achieved it. She had her father's nose also. But the rest of her features were delicately regular, and her quick blue eyes were those of a woman who told no falsehoods herself, and had little patience with other people's.

'My dear Alice, why do you believe doctors? They always tell you what you want to hear. I am sure you told Dr. Crother exactly what to say,' said Margaret, laughing, as she placed a chair by the bedside.

'Oh, of course I know you think everybody's a sham who isn't as strong as yourself!' said Mrs. Gaddesden, sinking back on her pillows with a soft sigh of resignation. 'Though I think you might have remembered the horribly hard work I've been doing lately.'

'Have you?' Mrs. Strang wrinkled her brow, as though in an effort to recollect. 'Oh, yes, I know. I have always been getting notices lately with your name on them, at the end of a long tail beginning with a Duchess, and stuffed with Countesses. And I always think—there's Alice doing the work, and the Countesses getting the glory. Do you really do the work?'

And Margaret, who did not often see her sister, and was of a genuinely inquiring turn of mind, turned upon her a penetrating look.

'Well, of course,' said Mrs. Gaddesden, a little confused, 'there are always the secretaries.'

'Ah-ha!' Mrs. Strang laughed—one might almost say crowed. 'Yes, indeed, if it weren't for the secretaries! By the way, what do you think about the specimen here?'

Mrs. Gaddesden lost her languid air at once. She sat up among her pillows, a reasonably pretty woman, not without some likeness to Pamela, in points that did not matter.

'My dear Margaret,' she said, with emphasis, 'this has got to be watched!—watched, I tell you.'

Mrs. Strang opened her eyes wide.

'What on earth do you mean?'

Alice Gaddesden smiled.

'Well, of course, you're much cleverer than I am, but I really do see further in practical matters than you do. Haven't you noticed,' she bent forward, looking mysterious and intent, 'how already father depends upon her, how she's beginning to run the whole show—and she hasn't been here much more than six weeks? My dear Margaret, with a secretary like that you never can tell!'

'Well,' said Mrs. Strang coolly, 'and what then?'

'Oh, well, of course, if you're prepared to see a person like that—in our mother's place!'

'"A person like that"—how dreadfully old-fashioned you are, Alice! She's a lady; she's much more highly educated than you or I, and if she gets her way, she'll perhaps keep father out of some of the scrapes he seems bent on. You know this business of the park is perfectly mad!'

For the first time in this conversation Margaret Strang's face was grave. And when it was grave, some people would have called it fine.

'And just think what it'll cost,' said Mrs. Gaddesden despondently, 'even if he had a case—which he probably hasn't—and if he were to win it. There'll be no money left for Aubrey or any of us soon.'

'But of course he hasn't a case, and of course he can't win!' cried Margaret Strang. 'It's not that I care about—or the money—it's the disgrace!'

'Yes,' murmured Alice doubtfully.

'When you think—'

Mrs. Strang paused; her bright blue eyes, alive with thoughts, were fixed absently on her sister. She seemed to see a number of shabby streets, where she was accustomed to work, with little shabby shops, and placards on them—'No butter,' 'No milk,' and apples marked 4d. each.

'Think what?' said Alice.

Mrs. Strang's mind returned to Alice, and Alice's very elaborate and becoming negligée.

'Only that, in my opinion, it's the duty of every landowner to produce every ounce of food he can, and to do what he's told! And father not only sets a shocking example, but he picks this absurd quarrel with the Chicksands. What on earth is Aubrey to do? Or poor Beryl?'

'Well, he comes to-night,' said Alice, 'so I suppose we shall hear. I can't make Aubrey out,' she added reflectively.

'Nobody can. I was talking to a brother-officer of his last week, a man who's awfully fond of him. He told me Aubrey did his work very well. He was complimented by Headquarters on his School only last month. But he's like an automaton. Nobody really knows him, nobody gets any forwarder with him. He hardly speaks to anybody except on business. The mess regard him as a wet blanket, and his men don't care about him, though he's a capital officer. Isn't it strange, when one thinks of what Aubrey used to be five years ago?'

Alice agreed. Perhaps he was still suffering from the effects of his wound in 1915.

'Anyway he can't give Beryl up,' said Margaret with energy, 'if he's a man of honour!'

Alice shrugged her shoulders.

'Then he'll give up the estate, according to father.'

'Desmond would give it back to him, if there's anything left of it, or if he wants it.'

'Margaret!'

'You think I don't care about the family—that there should always be a Mannering of Mannering? Yes, I do care, but there are so many other things now to care about,' added Mrs.

Strang slowly.

'Who's making me late now?' said Alice, looking at her watch.

Margaret took the hint and departed.

That same evening, in the September dusk, a dog-cart arrived at the Hall, bringing Major Mannering and a Gladstone bag.

Pamela and Desmond rushed out to meet him. Their elder sisters were dressing for dinner, and the Squire was in the library with Elizabeth. The twins dragged the newcomer into their own den, and shut the door upon him. There Desmond gave him a breathless survey of the situation, while Pamela sat on a stool at his feet, and put in explanatory words at intervals. Their father's extraordinary preparations for waging war against the County Committee; his violence on the subject of the Chicksands; Beryl's despairing letters to Pamela; a letter from Arthur Chicksands to Desmond,—all these various items were poured out on the newcomer, with an eagerness and heat which showed the extreme interest which the twins took in the situation.

Meanwhile Aubrey Mannering sat listening almost in silence. He was a delicately built, distinguished-looking man, who carried a large scar on his forehead, and had lost a finger of the left hand. The ribbons on his breast showed that he was both an M.C. and a D.S.O.—distinctions won at the second battle of Ypres and on the Somme. While the twins talked, his eyes travelled from one to the other, attentive, but curiously aloof.

He was saying to himself that Pamela was extremely pretty, and Desmond a splendid fellow. Then—in a moment—while he looked at his young brother, a vision, insistent, terrible, passed ghost-like between him and the boy. Again and again he tried to shake it off, and again and again it interposed.

'Oh, Aubrey, what will you do?' said Pamela despairingly, leaning her head against her brother's knee.

Her voice recalled him. He laid his hand upon her beautiful hair.

'Well, dear, there's only one thing, of course, for me to do—to stick to Beryl and let father do his worst.'

'Hurrah!' said Desmond. 'That's all right. And of course you know, Aubrey, that if father tries any hankey-pankey with the estate, and leaves it to me, I shall give it back to you next day.'

Aubrey smiled. 'Father'll live another twenty years, old man. Will there be any England then, or any law, or any estates to leave?'

The twins looked at him in amazement. Again he recovered himself quickly.

'I only meant that, in times like these, it's no good planning anything twenty years ahead. We've got to win the war, haven't we?—that's the first thing. Well, now, I must go and clean up. Who's here?'

'Alice and Margaret,' said Pamela. 'And father's new secretary.'

'You never told me about him,' said Aubrey indifferently, as he rose.

'"Him" indeed!' laughed Desmond. 'Nothing of the sort!'

Aubrey turned a puzzled look upon him.

'What! a lady?'

Desmond grinned.

'First Class in Mods, and an awful swell. Father can't let her out of his sight. Says he never had anybody so good.'

'And she'll end by bossing us all,' put in Pamela. 'She's begun it already. Now you really must go and dress.'

When the eldest son of the house entered the drawing-room, he found everybody gathered there but his father and the Rector, who was coming to dine. He was at once seized on by his married sisters, who saw him very rarely. Then Pamela led him up to a tall lady in pale blue.

'My eldest brother—Miss Bremerton.'

He looked at her with curiosity, and was glad when, after the arrival of his father and the Rector, it fell to him to take the new secretary in to dinner. His father's greeting to him had been decidedly cool—the greeting of a man who sees a fight impending and wishes to give away nothing to his opponent. In fact the two men had never been on really cordial terms since August 1914, when Aubrey had thrown up his post in the Foreign Office to apply for one of the first temporary commissions in the New Army. The news came at a moment when the Squire was smarting under the breakdown of a long-cherished scheme of exploration in the Greek islands, which was to have been realized that very autumn—a scheme towards which his whole narrow impetuous mind had been turned for years. No more Hellenic or Asia Minor excavations! no more cosmopolitan Wissenschaft! On that fatal August 4 a whole world went down submerged beneath the waves of war, and the Squire cared for no other. His personal chagrin showed itself in abuse of the bungling diplomats and 'swashbuckler' politicians who, according to him, had brought us into war. So that when Aubrey applied for a commission, the Squire, mainly to relieve his own general irritation, had quarrelled with him for some months, and was only outwardly reconciled when his son came home invalided in 1915.

During the summer of 1917, Aubrey, after spending three days' leave at Mannering, had gone on to stay at Chetworth with the Chicksands for a week. The result of that visit was a letter to his father in which he announced his engagement to Beryl. The Squire could make then no open opposition, since he was still on friendly terms with Sir Henry, who had indeed done him more than one good turn. But in reply to his son's letter, he stood entirely on the defensive, lest any claim should be made upon him which might further interfere with the passion of his life. He was not, he said, in a position to increase Aubrey's allowance—the Government robbers had seen to that—and unless Beryl was prepared to be a poor man's wife he advised them to wait till after the war. Then Sir Henry had ridden over to Mannering with a statement of what he was prepared to do for his daughter, and the Squire had given ungracious consent to a marriage in the spring. Chicksands knew his man too well to take offence at the Squire's manners, and Beryl was for a time too timidly and blissfully happy to be troubled by them.

'You have been here a few weeks,' said the newcomer to Elizabeth, when the party had settled down at table.

'About six weeks. It seems longer!' smiled Elizabeth.

'You are doing some work for my father?'

Elizabeth explained herself. Major Mannering listened attentively.

'So what you do for him is literary—and historical?'

'Oh no—I do accounts, and write letters too.'

'Accounts? I thought there was a housekeeper?'

'She went a month ago to the W.A.A.C.'s. Please!—do you mind?' And to his amazement, as he was putting out his hand automatically to a piece of bread lying on his left, Miss Bremerton's hand holding a fork neatly intercepted him, and moved the bread away.

'It's our "Self-denying Ordinance,"' explained the lady, colouring a little. 'The bread appears because—because your father doesn't think rations necessary. But no one touches it, and Forest collects it afterwards—for breakfast.'

A smile broke on Aubrey's grave and pensive face.

'I see. Mayn't I really have any?'

Elizabeth hesitated.

'Well, perhaps, as a guest, and a soldier. Yes, I think you may.' And she would have restored her prey had not her neighbour stopped her.

'Not at all. As a soldier I obey orders. My hat! how you've drilled them all!' For, looking round the table, he saw that not a single guest had touched the bread lying to their left.

'That's Pamela and Mr. Desmond! They've given everybody a menu for three days.'

'Good heavens—not my father!'

'Oh no, no! We don't think he suspects anything, and he has everything he likes.'

'And my married sisters?' Elizabeth hesitated again.

'Well, Mrs. Gaddesden is rather afraid of being starved. Mrs. Strang, on the other hand, thinks we're wickedly extravagant!'

Her neighbour was so much amused that conversation flowed on easily thenceforward; and Desmond opposite whispered to Pamela:

'Just look at Broomie! She's actually making Aubrey talk.'

The Major's rôle, however, was on the whole that of listener. For Elizabeth meant to talk—meant to explain herself to the son and heir, and, if she could, to drive him to an interest in the family affairs. To her trained, practical mind the whole clan seemed by now criminally careless and happy-go-lucky. The gardens were neglected; so was the house; so was the estate. The gardens ought to have been made self-supporting; there were at least a third too many servants in the house; and as for the estate, instead of being a profit-making and food-producing concern, as it should have been, it was a bye-word for bad management and neglected land. She did not pretend to know much about it yet; but what she did know roused her. England was at grips with a brutal foe. The only weapon that could defeat her was famine—the sloth and waste of her own sons. This woman, able, energetic, a lover of her country, could not conceal her scorn for such a fatal incompetence. Naturally, in talking to the eldest son, she made the agent her scapegoat for the sins of the owner. The Squire's responsibility was carefully masked. But Aubrey Mannering perfectly understood what she would be at. She was a clever woman who wanted things improved. Well, let her improve them. It did not matter to him.

But she appeared to him as a somewhat special type of the modern woman, with her advanced education and her clear brain; and for a time he observed her curiously. The graceful dress, pale blue with touches of black, which exactly became her fair skin, the bright gold of her hair, and the pleasant homeliness of her face—her general aspect indeed—attracted him greatly. She might know Greek; at heart, he believed, she was a good housewife; and when she incidentally mentioned Dutch relations, he seemed to see her with a background of bright pots and pans, mopping tiled floors.

But presently he ceased to pay much attention to her. His dreamy sense became aware of the scene as a whole; the long table; his father's fantastic figure at the head of it; Alice Gaddesden elaborately dressed and much made up on the one side, his sister Margaret in a high black gown, erect and honest, on the other; Desmond and Pamela together, chatting and chaffing with the Rector. It was the room so familiar to his childhood and youth, with the family pictures, the Gainsborough full-length of his very plain great-grandmother in white satin at the end, two or three Vandyck school-portraits of seventeenth-century Mannerings, and the beautiful Hogarth head—their best possession—that was so like Pamela. The furniture of the room was of many different dates—incongruous, shabby, and on the whole ugly. The Mannerings of the past had not been an artistic lot.

Nor had the room—the house indeed—many tender associations for him. His childhood had not been very happy. He had never got on with his father, and his mother, who had been the victim of various long illnesses during his boyhood, had never, unluckily, meant much to him. He knew that he was of a very old stock, which had played a long and considerable part in the world; but the fact brought him no thrill. 'That kind of thing is played out,' he thought. Let his father disinherit him—he was quite indifferent.

Then, as he fell silent beside his father's new secretary, the table vanished. He saw instead the wide Picardy flats, a group of poplars, a distant wood, and in front a certain hollow strewn with dead and dying men—one figure, in front of the rest, lying face downwards. The queer twisted forms, the blasted trees, the inexorable horror—the whole vision swept over him again, as it had done in the schoolroom. His nerves shrank and trembled under it.

Beryl—poor little Beryl! What a wretch he had been to propose to her—in a moment of moral and physical weakness, when it had seemed a simple thing to accept her affection and to pledge his own! But if she stood by him, he must stand by her. And he had had the kindest letter from Sir Henry, and some sweet tremulous words from her. Suppose she offered to release him? His heart leapt guiltily at the thought. What, indeed, had a man so haunted and paralysed to give to a girl like Beryl? It was an outrage—it ought to cease.

But as to his father, that was simple enough.

The Squire and his eldest son retreated to the library after dinner, and all the rest of the party waited uneasily to see what would happen. Elizabeth did her best to keep things going. It might have been noticed—it was noticed by at least two of the persons present—that quite unobtrusively, she was already the mistress of the house. She found a stool and a fire-screen for Mrs. Gaddesden; she held some wool for Mrs. Strang to wind; and a backgammon board was made ready for the Squire, in case he returned.

But he did not return. Aubrey came back alone, and found them all hanging on his entrance. Pamela put down her knitting and looked at him anxiously; so did the elder sisters. He went up absently to the chimney-piece, and stood leaning against it.

'Well?' said Pamela in a low voice, as she came to sit on a stool near him.

He smiled, but she saw that he was pale.

'Can you take me over to Chetworth to-morrow—early—in the pony-cart?'

'Yes, certainly.'

'Half-past ten?'

'Right you are.'

No more was said. Aubrey turned at once to Alice Gaddesden and proposed a round game. He played it with much more spirit than usual, and Desmond's antics in 'Animal Grab' put all serious notions to flight.

But when the game was over, and Forest brought in the candles, Margaret tried to get some information.

'You found the father reasonable?' she said to her brother in an undertone, as they stood together by the fire.

'Oh, yes,' was the indifferent answer, 'from his own point of view.'

And when he had lit their candles for his sisters, he excused himself at once on the ground of being dog-tired after a long day. The door closed upon him.

The family gathered together in a group, while the Rector and Elizabeth talked about the village at the further end of the room.

'They've quarrelled!' said Margaret decisively.

Alice Gaddesden, because it was Margaret's opinion, disagreed. There was nothing to show it, she said. Aubrey had been quite calm. Desmond broke out, 'Did you ever see Aubrey anything else?' Pamela said nothing, but she slipped out to tell Forest about the pony-cart.

Meanwhile the Rector had looked at his watch, and came up to take his leave.

'Has the Squire gone to bed?' he said cheerfully. 'I daresay. He works so hard. Give him my fare-wells.'

And he went off, quite aware, both from his knowledge of the family and of the Squire's recent actions, that there were storms brewing in the old house, but on the whole thinking more of the new secretary than of his old friends. A charming woman!—most capable! For the first time he might get some attention paid to the village people. That child with the shocking bow-legs. Poor little Pamela had tried to do her best. But this woman would see to it; she knew how to get things done.

Meanwhile, as the rest of the party dispersed, Forest brought a message to Elizabeth. 'The Squire would be glad if you would spare him a few minutes, Miss, in the library. He won't keep you long.'

Elizabeth went unwillingly.

The library was in darkness, except for one small lamp at the further end, and the Squire was walking up and down. He stopped abruptly as he saw his secretary.

'I won't keep you, Miss Bremerton, but do you happen to know at all where my will is?'

'Your will, Mr. Mannering?' said Elizabeth in amazement. 'No, indeed! I have never seen it.'

'Well, it's somewhere here,' said the Squire impatiently. 'I should have thought in all your rummagings lately you must have come across it. I took it away from those robbers, my old solicitors, and I wasn't going to give it to the new man—don't trust him particularly not to talk. So I locked it up here—somewhere. And I can't find it.' And he began restlessly to open drawer after drawer, which already contained piles of letters and documents, neatly and systematically arranged, with the proper dockets and sub-headings, by Elizabeth.

'Oh, it can't be there!' cried Elizabeth. 'I know everything in those drawers. Surely it must be in the office?' By which she meant the small and hideously untidy room on the ground floor into which masses of papers of all dates, still unsorted, had been carted down from London.

'It isn't in the office!' He was, she saw, on the brink of an outburst. 'I put it somewhere in this room my own self! And I should have thought by now you knew the geography of this place as well as I do!'

Elizabeth raised her eyebrows, but said nothing. The big room indeed was still full to her of unexplored territory, with caches of all kinds in it, new and ancient, waiting to be discovered. She looked round her in perplexity, not knowing where to begin. A large part of the room was walled with glass cases, holding vases, bronzes, and other small antiquities, down to about a yard from the floor, and the space below being filled by cupboards and drawers. Elizabeth made a vague movement towards a particular set of cupboards which she knew she had not yet touched, but the Squire irritably stopped her.

'It's certainly not there. That bit of the room hasn't been disturbed since the Flood! Now those drawers'—he pointed—'might be worth looking at.'

She hurried towards them. But the Squire, instead of helping her in her search, resumed his walk up and down, muttering to himself. As for her, she was on the verge of laughter, the laughter that comes from nerves and fatigue; for she had had a long day's work and was really tired. The first drawer she opened was packed with papers, a few arranged in something like order by her predecessor, the London University B.A., but the greater part of them in confusion. They mostly related to a violent controversy between the Squire and various archæological experts with regard to some finds in the Troad a year or two before the war, in which the Squire had only just escaped a serious libel suit, whereof indeed all the preliminaries were in the drawer.

On the very top of the drawer, however, was a conveyance of a small outlying portion of the Mannering estate, which the Squire had sold to a neighbour only a year before this date. Hopeless! If that was there, anything might be anywhere!

Was she to spend the night searching for the needle in this bottle of hay? Elizabeth's face began to twitch with uncomfortable merriment. Should she go and knock up the housekeeper and instal her as chaperon, or take a stand, and insist on going to bed like a reasonable woman?

She hunted through three drawers. The Squire meanwhile paced incessantly, sometimes muttering to himself. Every time he came within the circle of lamplight his face was visible to

Elizabeth, wrinkled and set, with angry eyes; and she saw him as a person possessed by a stubborn demon of self-will. Once, as he passed her, she heard him say to himself, 'Of course I can write another at once—half a sheet will do.'

She replaced the third drawer. Was the Squire to have a monopoly of stubbornness? She thought not. Waves of indefinite but strong indignation were beginning to sweep through her. Why was the Squire hunting for his will? What had he been saying to his son—his son who bore on his breast and on his body the marks of his country's service?

She rose to her feet.

'I can't find anything, Mr. Mannering. And I think, if you will allow me, I will go to bed.'

He looked at her darkly.

'I see. You are a person who stickles for your hours—you won't do anything extra for me.' There was a sneer in his tone.

Elizabeth felt her cheeks suddenly burn. In the dim light she looked amazingly tall, as she stood straightened to her full height, confronting this man who really seemed to her to be only half sane.

'I think I have done a great deal for you, Mr. Mannering. But if you don't think so we had better end my engagement!'

His countenance changed at once. He eagerly apologized. He was perfectly aware of her extraordinary merits, and should be entirely lost without her help. The fact was he had had a painful scene, and was overdone.

Elizabeth received his explanation very coldly, only repeating, 'May I go to bed?'

The Squire drew his hand across his eyes.

'It is not very late—not yet eleven.' He pointed to the grandfather clock opposite. 'If you will only wait while I write something?'—he pointed to a chair. 'Just take a book there, and give me a quarter of an hour, no more—I want your signature, that's all. We won't look any further for the will. I can do all I want by a fresh document. I have been thinking it over, and can write it in ten minutes. I know as much about it as the lawyers—more. Now do oblige me. I am ashamed of my discourtesy. I need not say that I regard you as indispensable—and—I think I have been able to do something for your Greek.'

He smiled—a smile that was like a foam-flake on a stormy sea. But he could put on the grand manner when he chose, and Elizabeth was to some extent propitiated. After all he and his ways were no longer strange to her. Very unwillingly she seated herself again, and he went rapidly to his writing-table.

Then silence fell, except for the scratching of the Squire's pen. Elizabeth sat pretending to read, but in truth becoming every moment the prey of increasing disquiet. What was he going to ask her to sign? She knew nothing of his threat to his eldest son—nothing, that is, clear or direct, either from himself or from the others; but she guessed a good deal. It was impossible to live even for a few weeks in close contact with the Squire without guessing at most things.

In the silence she became aware of the soft autumn wind—October had just begun—playing with a blind on a distant window. And through the window came another sound—Desmond and

Pamela, no doubt, still laughing and talking in the schoolroom.

The Squire rose from his seat.

'I shall be much obliged,' he said formally, 'if you will kindly come here. We shall want another witness, of course. I will call Forest.'

Elizabeth approached, but paused a yard or two from him. He saw her in the light—her gold hair and brilliant dress illuminated against the dark and splendid background of the Nikê in shadow.

She spoke with hesitation.

'I confess I should like to know, Mr. Mannering, what it is you are asking me to sign.'

'That doesn't matter to a witness. It is nothing which will in any way compromise you.'

'No—but'—she drew herself up—'I should blame myself if I made it easier for you to do something you would afterwards regret.'

'What do you mean?'

She summoned all her courage.

'Of course I must know something. You have not kept your affairs very secret. I guess that you are angry with your son, with Major Mannering. If this thing you ask me to sign is to hurt—to injure him—if it is—well, then—I refuse to sign it!'

And with a sudden movement she threw both her hands behind her back and clasped them there.

'You refuse?'

'If you admit my description of that paper.' She motioned towards it as it lay on the writing-table.

'I have no objection whatever to your knowing what it is—as you seem determined to know,' he said sarcastically. 'It is a codicil revoking my will in favour of my eldest son, and leaving all the property of which I die possessed, and which is in my power to bequeath, to my younger son Desmond. What have you to do with that? What possible responsibility can you have?'

Elizabeth wavered, but held her ground, though in evident distress.

'Only that—if I don't sign it—you would have time to consider it again. Mr. Mannering—isn't it—isn't it—very unjust?'

The Squire laughed.

'How do you know that in refusing you are not unjust to Desmond?'

'Oh no!' she said fervently. 'Mr. Desmond would never wish to supplant his brother—and for such a reason. And especially—' she paused.

There were tears rising in her throat.

'Especially—what? Upon my word, you claim a rather remarkable knowledge of my family—in six weeks!'

'I do know something of Desmond!' Her voice showed her agitation. 'He is the dearest, the most generous boy. In a few months he will be going out—he will be saying good-bye to you all.'

'And then?'

'Is this a time to make him unhappy—to send him out with something on his mind?—something that might even—'

'Well, go on!'

'Might even make him wish'—her voice dropped—'not to come back.'

There was silence. Then the Squire violently threw down the pen he was holding on the table beside him.

'Thank you, Miss Bremerton. That will do. I bid you good-night!'

Elizabeth did not wait to be told twice. She turned and fled down the whole length of the library. The door at the further end closed upon her.

'A masterful young woman!' said the Squire after a moment, drawing a long breath. Then he took up the codicil, thrust it into a drawer of his writing-table, lit a cigarette, and walked up and down smoking it. After which he went to bed and slept remarkably well.

Elizabeth cried herself to sleep. No comforting sprite whispered to her that she had won the first round in an arduous campaign. On the contrary, she fully expected dismissal on the morrow.

CHAPTER V

It was a misty but warm October day, and a pleasant veiled light lay on the pillared front of Chetworth House, designed in the best taste of a fastidious school. The surroundings of the house, too, were as perfect as those of Mannering were slatternly and neglected. All the young men had long since gone from the gardens, but the old labourers and the girls in overalls who had taken their places, under the eye of a white-haired gardener, had been wonderfully efficient so far. Sir Henry supposed he ought to have let the lawns stand for hay, and the hedges go unclipped; but as a matter of fact the lawns had never been smoother, or the creepers and yew hedges more beautifully in order, so that even the greatest patriot fails somewhere.

Beryl Chicksands was walking along a stone-flagged path under a yew hedge, from which she commanded the drive and a bit of the road outside. Every now and then she stopped to peer into the sunlit haze that marked the lower slopes of the park, and the delicate hand that shaded her eyes shook a little.

Aubrey was coming—and she was going seriously to offer to give him up—to try to persuade him indeed to break it off. Since her first agitated letter to him begging him not to think of her, but to decide only what was best for his own future, she had received a few words from him.

'DEAREST BERYL—Nothing has happened to interfere with what we promised each other last summer—nothing at all! My poor father seems to be half out of his mind under the stress of war. If he does what he threatens, it will matter very little to me; but of course you must consider it carefully, for I shall have uncommonly little in the worldly way to offer you. Your father has written very kindly, and your dear little note is just like you. But you must consider.

'I sometimes doubt whether my father will do what he threatens, but we should have to take the risk. Anyway we shall meet directly, and I am always, and unalterably, your devoted

'AUBREY.'

That had been followed by a boyish note from Desmond—dear, jolly fellow!

'My father's clean daft! Don't bother, my dear Beryl. If he tries to leave me this funny old place, instead of Aubrey, well, there are two can play at that game. I wouldn't touch it with a barge-pole. You and A. have only got to stick it a little, and it'll be all right.

'I've given him a bit of my mind about the park and the farm. He stands it from me and only chaffs. That's because he always treats me like a baby.

'Very sorry I can't come on Tuesday with Aubrey, but there's some good-bye calls I must pay. Hope Arthur will be about. I want awfully to see him. Hard luck his being hit like that, after all the rest. Snipers are beasts!

'P.S.—You can't think what a brainy young woman father's got for his new secretary. And she's not half bad either. Pamela's rather silly about her, but she'll come round.'

Beryl paid small attention to the postscript. She had heard a good deal from Pamela about the newcomer, but it did not concern her. As to the business aspect of the Squire's behaviour, Beryl was well aware that she was an heiress. Aubrey would lose nothing financially by giving up the Mannering estate to marry her. Personally she cared nothing about Mannering, and she had enough for both. But still there was the old name and place. How much did he care about it? how much would he regret it? Supposing his extraordinary father really cut him off?

Beryl felt she did not know. And therewith came the recurrent pang—how little she really knew about the man to whom she was engaged! She adored him. Every fibre in her slight sensitive body still remembered the moment when he first kissed her, when she first felt his arm about her. But since—how often there had been moments when she had been conscious of a great distance between them—of something that did not fit—that jarred!

For herself, she could never remember a time since she was seventeen when Aubrey Mannering had not meant more to her than any one else in the world. On his first departure to France, she had said good-bye to him with secret agonies of spirit, which no one guessed but her mother, a colourless, silent woman, who had a way of knowing unexpectedly much of the people about her. Then when he was badly wounded in some fighting near Festubert, in May 1915, and came home for two months' leave, he seemed like a stranger, and Beryl had not known what to be at with him. She was told that he had suffered very much—it had been a severe thigh wound implicating the sciatic nerve—and that he had been once, at least, very near to death. But when she tried to express sympathy with what he had gone through, or timidly to question him about it, her courage fled, her voice died in her throat. There was something unapproachable in her old playfellow, something that held her, and indeed every one else, at bay.

He was always courteous, and mostly cheerful. But his face in repose had an absent, haunted look, the eyes alert but fixed on vacancy, the brow overcast and frowning. In the old days Aubrey's smile had been his best natural gift. To win a smile from him in her childhood, Beryl would have done anything—have gone on her knees up the drive, or offered up the only doll she cared for, or gone without jam for a week. Now when he came home invalided, she had the same craving; but what she craved for came her way very rarely. He would laugh and talk with her as with other people. But that exquisite brightness of eye and lip, which seemed to be for one person only, and, when it came, to lift that person to the seventh heaven, she waited for in vain.

Then he went back to France, and in due course came the Somme. Aubrey Mannering went through the whole five months without a scratch. He came back with a D.S.O. and a Staff appointment for a short Christmas leave, everybody, except his father, turning out to welcome him as the local hero. Then, for a time, he went to Aldershot as the head of an Officers' School there, and was able to come down occasionally to Chetworth or Mannering.

During that first Christmas leave he paid several visits to Chetworth, and evidently felt at home there. To Lady Chicksands, whom most people regarded as a tiresome nonentity, he was particularly kind and courteous. It seemed to give him positive pleasure to listen to her garrulous housekeeping talk, or to hold her wool for her while she wound it. And as she, poor lady, was not accustomed to such attention from brilliant young men, his three days' visit was to her a red-letter time. With Sir Henry also he was on excellent terms, and made just as good a listener to the details of country business as to Lady Chicksands' domestic tales.

And yet to Beryl he was in some ways more of a riddle than ever. He talked curiously little about the war—at least to her. He had a way of finding out, both at Chicksands and Mannering, men who had lost sons in France, and when he and Beryl took a walk, it seemed to Beryl as though they were constantly followed by friendly furtive looks from old labourers who passed them on the road, and nodded as they went by. But when the daily war news was being discussed he had a way of sitting quite silent, unless his opinion was definitely asked. When it was, he would answer, generally in a rather pessimistic spirit, and escape the conversation as soon as he could. And the one thing that roused him and put him out of temper was the easy complacent talk of people who were sure of speedy victory and talked of 'knock-out' blows.

Then six months later, after the capture of the Messines Ridge, in which he took part, he reappeared, and finding his father, apparently, almost intolerable, and Pamela and Desmond away, he migrated to Chetworth. And there he and Beryl were constantly thrown together. He never talked to her with much intimacy; he certainly never made love to her. But suddenly she became aware that she had grown very necessary to him, that he missed her when she was away, that his eyes lit up when she came back. A special relation was growing up between them. Her father perceived it; so did her brother Arthur; and they had both done their best to help it on. They were both very fond of Aubrey; and nothing could be more natural than that she should marry one who had been her neighbour and playmate from childhood.

The thing drifted on, and one day, in the depths of a summer beechwood, some look in the girl's eyes, some note of tremulous and passionate sweetness, beyond her control, in her deep quiet voice, touched something irrepressible in him, and he turned to her with a face of intense, almost hungry yearning, and caught her hands—'Dear—dearest Beryl, could you—?'

The words broke off, but her eyes spoke in reply to his, and her sudden whiteness. He drew her to him, and folded her close.

'I don't think I ought'—the faltering, broken voice startled her—'I don't know whether I can make you happy. Dear, dear little Beryl!'

At that she put up her mouth instinctively, only to shrink back under the energy of his kiss. Then they had walked on together, hand in hand; but she remembered that, even before they left the wood, something seemed to have dimmed the extraordinary bliss of the first moment—some restlessness in him—some touch of absent-mindedness, as though he grudged himself his own happiness.

And so it had been ever since. He had resumed his work at Aldershot, and owing to certain consequences of the wound in 1915 was not likely, in spite of desperate efforts on his own part, to be sent back to the front. His letters varied just as his presence did. Something always seemed to be kept back from her—was always beyond her reach. Sometimes she supposed she was not clever enough, that he found her inadequate and irresponsive. Sometimes, with a sudden, half-guilty sense of disloyalty to him, she vaguely wondered whether there was some secret in his life—some past of which she knew nothing. How could there be? A man of stainless and brilliant reputation—modest, able, foolhardily brave, of whom all men spoke warmly; of a sensitive refinement too, which made it impossible to think of any ordinary vulgar skeleton in the background of his life.

Yet her misgivings had grown and grown upon her, till now they were morbidly strong. She did not satisfy him; she was not making him happy; it would be better for her to set him free. This action of his father's offered the opportunity. But as she thought of doing it—how she would do it, and how he might possibly accept it—she was torn with misery.

She and her girl-friend Pamela were very different. She was the elder by a couple of years, and much more mature. But Pamela's undeveloped powers, the flashes of daring, of romance, in the awkward reserved girl, the suggestion in her of a big and splendid flowering, fascinated Beryl, and in her humility she never dreamt that she, with her delicate pensiveness, the mingled subtlety and purity of her nature, was no less exceptional. She had been brought up very much alone. Her mother was no companion for her, and the brother nearest her own age and nearest her heart had been killed at the opening of the war. Arthur and she were very good friends, but not altogether congenial. She was rather afraid of him—of his critical temper, and his abrupt intolerant way, with people or opinions he disliked. Beryl was quite aware of his effect on Pamela Mannering, and it made her anxious. For she saw little chance for Pamela. Before the war, Arthur in London had been very much sought after, in a world where women are generally good-looking, and skilled besides in all the arts of pursuit. His standards were ridiculously high. His women friends were many and of the best. Why should he be attracted by anything so young and immature as Pamela?

At last! A pony-cart coming up from the lodge, with two figures in it—Aubrey and Pamela. So poor Pam had at last got hold of something in the nature of an animal!

Beryl gripped the balustrading which bordered one side of the path, and stood watching intently—a slender creature, in a broad purple hat, shading her small, distinguished face.

Presently, as the visitors approached the house, she waved to them, and they to her. They disappeared from view for a minute. Then a man's figure emerged alone from a garden door opening on the flagged path.

He came towards her with outstretched hands, looked round him smiling to see that no one was in sight, and then kissed her. Beryl knew she ought to have resisted the kiss; she had meant to do it; but all the same she submitted.

'Your father met us at the door. Arthur has carried Pamela off somewhere. Very sporting of them, wasn't it? So I've got you alone! How nice you look! And what a jolly place this is!'

He first looked her up and down with admiring eyes, and then made a gesture towards the beautiful modern house, and the equally beautiful and modern gardens in which it stood, with their still unspoilt autumn flowers, their cunning devices in steps and fountains and pergolas.

'How on earth do you keep it so trim?' He put a hand through her arm, and drew her on towards the wood-walk which opened beyond the formal garden and the lawn.

'With two or three old men, and two girls from the village,' said Beryl. 'Father doesn't mind what he gives up so long as it isn't the garden.'

'It's his pet vice!' laughed Aubrey—'his public-house, like my father's Greek pots. I say— you've heard of the secretary?'

It seemed to Beryl that he was fencing with her—delaying their real talk. But she accepted his lead.

'Yes, Desmond seems to like her. I don't gather that Pamela cares very much about her.'

'Oh, Pamela takes time. But what do you think the secretary did last night?'

'What?' They had paused under a group of limes clad in a glory of yellow leaf, and she was looking up in surprise at the unusual animation playing over the features of the man beside her.

'She refused to sign a codicil to my father's will, disinheriting me, and came to tell me so this morning! You should have heard her! Very formal and ceremonious—very much on her dignity! But such a brick!'

Mannering's deep-set eyes under his lined thinker's brow shone with amusement. Beryl, with the instinctive jealousy of a girl in love, was conscious of a sudden annoyance that Miss Bremerton should have been mixed up in Aubrey's personal affairs.

'What do you mean?'

Aubrey put an arm round her shoulder. She knew she ought to shake it off, but the pressure of it was too welcome. They strolled on.

'I had my talk with father last night. I told him he was absurd, and I was my own master. That you were perfectly free to give me up—that I had begged you to consider it—but I didn't think you would,' he smiled down upon her, but more gravely; 'and failing dismissal from you, we should be married as soon as it was reasonably possible. Was that right, darling?'

She evaded the question.

'Well—and then?'

'Then he broke out. Sir Henry of course was the bête noire. You can imagine the kind of things he said, I needn't repeat them. He is in a mood of perfectly mad opposition to all this war legislation, and it is not the least good arguing with him. Finally he told me that my allowance would be stopped, and Mannering would be left to Desmond, if we married. "All right!" I said, "I daresay, if he and I survive you, Desmond will let me look round sometimes." Not very respectful, perhaps, but by that time I was fed up. So then I wished him good-night, and went back to the drawing-room. In a few minutes he sent for Miss Bremerton—nobody knew why. I was dog-tired, and went to bed, and didn't I sleep!—nine good hours. Then this morning, just after breakfast, when I was strolling in the garden with a cigarette waiting for Pamela, who should come out but Miss Bremerton! Have you seen her?'

'Only in the distance.'

'Well, she's really a very fine creature, not pretty exactly—oh, not pretty at all—but wonderfully well set up, with beautiful hair, and a general look of—what shall I say?—dignity, refinement, knowing her own mind. You feel she would set you down in a moment if you took the smallest liberty. I could not think what she wanted. But she came up to me—of course we had made acquaintance the night before—"May I speak to you, Major Mannering? I wish to say something private. Shall we walk down to the kitchen garden?" So we walked down to the kitchen garden, and then she told me what had happened after dinner, when my father sent for her. She told it very stiffly, rather curtly in fact, as though she were annoyed to have to bother about such unprofessional things, and hated to waste her time. "But I don't wish, I don't intend," she said, "to have the smallest responsibility in the matter. So after thinking it over, I decided to inform you—and Mr. Desmond too, if you will kindly tell him—as to what I had done. That is all I have to say," with her chin very much in the air! "I did it, of course, because I did not care to be mixed up in any private or family affairs. That is not my business." I was taken aback, as you can imagine! But, of course, I thanked her—'

'Why, she couldn't have done anything else!' said Beryl with vivacity.

'I don't know that. Anybody may witness anything. But she seems to have guessed. Of course my father never keeps anything to himself. Anyway she didn't like being thanked at all. She turned back to the house at once. So then I asked her if she knew what had happened to the precious codicil. And she flushed up and said, with the manner of an icicle, "Mr. Mannering sent me to the drawer this morning, where he had put it away. It was lying on the top, and I saw it." "Signed?" I said. "No, not signed." Then she began to hurry, and I thought I had offended her in some way. But it dawned upon me, presently, that she was really torn between her feeling of chivalry towards me—she seems to have a kindness for soldiers! her brother is fighting somewhere—and her professional obligations towards my father. Wasn't it odd? She hated to be indiscreet, to give him away, and yet she could not help it! I believe she had been awake half the night. Her eyes looked like it. I must say I liked her very much. A woman of a great deal of character! I expect she has a rough time of it!'

'But of course,' said Beryl, 'it may be all signed and witnessed by now!'

'Most probably!' The Major laughed. 'But she did her best anyway, and I shan't ask her any more questions. We had better take it for granted. My father is as obstinate as they make 'em. Well now, dear Beryl, have you—have you thought it over?'

He pointed to a seat, and sat down by her. The brightness of his look had passed away. The thin, intellectual face and lined brow had resumed the expression that was familiar to Beryl. It was an expression of fatigue—not physical now, for he had clearly recovered his health, but moral; as though the man behind it were worn out by some hidden debate with his own mind, into which he fell perpetually, when left to himself. It was the look which divided him from her.

'Yes,' she said slowly, 'I've been thinking a great deal.' She stopped; then lifting her eyes, which were grey and fringed with dark lashes—beautiful eyes, timid yet passionately honest—she said, 'You'd better give me up, Aubrey!'

He made a restless movement, then took her hands and raised them to his lips.

'I don't feel like it!' he said, smiling. 'Tell me what you mean.'

She looked down, plucking at the fringed belt of her sports coat. Her lips trembled a little.

'I don't think, Aubrey, I can make you happy! I've been feeling often—that I don't seem to make much difference to you. And now this is very serious—giving up Mannering. You may mind it much more than you think. And if—'

'If what? Go on!'

She raised her eyes again and looked at him straight.

'If I can't make up?'

The colour flooded into his face, as though, far within, something stirred 'like a guilty thing surprised.' But he said tenderly:

'I don't care that, Beryl'—he snapped his fingers—'for Mannering in comparison with you.'

Her breath fluttered a little, but she went on resolutely. 'But I must say it—I must tell you what I feel. It seems the right opportunity. So often, Aubrey, I don't seem to understand you! I say the wrong thing. I'm not clever. I haven't any deep thoughts—like you or Arthur. It would be terrible if you married me, and then—I felt you were disappointed.'

He moved a little away from her and, propping his chin on his hands, looked gravely through the thinning branches of the wood.

'I wonder why you say that—I wonder what I've done!'

'Oh, you've done nothing!' cried Beryl. 'It's only I feel—sometimes—that—that you don't let me know things—share things. You seem sometimes so sad—and I can't be any help—you won't let me! That's what I mind so much—so dreadfully!'

He was silent a moment. Then without any attempt at caresses, he said, 'I wonder, Beryl, whether you—whether you—ever realize—what we soldiers have seen? No!—thank God!—you don't—you can't.'

She pressed her hands to her eyes, and shuddered.

'No, of course I can't—of course I can't!' she said passionately.

Then, while her eyes were still hidden, there passed through his worn features a sharp spasm, as of some uncontrollable anguish—passed and was gone.

He turned towards her, and she looked up. If ever love, all-giving, self-forgetting, was written on a girl's face, it was written on Beryl's then. Her wild-rose colour came and went; her eyes were full of tears. She had honestly made her attempt, but she could not carry it through, and he saw it. Some vague hope—of which he was ashamed—died away. Profoundly touched, he put out his arms, and making nothing of her slight resistance, gathered her close to him.

'Did you ever read Sintram, Beryl?'

'Yes, years ago.'

'Do you remember his black fits—how they came upon him unexpectedly—and only Verena could help him? It's like that with me sometimes. Things I've seen—horrible sufferings and death—come back on me. I can't get over it—at least not yet. But I'll never let it come really between us. And perhaps—some day'—he hesitated and his voice dropped—'you shall help me—like Verena!'

She clung to him, not knowing what he meant, but fascinated by his deep voice, and the warm shelter of his arms. He bent down to kiss her, in the most passionate embrace he had ever given her.

Then he released her, and they both looked at each other with a new shyness.

'So that's all right!' he said, smiling. 'You see you can't drop me as easily as you think. I stick! Well, now, you take me as a pauper—not exactly a pauper—but still—I've got to settle things with your father, though!'

Beryl proposed that they should go and look for the others.

They went hand in hand.

Sir Henry meanwhile was engaged in the congenial occupation of inspecting and showing his kitchen gardens. His son Arthur and Pamela Mannering were following him round the greenhouses, finding more amusement in the perplexities of Sir Henry's conscience than interest in the show itself.

'You see they've brought in the chrysanthemums. Just in time! There was a frost last night,' said Sir Henry, throwing open a door, and disclosing a greenhouse packed with chrysanthemums in bud.

'My hat—what a show!' said his son.

'Not at all, Arthur, not at all,' said his father, annoyed. 'Not a third of what we had last year.'

Arthur raised his eyebrows, and behind his father's back he and Pamela exchanged smiles. The next house showed a couple of elderly men at work pruning roses intended to flower in February and March.

'This is almost my favourite house,' exclaimed Sir Henry. 'Such a wonderful result for so little labour!' He strolled on complacently.

'How long does this take you, Grimes?' Arthur inquired discreetly of one of the gardeners.

'Oh, a good while, Mr. Arthur—what with the pruning, and the syringing, and the manuring,' said the man addressed, stopping to wipe his brow, for the day was mild.

Arthur's look darkened a little. He fell into a reverie, while Pamela was conscious at every step of his tall commanding presence, of the Military Cross on his khaki breast, and the pleasant, penetrating eyes under his staff cap. Arthur, she thought, must be now over thirty. Before his recent wound he had been doing some special artillery work on the Staff of an Army Corps, and was a very rising soldier. He was now chafing hotly against the ruling of his Medical Board, who were insisting that he was not yet fit to go back to France.

Pamela meanwhile was going through moments of disillusion. After these two years she had looked forward to the meeting with such eagerness, such hidden emotion! And now—what was there to have been eager about? They seemed to be talking almost as strangers. The soreness of it bewildered her.

Presently, as they were walking back to the house, leaving Sir Henry in anxious consultation over the mushroom-house with the grey-haired head gardener, her companion turned to her abruptly.

'I suppose that's all right!' He pointed to some distant figures on the fringe of a wood.

'Beryl and Aubrey? Yes—if Aubrey can make her see that she isn't doing him any harm by letting him go on.'

'Good heavens! how could she do him any harm?'

'Well, there's Mannering. As if that mattered!' said the girl scornfully. 'And then—Beryl's too dreadfully humble!'

'Humble! About what? No girl ought to be humble—ever!'

Pamela's eyes recovered their natural brilliance under his peremptory look. And he, who had begun the walk with no particular consciousness at all about his companion, except that she was a nice, good-looking child, whom he had known from a baby, with equal suddenness became aware of her in a new way.

'Why shouldn't we be humble, please?' she said, with a laugh.

'Because it's monstrous that you should. Leave that to us!'

'There wouldn't be much of it about, if we did!' The red danced in her cheek.

'Much humility? Oh, you're quite mistaken. Men are much more humble than you think. But we're human, of course. If you tempt us, you soon put the starch into us.'

'Well, you must starch Beryl!' said Pamela, with emphasis. 'She will think and say that she's not worthy of Aubrey, that she knows she'll disappoint him, that she wouldn't mind his giving up Mannering if only she were sure she could make him happy—and heaps of things like that! I'm sure she's saying them now!'

'I never heard such nonsense in my life!' The masculine face beside her was all impatience. 'One can't exactly boast about one's sister, but you and I know very well what Beryl is worth!'

Pamela agreed fervently. 'Besides, Desmond would give it back.'

'Hm—' her companion demurred. 'Giving back isn't always easy. As to pounds, shillings, and pence, if one must talk of them, it's lucky that Beryl has her "bit." But I shouldn't wonder if your father thought better of it after all.'

Pamela flushed indignantly.

'He all but signed a codicil to his will last night! He's in a tearing hurry about it. He called in Miss Bremerton and wanted her to witness it. And she refused. So father threw it into a drawer, and nobody knows what has happened.'

'Miss Bremerton? The new secretary?' The tone expressed both amusement and curiosity. 'Ah! I hear all sorts of interesting things about her.'

Pamela straightened her shoulders defiantly.

'Of course she's interesting. She's terribly clever and up to date, and all the rest of it. She's beginning to boss father, and very soon she'll boss all the rest of us.'

'Perhaps you wanted it!' said Captain Chicksands, smiling.

'Perhaps we did,' Pamela admitted. 'But one needn't like it all the same. Well, she's rationed us—that's one good thing—and father really doesn't guess! And now she's begun to take an interest in the farms! I believe she's walked over to the Holme Wood farm to-day, to see for herself what state it's in. Father's in town. And she's trying hard to keep father out of a horrible row with the County Committee.'

'About ploughing up the park?'

Pamela nodded.

'Plucky woman!' said Arthur Chicksands heartily. 'I'm sure you help her, Pamela, all you can?'

'I don't like being managed,' said the girl stubbornly, rather resenting his tone.

A slight shade of sternness crossed the soldier's face.

'You know it's no good playing with this war,' he said drily. 'It's as much to be won here as it is over seas. Food!—that'll be the last word for everybody. And it's women's work as much as men's.'

She saw that she had jarred on him. But an odd jealousy—or perhaps her hidden disappointment—drove her on.

'Yes, but one doesn't like strangers interfering,' she said childishly.

The soldier threw her a side-glance, while his lip twitched a little. So this was Pamela—grown-up. She seemed to him rather foolish—and very lovely. There was no doubt about that! She was going to be a beauty, and of a remarkable type. He himself was a strong, high-minded, capable fellow, with an instinctive interest in women, and a natural aptitude for making friends with them. He was inclined, always, to try and set them in the right way; to help them to some of the mental training which men got in a hundred ways, and women, as it seemed to him, were often so deplorably without. But this schoolmaster function only attracted him when there was opposition. He had been quite sincere in denouncing humility in women. It never failed to warn him off.

'Do you think she really wants to interfere?' he asked, smiling. 'I expect it's only that she's got a bit of an organizing gift—like the women who have been doing such fine things in the war.'

'There's no chance for me to do fine things in the war,' said Pamela bitterly.

'Take up the land, and see! Suppose you and Miss Bremerton could pull the estate together!'

Pamela's eyes scoffed.

'Father would never let me. No, I think sometimes I shall run away!'

He lifted his eyebrows, and she was annoyed with him for taking her remark as mere bluff.

'You'll see,' she insisted. 'I shall do something desperate.'

'I wouldn't,' he said, quietly. 'Make friends with Miss Bremerton and help her.'

'I don't like her enough,' she said, drawing quick breath.

He saw now she was in a mood to quarrel with him outright. But he didn't mean to let her. With those eyes—in such a fire—she was really splendid. How she had come on!

'I'm sorry,' he said mildly. 'Because, you know—if you don't mind my saying so—it'll really take the two of you to keep your father out of gaol. The Government's absolutely determined about this thing—they can't afford to be anything else. We're being hammered, and gassed, and blown to pieces over there'—he pointed eastward. 'It's the least the people over here can do—to play up—isn't it?' Then he laughed. 'But I mustn't be setting you against your father. I didn't mean to.'

Pamela shrugged her shoulders, in silence. She really longed to ask him about his wound, his staff work, a thousand things; but they didn't seem, somehow, to be intimate enough, to be hitting it off enough. This meeting, which had been to her a point of romance in the distance, was turning out to be just nothing—only disappointment. She was glad to see how quickly the other pair were coming towards them, and at the same time bitterly vexed that her tête-à-tête with Arthur was at an end.

CHAPTER VI

Meanwhile Elizabeth Bremerton was sitting pensive on a hill-side about mid-way between Mannering and Chetworth. She had a bunch of autumn berries in her hands. Her tweed skirt and country boots showed traces of mud much deeper than anything on the high road; her dress was covered with bits of bramble, dead leaves, and thistledown; and her bright gold hair had been pulled here and there out of its neat coils, as though she had been pushing through hedges or groping through woods.

'It's perfectly monstrous!' she was thinking. 'It oughtn't to be allowed. And when we're properly civilized, it won't be allowed. No one ought to be free to ruin his land as he pleases! It concerns the State. "Manage your land decently—produce a proper amount of food—or out you go!" And I wouldn't have waited for war to say it! Ugh! that place!'

And she thought with disgust of the choked and derelict fields, the ruined gates and fences, the deserted buildings she had just been wandering through. After the death of an old miser, who, according to the tale she had heard in a neighbouring village, had lived there for forty years, with a decrepit wife, both of them horribly neglected and dirty, and making latterly no attempt to work the farm, a new tenant had appeared who would have taken the place, if the Squire would have rebuilt the house and steadings, and allowed a reasonable sum for the cleansing and recovering of the land. But the Squire would do nothing of the kind. He 'hadn't a farthing to spend on expensive repairs,' and if the new tenant wouldn't take the farm on the old terms, well, he might leave it alone.

The place had just been investigated by the County Committee, and a peremptory order had been issued. What was the Squire going to do?

Elizabeth fell to thinking what ought to be done with the Squire's twelve thousand acres, if the Squire were a reasonable man. It was exasperating to her practical sense to see a piece of business in such a muddle. As a child and growing girl she had spent long summers in the country with a Dorsetshire uncle who farmed his own land, and there had sprung up in her an instinctive sympathy with the rich old earth and its kindly powers, with the animals and the crops, with the labourers and their rural arts, with all the interwoven country life, and its deep rooting in the soil of history and poetry.

Country life is, above all, steeped in common sense—the old, ancestral, simple wisdom of primitive men. And Elizabeth, in spite of her classical degree, and her passion for Greek pots, believed herself to be, before everything, a person of common sense. She had always managed her own family's affairs. She had also been the paid secretary of an important learned society in her twenties not long after she left college, and knew well that she had been a conspicuous success. She had a great love, indeed, for any sort of organizing, large and small, for putting things straight, and running them. She was burning to put Mannering straight—and run it. She knew she could. Organizing means not doing things yourself, but finding the right people to do them. And she had always been good at finding the right people—putting the round pegs into the round holes.

All very well, however, to talk of running the Squire's estate! What was to be done with the Squire?

Take the codicil business. First thing that morning he had sent her to that very drawer to look for something, and there lay the precious document—unsigned and unwitnessed—for any one to see. He made no comment, nor of course did she. He would probably forget it till the date of his son's marriage was announced, and then complete it in a hurry.

Take the farms and the park. As to the farms there were two summonses now pending against him with regard to 'farms in hand'—Holme Wood and another—besides the action in the case of the three incompetent men, Gregson at their head, who were being turned out. With regard to ploughing up the park, all his attempts so far to put legal difficulties in the way of the County Committee had been quite futile. The steam plough was coming in a week. Meanwhile the gates were to be locked, and two old park-keepers, who were dithering in their shoes, had been told to defend them.

At bottom, Elizabeth was tolerably convinced that the Squire would not land himself in gaol, cut off from his books and his bronzes, and reduced to the company of people who had never heard of Pausanias. But she was alarmed lest he should 'try it on' a little too far, in these days when the needs of war and the revolutionary currents abroad make the setting down of squires especially agreeable to the plebeians who sit on juries or county committees. Of course he must—he certainly would—climb down.

But somebody would have to go through the process of persuading him! That was due to his silly dignity! She supposed that somebody would be herself. How absurd! She, who had just been six weeks on the scene! But neither of the married daughters had the smallest influence with him; Sir Henry Chicksands had been sent about his business; Major Mannering was out of favour, and Desmond and Pamela were but babes.

Then a recollection flashed across the contriving mind of Elizabeth which brought a decided flush to her fair skin—a flush which was half amusement, half wrath. That morning a rather curious incident had happened. After her talk with Major Mannering, and because the morning was fine and the Squire was away, she had dragged a small table out into the garden, in front of the library, and set to work there on a part of the new catalogue of the collections, which she and Mr. Levasseur were making. She did not, however, like Mr. Levasseur. Something in her, indeed, disapproved of him strongly. She had already managed to dislodge him a good deal from his former intimacy with the Squire. Luckily she was a much better scholar than he, though she admitted that his artistic judgment was worth having.

As a shelter from a rather cold north wind, she was sitting in full sun under the protection of a yew hedge of ancient growth, which ran out at right angles to the library, and made one side of a quadrangular rose-garden, planted by Mrs. Mannering long ago, and now, like everything else, in confusion and neglect.

Presently she heard voices on the other side of the hedge—Mrs. Strang, no doubt, and Mrs. Gaddesden. She did not take much to either lady. Mrs. Strang seemed to her full of good intentions, but without practical ability to fit them. For Mrs. Gaddesden's type she had an instinctive contempt, the contempt of the clever woman of small means who has had to earn her own living, and to watch in silence the poses and pretences of rich women playing at philanthropy. But, all the same, she and the servants between them had made Mrs. Gaddesden extremely comfortable, while at the same time rationing her strictly. 'I really can be civil to anybody!' thought Elizabeth complacently.

Suddenly, her own name, and a rush of remarks on the other side of this impenetrable hedge, made her raise her head, startled, from her work, eyes and mouth wide open.

It was Mrs. Gaddesden speaking.

'Yes, she's gone out. I went into the library just now to ask her to look out a train for me. She's wonderfully good at Bradshaw. Oh, of course, I admit she's a very clever woman! But she wasn't there. Forest thinks she's gone over to Holme Wood, to get father some information he wants. She asked Forest how to get this this morning. My dear Margaret,' with great emphasis, 'there's no question about it! If she chooses, she'll be mistress here before long. She's steadily getting father into her hands. She was never engaged, was she, to look after accounts and farms? and yet here she is, taking everything on. He'll grow more and more dependent upon her, and you'll see!—I believe he's been inclined for some time to marry again. He wants somebody to look after Pamela, and set him free for his hobbies. He'll very soon find out that this woman fills the part, and that, if he marries her, he'll get a classical secretary besides.'

Mrs. Strang's voice—a deep husky voice—interposed.

'Miss Bremerton's not a woman to be married against her will, that you may be sure of, Alice.'

'No, but, my dear,' said the other impatiently, 'every woman over thirty wants a home—and a husband. She'd get that here anyway, however bad father's affairs may be. And, of course, a position.'

The voices passed on out of hearing. Elizabeth remained transfixed. Then with a contemptuous shake of the head, and a bright colour, she returned to her work.

But now, as she sat meditating on the hill-side, this absurd conversation recurred to her. Absurd, and not absurd! 'Most women of my sort can do what they have a mind to do,' she thought to herself, with perfect sang-froid. 'If I thought it worth while to marry this elderly lunatic—he's an interesting lunatic, though!—I suppose I could do it. But it isn't worth while—not the least. I've done with being a woman! What interests me is the bit of work—national work! Men find that kind of thing enough—a great many of them. I mean to find it enough. A fig for marrying!'

All the same, as she returned to her schemes both for regenerating the estate and managing the Squire—schemes which were beginning to fascinate her, both by their difficulty and their scale—she found her thoughts oddly interfered with, first by recollections of the past—bitter, ineffaceable memories—and then by reflections on the recent course of her relations with the Squire.

He had greeted her that morning without a single reference to the incidents of the night before, had seemed in excellent spirits, and before going up to town had given her in twenty minutes, à propos of some difficulty in her work, one of the most brilliant lectures on certain points of

Homeric archaeology she had ever heard—and she was a connoisseur in lectures.

Intellectually, as a scholar, she both admired and looked upon him—with reverence, even with enthusiasm. She was eager for his praise, distressed by his censure. Practically and morally, patriotically, above all, she despised him, thought him 'a worm and no man'! There was the paradox of the situation and as full of tingling challenge and entertainment as paradoxes generally are.

At this point she became aware of a group on the high road far to her right. A pony-cart—a girl driving it—a man in khaki beside her; with a second girl-figure and another khaki-clad warrior, walking near.

She presently thought she recognized Pamela's pony and Pamela herself. Desmond, who was going off that very evening to his artillery camp, had told her that 'Pam' was driving Aubrey over to Chetworth, and that he, Desmond, was 'jolly well going to see to it that neither old Aubrey nor Beryl were bullied out of their lives by father,' if he could help it. So no doubt the second girl-figure was that of Beryl Chicksands, and the other gentleman in khaki was probably Captain Chicksands, for whom Desmond seemed to cherish a boyish hero-worship. They had been all lunching together at Chetworth, she supposed.

She watched them coming, with a curious mingling of interest in them and detachment from them. She was to them merely the Squire's paid secretary. Were they anything to her? A puckish thought crossed her mind, sending a flash of slightly cynical laughter through her quiet eyes. If Mrs. Gaddesden's terrors—for she supposed they were terrors—were suddenly translated into fact, why, all these people would become in a moment related to her!—their lives would be mixed up with hers—she and they would matter intimately to each other!

She sat smiling and dreaming a few more minutes, the dimples playing about her firm mouth and chin. Then, as the sound of wheels drew nearer, she rose and went towards the party.

The party from Chetworth soon perceived Elizabeth's approach. 'So this is the learned lady?' said the Captain in Pamela's ear. She had brought him in her pony-carriage so far, as he was not yet able for much physical exertion, and he and Beryl were to walk back from Holme Wood Hill.

He put up his eye-glass, and examined the figure as it came nearer.

'She's just come up, I suppose, from the farm,' said Pamela, pointing to some red roofs among the trees, in the wide hollow below the hill.

'"Athêne Ageleiê"!' murmured the Major, who had been proxime for the Ireland, and a Balliol man. 'She holds herself well—beautiful hair!'

'Beryl, this is Miss Bremerton,' said Aubrey Mannering, with a cordial ring in his voice, as he introduced his fiancée to Elizabeth. The two shook hands, and Elizabeth thought the girl's manner a little stand-off, and wondered why.

The pony had soon been tied up, and the party spread themselves on the grass of the hill-side; for Holme Wood Hill was a famous point of view, and the sunny peace of the afternoon invited loitering. For miles to the eastward spread an undulating chalk plain, its pale grey or purplish soil showing in the arable fields where the stubbles were just in process of ploughing, its monotony broken by a vast wood of oak and beech into which the hill-side ran down—a wood of historic fame, which had been there when Senlac was fought, had furnished ship-timber for the Armada, and sheltered many a cavalier fugitive of the Civil Wars.

The wood indeed, which belonged to the Squire, was a fragment of things primeval. For generations the trees in it had sprung up, flourished, and fallen as they pleased. There were corners of it where the north-west wind sweeping over the bare down above it had made pathways of death and ruin; sinister places where the fallen or broken trunks of the great beech trees, as they had crashed down-hill upon and against each other, had assumed all sorts of grotesque and phantasmal attitudes, as in a trampled mêlée of giants; there were other parts where slender plumed trees, rising branchless to a great height above open spaces, took the shape from a distance of Italian stone palms, and gave a touch of southern or romantic grace to the English midland scene; while at their feet, the tops of the more crowded sections of the wood lay in close, billowy masses of leaf, the oaks vividly green, the beeches already aflame.

'Who says there's a war?' said Captain Chicksands, sinking luxuriously into a sunny bed of dry leaves, conveniently placed in front of Elizabeth. 'Miss Bremerton, you and I were, I understand, at the same University?'

Elizabeth assented.

'Is it your opinion that Universities are any good?—that after the war there are going to be any Universities?'

'Only those that please the Labour Party!' put in Mannering.

'Oh, I'm not afraid of the Labour Party—awfully good fellows, many of them. The sooner they make a Government the better. They've got to learn their lessons like the rest of us. But I do want to know whether Miss Bremerton thinks Oxford was any use—before the war—and is going to be any use after the war? It's all right now, of course, for the moment, with the Colleges full of cadets and wounded men. But would you put the old Oxford back if you could?'

He lay on his elbows looking up at her. Elizabeth's eyes sparkled a little. She realized that an able man was experimenting on her, putting her through her paces. She asked what he meant by 'the old Oxford,' and an amusing dialogue sprang up between them as to their respective recollections of the great University—the dons, the lectures, the games, the Eights, 'Commem.' and the like. The Captain presently declared that Elizabeth had had a much nicer Oxford than he, and he wished he had been a female student.

'Didn't you—didn't you,' he said, his keen eyes observing her, 'get a prize once that somebody had given to the Women's Colleges for some Greek iambics?'

'Oh,' cried Elizabeth, 'how did you hear of that?'

'I was rather a dab at them myself,' he said lazily, drawing his hat over his eyes as he lay in the sun, 'and I perfectly remember hearing of a young lady—yes, I believe it was you!—whose translation of Browning's "Lost Leader" into Greek iambics was better than mine. They set it in the Ireland. You admit it? Capital! As to the superiority of yours, I was, of course, entirely sceptical, though polite. Remind me, how did you translate "Just for a ribbon to put on his coat"?'

With a laughing mouth, Elizabeth at once quoted the Greek.

The Captain made a wry face.

'It sounds plausible, I agree,' he said slowly, 'but I don't believe a Greek would have understood a word of it. You remember that in the dim Victorian ages, when one great Latin scholar gave, as he thought, the neatest possible translation of "The path of glory leads but to the grave," another great Latin scholar declared that all a Roman could have understood by it would have been "The path of a public office leads to the jaws of the hillock"?'

The old Oxford joke was new in the ears of this Georgian generation, and when the laugh subsided, Elizabeth said mildly:

'Now, please, may I have yours?'

'What—my translation? Oh—horribly unfair!' said the Captain, chewing a piece of grass. 'However, here it is!'

He gave it out—with unction.

Elizabeth fell upon it in a flash, dissected and quarrelled with every word of it, turned it inside out in fact, while the Captain, still chewing, followed her with eyes of growing enjoyment.

'Well, I'll take a vote when I get back to the front,' he said, when she came to an end. 'Several firsts in Mods on our staff. I'll send you the result.'

The talk dropped. The mention of the front reminded every one of the war, and its bearing on their own personal lot. Desmond was going into camp that evening. In a few months he would be a full-blown gunner at the front. Beryl, watching Aubrey's thin face and nervous frown, proved inwardly that the Aldershot appointment might go on. And Elizabeth's thoughts had flown to her brother in Mesopotamia.

Pamela, sitting apart, and deeply shaded by a great beech with drooping branches that rose behind the group, was sharply unhappy, and filled with a burning jealousy of Elizabeth, who queened it there in the middle of them—so self-possessed, agreeable, and competent. How well Arthur had been getting on with her! What a tiresome, tactless idiot she, Pamela, must seem in comparison! The memory of her talk with him made her cheeks hot. So few chances of seeing him!—and when they came, she threw them away. She felt for the moment as though she hated Elizabeth. Why had her father saddled her upon them? Life was difficult enough before. Passionately she began to think of her threat to Arthur. It had been the merest 'idle word.' But why shouldn't she realize it—why not 'run away'? There was work to be done, and money to be earned, by any able-bodied girl. And perhaps then, when she was on her own, and had proved that she was not a child any longer, Arthur would respect her more, take more interest in her.

'What do you prophesy?' said Elizabeth suddenly, addressing Arthur Chicksands, who seemed to be asleep in the grass. 'Will it end—by next summer?'

'What, the war?' he said, waking up. 'Oh dear, no. Next year will be the worst of any—the test of us all—especially of you civilians at home. If we stick it, we shall save ourselves and the world. If we don't—'

He shrugged his shoulders. His voice was full and deep. It thrilled the girl sitting in the shade—partly with fear. In three weeks or so, the speaker would be back in the full inferno of the front, and because of her father's behaviour she would probably not be able to see him in the interval. Perhaps she might never see him again. Perhaps this was the last time. And he would go away without giving her a thought. Whereas, if she had played her cards differently, this one last day, he might at least have asked her to write to him. Many men did—even with girls they hardly knew at all.

Just then she noticed a movement of Beryl's, and saw her friend's small bare hand creep out and slip itself into Aubrey Mannering's, as he sat beside her on the grass. The man's hand enfolded the girl's—he turned round to smile at her in silence. A pang of passionate envy swept through Pamela. It was just so she wished to be enfolded—to be loved.

It was Elizabeth—as the person who had business to do and hours to keep—who gave the signal for the break-up of the party. She sprang to her feet, with a light, decided movement, and all the others fell into line. Arthur and Beryl still accompanied the Mannering contingent a short distance, the Captain walking beside Elizabeth in animated conversation. At last Beryl peremptorily recalled him to the pony-carriage, and the group halted for good-byes.

Pamela stood rather stiffly apart. The Captain went up to her.

'Good-bye, Pamela. Do write to me sometimes! I shall be awfully interested about the farms!'

With vexation she felt the colour rush to her cheeks.

'I shan't have much to say about them,' she said stiffly.

'I'm sure you will! You'll get keen! But write about anything. It's awfully jolly to get letters at the front!'

His friendly, interrogating eyes were on her, as though she puzzled him in this new phase, and he wanted to understand her. She said hurriedly, 'If you like,' hating herself for the coolness in her voice, and shook hands, only to hear him say, as he turned finally to Elizabeth, 'Mind, you have promised me "The Battle of the Plough"! I'm afraid you'll hardly have time to put it into iambics!'

So he had asked Miss Bremerton to write to him too! Pamela vowed inwardly that in that case she would not write him a line. And it seemed to her unseemly that her father's secretary should be making mock of her father's proceedings with a man who was a complete stranger to her. She walked impetuously ahead of Aubrey and Elizabeth. Towards the west the beautiful day was dying, and the light streamed on the girl's lithe young figure and caught her golden-brown hair. Clouds of gnats rose in the mild air; and a light seemed to come back from the bronzed and purple hedgerows, making a gorgeous atmosphere, in which the quiet hill-top and the thinning trees swam transfigured. A green woodpecker was pecking industriously among some hedgerow oaks, and Pamela, who loved birds and watched them, caught every now and then the glitter of his flight. The world was dropping towards sleep. But she was burningly awake and alive. Had she ever been really alive before?

Then—suddenly she remembered Desmond. He was to be home from some farewell visits between five and six. She would be late; he might want her for a hundred things. His last evening! Her heart smote her. They had reached the park gates. Waving her hand to the two behind, with the one word 'Desmond!' she began to run, and was soon out of their sight.

Elizabeth and Aubrey were not long behind her. They found the house indeed pervaded with Desmond, and Desmond's going. Aubrey also was going up to town, but of him nobody took any notice. Pamela and Forest were in attendance on the young warrior, who was himself in the wildest spirits, shouting and whistling up and downstairs, singing the newest and most shocking of camp songs, chaffing Forest, and looking with mischievous eyes at the various knitted 'comforts' to which his married sisters were hastily putting the last stitches.

'I say, Pam—do you see me in mittens?' he said to her in the hall, thrusting out his two splendid hands with a grin. 'And as for that jersey of Alice's—why, I should stew to death in it. Oh, I know—I can give it to my batman. The fellows tell me you can always get rid of things to your batman. It's like sending your wedding-presents to the pawn-shop. But where is father?' The boy looked discontentedly at his watch. 'He vowed he'd be here by five. I must be off by a few minutes after eight.'

'The train's late. He'll be here directly,' said Pamela confidently; 'and I say—don't you hurt Alice's feelings, old man.'

'Don't you preach, Pam!' said the boy, laughing. And a few minutes afterwards Pamela, passing the open door of the drawing-room, heard him handsomely thanking his elder sisters. He ran into her as he emerged with his arms full of scarves, mittens, and the famous jersey which had taken Alice Gaddesden a year to knit.

'Stuff 'em in somewhere, Pam!' he said in her ear. 'They can go up to London anyway.' And having shovelled them all off on to her, he raced along the passage to the library in search of Elizabeth.

'I say, Miss Bremerton, I want a book or two.'

Elizabeth looked up smiling from her table. She was already of the same mind as everybody outside and inside Mannering—that Desmond did you a kindness when he asked you to do him one.

'What kind of a book?'

'Oh, I've got some novels, and some Nat Goulds, and Pamela's given me some war-books. Don't know if I shall read 'em!—Well, I'd like a small Horace, if you can find one. "My tutor" was an awfully good hand at Horace. He really did make me like the old chap! And have you got such a thing as a Greek Anthology that wouldn't take up much room?'

Elizabeth went to the shelves to look. Desmond as the possessor of literary tastes was a novelty to her. But, after all, she understood that he had been a half in the Sixth at Eton, before his cadet training began. She found him two small pocket editions, and the boy thanked her gratefully. He began to turn over the Anthology, as though searching for something.

'Can I help you to find anything?' she asked him.

'No—it's something I remember,' he said absently, and presently hit upon it, with a look of pleasure.

'They did know a thing or two, didn't they? That's fine anyway?' He handed her the book. 'But I forget some of the words. Do you mind giving me a construe?' he said humbly.

Elizabeth translated, feeling rather choky.

'"On the Spartans at Thermopylæ.

'"Him—"'

'That's Xerxes, of course,' put in Desmond.

'"Him, who changed the paths of earth and sea, who sailed upon the mainland, and walked upon the deep—him did Spartan valour hold back, with just three hundred spears. Shame on you, mountains and seas!"'

'Well, that's all right, isn't it?' said the boy simply, looking up. 'Couldn't put it better if you tried, could you?' Then he said, hesitating a little as he turned down the leaf, and put the book in his pocket, 'Five of the fellows who were in the Sixth with me this time last year are dead by now. It makes you think a bit, doesn't it?—Hullo, there is father!'

He turned joyously, his young figure finely caught in the light of Elizabeth's lamp against the background of the Nikê.

'Well, father you have been a time! I thought you'd forgotten altogether I was off to-night.'

'The train was abominably late. Travelling is becoming a perfect nuisance! I gave the station-master a piece of my mind,' said the Squire angrily.

'And I expect he said that you civilians jolly well have to wait for the munition trains!'

'He muttered some nonsense of that sort. I didn't listen to him.' The Squire threw himself down in an arm-chair. Desmond perched on the corner of a table near. Elizabeth discreetly took up her work and disappeared.

'How much time have you got?' asked the Squire abruptly.

'Oh, a few minutes. Aubrey and I are to have some supper before I go. But Forest'll come and tell me.'

'Everything ready? Got money enough?'

'Rather! I shan't want anything for an age. Why, I shall be buying war-loan out of my pay!'

He laughed happily. Then his face grew suddenly serious.

'Look here, father—I want awfully to say something. Do you mind?'

'If you want to say it, I suppose you will say it.'

The Squire was sitting hunched up, looking old and tired, his thick white hair piled fantastically above his eyes.

Desmond straightened his shoulders with the air of one going over the parapet.

'Well, it's this, father. I do wish you'd give up that row about the park!'

The Squire sat up impatiently.

'That's not your business, Desmond. It can't matter to you.'

'Yes, but it does matter to me!' said the boy with energy. 'It'll be in all the papers—the fellows will gas about it at mess—it's awfully hard lines on me. It makes me feel rotten!'

The Squire laughed. He was reminded of a Fourth of June years before, when Desmond had gone through agonies of shame because his father was not, in his eyes, properly 'got-up' for the occasion—how he had disappeared in the High Street, and only joined his people again in the crowd at the fireworks.

'I recommend you to stick it, Desmond. It won't last long. I've got my part to play, and you've got yours. You fight because they make you.'

'I don't!' said the boy passionately. 'I fight because—'

Then his words broke down. He descended from the table.

'Well, all right, father. I suppose it's no good talking. Only if you think I shan't mind if you get yourself put in quad, you're jolly well mistaken. Hullo, Forest! I'm coming!'

He hurried off, the Squire moving slowly after him. In the hour before the boy departed he was the spoilt darling of his sisters and the servants, who hung round him, and could not do enough for him. He endured it, on the whole, patiently dashing out at the very end to say good-bye to an old gardener, once a keeper, with whom he used to go ferreting in the park. To his father alone his manner was not quite as usual. It was the manner of one who had been hurt. The Squire felt it.

As to his elder son, he and Aubrey parted without any outward sign of discord, and on the way to London Aubrey, with the dry detachment that was natural to him in speaking of himself, told the story of the preceding twenty-four hours to the eager Desmond's sympathetic ears. 'Well done, Broomie!' was the boy's exultant comment on the tale of the codicil.

The house after Desmond's departure settled dreamily down. Pamela, with red eyes, retreated to the schoolroom, and began to clear up the debris left by the packing; Alice Gaddesden went to sleep in the drawing-room; Mrs. Strang wrote urgent letters to registry offices, who now seldom answered her; the Squire was in the library, and Elizabeth retreated early to her own room. She spent a good deal of time in writing up a locked diary, and finishing up a letter to her mother. Then she saw to her astonishment that it was nearly one o'clock, and began to feel sleepy.

The night was warm, and before undressing she put out her light, and threw up her window. There was a moon nearly at the full outside, and across the misty stretches of the park the owls were calling.

Suddenly she heard a distant footstep, and drew back from the window. A man was pacing slowly up and down an avenue of pollarded limes which divided the rose-garden from the park. His figure could only be intermittently seen; but it was certainly the Squire.

She drew the curtains again without shutting the window; and for long after she was in bed she still heard the footstep. It awakened many trains of thought in her—of her own position in this household where she seemed to have become already mistress and indispensable; of Desmond's last words with her; of the relations between father and son; of Captain Chicksands and his most agreeable company; of Pamela's evident dislike of her, and what she could do to mend it.

As to Pamela, Elizabeth's thoughts went oddly astray. She was vexed with the girl for what had seemed to the elder woman her young rudeness to a gallant and distinguished man. Why, she had scarcely spoken a word to him during the sitting on the hill! In some way, Elizabeth supposed, Captain Chicksands had offended her—had not made enough of her perhaps? But girls must learn now to accept simpler and blunter manners from their men friends. She guessed that Pamela was in that self-conscious, exalté mood of first youth which she remembered so well in herself—fretting too, no doubt, poor child! over the parting from Desmond. Anyway she seemed to have no particular interest in Arthur Chicksands, nor he in her, though his tone in speaking to her had been, naturally, familiar and intimate. But probably he was one of those able men who have little to say to the young girl, and keep their real minds for the older and experienced woman.

At any rate, Elizabeth dismissed from her mind whatever vague notion or curiosity as to a possible love-affair for Pamela in that direction might have been lurking in it. And that being so, she promptly, and without arrière pensée of any sort, allowed herself the pleasant recollection of half an hour's conversation which had put her intellectually on her mettle, and quickened those infant ambitions of a practical and patriotic kind which were beginning to rise in her.

But the Squire's coming escapade! How to stop it?—for Desmond's sake chiefly.

Dear boy! It was on a tender, almost maternal thought of him that she at last turned to sleep. But the footstep pursued her ear. What was the meaning of this long nocturnal pacing? Had the Squire, after all, a heart, or some fragment of one? Was it the parting from Desmond that thus kept him from his bed? She would have liked to think it—but did not quite succeed!

CHAPTER VII

A week or two had passed.

The Squire was on his way to inspect his main preparations for the battle at the park gates, which he expected on the morrow. He had been out before breakfast that morning, on horseback, with one of the gardeners, to see that all the gates on the estate, except the Chetworth gate, were locked and padlocked. For the Chetworth gate, which adjoined the land to be attacked, more serious defences were in progress.

All his attempts to embarrass the action of the Committee had been so far vain. The alternatives he had proposed had been refused. Fifty acres at the Chetworth end of Mannering Park, besides goodly slices elsewhere, the County Committee meant to have. As the Squire would not plough them himself, and as the season was advancing, he had been peremptorily informed that the motor plough belonging to the County Committee would be sent over on such a day, with so many men, to do the work; the land had been surveyed; no damage would be done to the normal state of the property that could be avoided; et cetera.

So the crisis was at hand. The Squire felt battle in his blood.

As he walked along through his domain, exhilarated by the bright frosty morning, and swinging his stick like a boy, he was in the true Quixotic mood, ready to tilt at any wind-mill in his path. The state of the country, the state of the war, the state of his own affairs, had produced in him a final ferment of resentment and disgust which might explode in any folly.

Why not go to prison? He thought he could bear it. A man must stand by his opinions—even through sacrifice. It would startle the public into attention. Such outrages on the freedom, on the ancient rights of Englishmen, must not pass without protest. Yes—he felt it in him to be a martyr! They would hardly refuse him a pocket Homer in prison.

What, a month? Three weeks, in actual practice. Luckily he cared nothing at all about food—though he refused to be rationed by a despotic Government. On a handful of dates and a bit of coarse bread he had passed many a day of hard work when he was excavating in the East. One can always starve—for a purpose! The Squire conceived himself as out for Magna Charta—the root principles of British liberty. As for those chattering fellows of the Labour Party, let them conquer England if they could. While the Government ploughed up his land without leave, the Socialists would strip him of it altogether. Well, nothing for it but to fight! If one went down, one went down—but at least honourably.

In the Times that morning there was a report of a case in the north, a landowner fined £100, for letting a farm go to waste for the game's sake. And Miss Bremerton had been holding up the like fate to him that morning—because of Holme Wood. A woman of parts that!—too clever!—a disputatious creature, whom a man would like to put down. But it wasn't easy; she slipped out of your grip—gave you unexpected tits for tats. One would have thought after that business with the will, she would be anxious to make up—to show docility. In such a relation one expected docility. But not a bit of it! She grew bolder. The Squire admitted uncomfortably that it was his own fault—only, in fact, what he deserved for making a land-agent, accountant, and legal adviser out of a poor lady who had merely engaged herself to be his private secretary for classical purposes.

All the same he confessed that she had never yet neglected the classical side of her duties. His thoughts contrasted the library and the collections as they were now, with what they had been a couple of months before. Now he knew where books could be found; now one could see the precious things he possessed. Her taste—her neatness—her diligence—nothing could beat them. And she moved so quietly—had so light a foot—and always a pleasant voice and smile. Oh yes, she had been a great catch—an astonishing catch—no doubt of that. All the same he was not going to be entirely governed by her! And again he thought complacently of the weak places in her scholarship—the very limited extent of her reading—compared to his. 'By Zeus!—ει ποτ' εστιν—if it weren't for that, I should never keep the whip-hand of her at all!'

She had made a forlorn attempt again, that morning, to dissuade him from the park adventure. But there he drew the line. For there really was a line, though he admitted it might be difficult to see, considering all that he was shovelling upon her. He had been very short—perhaps she would say, very rude—with her. Well, it couldn't be helped! When she saw what he was really prepared to face, she would at least respect him. And if he was shut up, she could get on with the catalogue, and keep things going.

Altogether the Squire was above himself. The tonic air and scents of the autumn, the crisp leaves underfoot, the slight frost on the ruts, helped his general intoxication. He, the supposed scholar and recluse, was about to play a part—a rattling part. The eye of England would be upon him! He already tasted the prison fare, and found it quite tolerable.

As to Desmond—

But the thought of him no sooner crossed the Squire's mind than he dismissed it. Or rather it survived far within, as a volcanic force, from which the outer froth and ferment drew half its strength. He was being forcibly dispossessed of Desmond, just as he was being forcibly dispossessed of his farms and his park; or of his money, swallowed up in monstrous income tax.

Ah, there were Dodge and Perley, the two park-keepers, one of whom lived in the White Lodge, now only a hundred yards away. Another man who was standing by them, near the park wall, looked to the Squire like Gregson, his ejected farmer. And who was that black-coated fellow coming through the small wicket-gate beside the big one? What the devil was he doing in the park? There was a permanent grievance in the Squire's mind against the various rights-of-way through his estate. Why shouldn't he be at liberty to shut out that man if he wanted to? Of course by the mere locking and barricading of the gates, as they would be locked and barricaded on the morrow, he was flouting the law. But that was a trifle. The gates were his own anyway.

The black-coated man, however, instead of proceeding along the road, had now approached the group of men standing under the wall, and was talking with them. They themselves did not seem to be doing anything, although a large coil of barbed wire and a number of hurdles lay near them.

'Hullo, Dodge!'

At the Squire's voice the black-coated man withdrew a little distance to the roadway, where he stood watching. Of the three others the two old fellows, ex-keepers both of them, stood sheepishly silent, as the Squire neared them.

'Well, my men, good-morning! What have you done?' said the Squire peremptorily.

Dodge looked up.

'We've put a bit of wire on the gate, Squoire, an' fastened the latch of it up—and we've put a length or two along the top of the wall,' said the old man slowly—'an' then—' He paused.

'Then what?—what about the hurdles? I expected to find them all up by now!'

Dodge looked at Perley. And Perley, a gaunt, ugly fellow, who had been a famous hunter and trapper in his day, took off his hat and mopped his brow, before he said, in a small, cautious voice, entirely out of keeping with the rest of him:

'The treuth on it is, Squoire, we don't loike the job. We be afeard of their havin' the law on us.'

'Oh, you're afraid, are you?' said the Squire angrily. 'You won't stand up for your rights, anyway!'

Perley looked at his employer a little askance.

'They're not our rights, if you please, Muster Mannering. We don't have nothing to say to 'un.'

'They are your rights, you foolish fellow! If this abominable Government tramples on me to-day, it'll trample on you to-morrow.'

'Mebbe, Squoire, mebbe,' said Perley mildly. 'But Dodge and I don't feel loike standing up to 'un. We was engaged to mind the roads an' the leaves, an' a bit rabbitin', an' sich like. But this sort of job is somethin' out o' the common, Muster Mannering. We don't hold wi' it. The County they've got a powerful big road-engine, Squoire. They'll charge them gates to-morrow—there 'll be a terr'ble to do. My wife, she's frightened to death. She's got a cart from Laycocks, and she's takin' all our bit things over to her mother's. She won't stay, she says, to be blowed up, not for no one. Them Governments is terr'ble powerful, Squoire. If they was to loose a bit o' gas on us—or some o' they stuffs they put into shells? Noa, Noa, Squoire'—Perley shook his head resolutely, imitated exactly by Dodge—'we'll do our dooty in them things we was engaged to do. But we're not foightin' men!'

'You needn't tell me that!' said the Squire, exasperated. 'The look of you's enough. So you refuse to barricade those gates?'

'Well, we do, Squoire,' said Perley, in a tone of forced cheerfulness.

'Yes, we do,' said Dodge slowly, copying the manner of his leader.

All this time Gregson had been standing a little apart from the rest. His face showed traces of recent drinking, his hands wandered restlessly from his coat-collar to his pockets, his clothes were shabby and torn. But when the Squire looked round him, as though invoking some one or something to aid him against these deserters, Gregson came forward.

'If you want any help, Mr. Mannering, I'm your man. I suppose these fellows'll lend a hand with carrying these things up to the gates. They'll not risk their precious skins much by doing that!'

Perley and Dodge replied with alacrity that so far they would gladly oblige the Squire, and they began to shoulder the hurdles.

It was at that moment that the Squire caught the eye of the black-coated man, who had been observing the whole proceedings from about ten yards off. The expression of the eye roused in Mannering an itching desire to lay immediate hands on its possessor. He strode up to him.

'I don't know, sir, why you stand there, looking on at things that are no business of yours,' he said angrily. 'If you want to know your way anywhere, one of my men here will show you.'

'Oh, thank you,' said the other tranquilly. 'I know my way perfectly.' He held up an ordnance map, which he carried in his hand. 'I'm an engineer. I come from London, and I'm bound for a job at Crewe. But I'm very fond of country walking when the weather's good. I've walked about a good bit of England, in my time, but this part is a bit I don't know. So, as I had two days' holiday, I thought I'd have a look at your place on the road. And as you are aware, Mr. Mannering'—he pointed to the map—'this is a right-of-way, and you can't turn me out.'

'All the same, sir, you are on my property,' said the Squire hotly, 'and a right-of-way only means a right of passing through. I should be much obliged if you would hurry yourself a little.'

The other laughed. He was a slim fellow, apparently about thirty, in a fresh, well-cut, serge suit. A book was sticking out of one pocket; he returned the map to the other. He had the sallow look of one who has spent years in hot workshops, and a slight curvature of the spine; but his eyes were singularly, audaciously bright, and all his movements alert and decided.

'It's not often one sees such a typical bit of feudalism as this,' he said, without the smallest embarrassment, pointing to the old men, the gates, the hurdles, which Gregson was now placing in position, and finally the Squire himself. 'I wouldn't have missed it for worlds. It's as good as a play. You're fighting the County Agricultural War Committee, I understand from these old fellows, because they want a bit of your park to grow more food?'

'Well, sir, and how does it matter to you?'

'Oh, it matters a great deal,' said the other, smiling. 'I want to be able to tell my grandchildren—when I get 'em—that I once saw this kind of thing. They'll never believe me. For in their day, you see, there'll be no squires, and no parks. The land 'll be the people's, and all this kind of thing—your gates, your servants, your fine house, your game-coverts, and all the rest of it—will be like a bit of history out of Noah's Ark.'

The Squire looked at him attentively.

'You're a queer kind of chap,' he said, half contemptuously. 'I suppose you're one of those revolutionary fellows the papers talk about?'

'That's it. Only there are a good many of us. When the time comes,' he nodded pleasantly, 'we shall know how to deal with you.'

'It'll take a good deal longer than you think,' said the Squire coolly; 'unless indeed you borrow the chap from Russia who's invented the machine for cutting off five hundred heads at once, by electricity. That might hasten matters a little!'

He had by now entirely recovered his chaffing, reckless temper, and was half enjoying the encounter.

'Oh, not so long,' said the other. 'You're just passing a Franchise Bill that will astonish you when you see the results! You perhaps may just live it out—yes, you may die peaceably in that house yonder. But your son, if you have one—that'll be another pair of boots!'

'You and your pals would be much better employed in stopping this accursed war than in talking revolutionary drivel like that,' said the Squire, with energy.

'Oh ho! so you want to stop the war?' said the other, lifting his eyebrows. 'I should like to know why.'

The Squire went off at once into one of his usual tirades as to 'slavery' and 'liberty.' 'You're made to work, or fight! willy-nilly. That man's turned out of his farm—willy-nilly. I'm made to turn him out—willy-nilly. The common law of England's trampled under foot. What's worth it? Nothing!'

The Squire's thin countenance glowed fanatically. With his arms akimbo he stood towering over the younger man, his white hair glistening in the sun.

The other smiled, as he looked his assailant up and down.

'Who's the revolutionist now?' he said quietly. 'What's the war cost you, Mr. Mannering, compared to what it's cost me and my pals? This is the first holiday I've had for three years. Twice I've dropped like dead in the shop—strained heart, says the doctor. No time to eat!—no time to sleep!—come out for an hour, wolf some brandy down and go back again, and then they tell you you're a drunken brute! "Shells and guns!" says the Government—"more shells!—more guns!—deliver the goods!" And we've delivered 'em. My two brothers are dead in France. I shall be "combed" out directly, and a "sniper" will get me, perhaps, three days after I get to the trenches, as he did my young brother. What then? Oh, I know, there's some of us—the young lads mostly—who've got out of hand, and 'll give the Government trouble perhaps before they've done. Who can wonder, when you see the beastly towns they come out of, and the life they were reared in! And none of us are going to stand profiteering, and broken pledges, and that kind of thing!'—a sudden note of passion rushed into the man's voice. 'But after all, when all's said and done, this is England!' he turned with a fine, unconscious gesture to the woods and green spaces behind him, and the blue distances of plain—'and we're Englishmen—and it's touch and go whether England's going to come out or go under; and if we can't pay the Huns for what they've done in Belgium—what they've done in France!—what they've done to our men on the sea!— well, it's a devil's world!—and I'd sooner be quit of it, it don't matter how!'

The man's slight frame shook under the force of his testimony. His eyes held the Squire, who was for the moment silenced. Then the engineer turned on his heel with a laugh:

'Well, good-day to you, Mr. Mannering. Go and fasten up your gates! If I'm for minding D.O.R.A. and winning the war, I'm a good Socialist all the same. I shall be for making short work with you, when our day comes.' And touching his hat, he walked rapidly away.

The Squire straightened his shoulders, and looked round to see whether they had been overheard. But the labourers carrying the hurdles, and Gregson burdened with the coil of wire, had not been listening. They stood now in a group close to the main gate waiting for their leader. The Squire walked up to them, picking his way among various articles of furniture, a cradle, some bedding, a trunk or two, which lay scattered in the road in front of the white casemented lodge. The wife of old Perley, the lodge-keeper, was standing on her doorstep.

'Well, no offence, Muster Mannering, but Perley and me's going over to my sister's at Wood

End to-night, afore the milingtary come.' The black-browed elderly woman spoke respectfully but firmly.

'What silly nonsense have you got into your heads?' shouted the Squire. 'You know very well all that's going to happen is that the County Council are going to send their motor-plough over, and they'll have to break down the gates to get in, so that the law can settle it. What's come to you that you're all scuttling like a pack of rabbits? It's not your skins that'll pay for it—it's mine!'

'We're told—Perley an' me—as there'll be milingtary,' said Mrs. Perley, unmoved. 'Leastways, they'll bring a road-engine, Perley says, as'll make short work o' them gates. And folks do say as they might even bring a tank along; you know, sir, as there's plenty of 'em, and not fur off.' She nodded mysteriously towards a quarter, never mentioned in the neighbourhood, where these Behemoths of war had a training-ground. 'And Perley and me, we can't have nowt to do wi' such things. We wasn't brought up to 'em.'

'Well, if you go, you don't come back!' said the Squire, shaking a threatening hand.

'Thank you, sir. But there's work for all on us nowadays,' said the woman placidly.

Then the Squire, with Gregson's help, set himself fiercely to the business. In little more than an hour, and with the help of some pieces of rope, the gate had been firmly barricaded with hurdles and barbed wire, wicket-gate and all, and the Squire, taking a poster in large letters from his pocket, affixed it to the outside of the gate. It signified to all and sundry that the Chetworth gate of Mannering Park could now only be opened by violence, and that those offering such violence would be proceeded against according to law.

When it was done, the Squire first addressed a few scathing words to the pair of park-keepers, who smoked imperturbably through them, and then transferred a pound-note to the ready palm of Gregson, who was, it seemed, on the point of accepting work as a stock-keeper from another of the Squire's farmers—a brother culprit, only less 'hustled' than himself by the formidable County Committee, which was rapidly putting the fear of God into every bad husbandman throughout Brookshire. Then the Squire hurried off homewards.

His chief thought now was—what would that most opinionated young woman at home say to him? He was at once burning to have it out with her, and—though he would have scorned to confess it—nervous as to how he might get through the encounter.

Fate, however, ordained that his thoughts about the person who had now grown so important to his household should be affected, before he saw her again, from a new quarter. The Rector, Mr. Pennington, quite unaware of the doughty deeds that had been done at the Chetworth gate, and coming from his own house which stood within the park enclosure, ran into the Squire at a cross-road.

The Squire looked at him askance, and kept his own counsel. The Rector was a man of peace, and had once or twice tried to dissuade the Squire from his proposed acts of war. The Squire, therefore, did not mean to discuss them with him. But, in general, he and the Rector were good friends. The Rector was a bit of a man of the world, and never attempted to put a quart into a pint-pot. He took the Squire as he found him, and would have missed the hospitalities of the Hall—or rather the conversation they implied—if he had been obliged to forgo them. The Squire on his side had observed with approval that the Rector was a fair scholar, and a bad beggar. He could take up quotations from Horace, and he was content with such parish subscriptions as the Squire had given for twenty years, and was firmly minded not to increase.

But here also the arrival of Elizabeth had stirred the waters. For the Rector was actually on his way to try and get a new subscription out of the Squire; and it was Elizabeth's doing.

'You remember that child of old Leonard the blacksmith?' said the Rector eagerly; 'a shocking case of bow-legs, one of the worst I ever saw. But Miss Bremerton's taken endless trouble. And now we've got an admission for him to the Orthopaedic hospital. But there's a few pounds to be raised for his maintenance—it will be a question of months. I was just coming over to see if you would give me a little,' he wound up, in a tone of apology.

The Squire, with a brow all clouds, observed that when children were bow-legged it was entirely the fault of their mothers.

'Ah, yes,' said the Rector, with a sigh. 'Mrs. Leonard is a slatternly woman—no doubt of that. But when you've said that you haven't cured the child.'

The Squire ungraciously said he would consider it; and the Rector, knowing well that he would get no more at a first assault, let the child alone, and concentrated on the topic of Elizabeth.

'An extraordinarily capable creature,' he said warmly, 'and a good heart besides. You were indeed lucky to find her, and you are very wise to give her her head. The village folk can't say enough about her.'

The Squire felt his mouth twitching. With some horses, is there any choice—but Hobson's—as to 'giving' them their head?

'Yes, she's clever,' he said grudgingly.

'And it was only to-day,' pursued the Rector, 'that I heard her story from a lady, a friend of my wife's, who's been spending Sunday with us. She seems to have met Miss Bremerton and her family at Richmond a year or so ago, where everybody who knew them had a great respect for them. The mother was a nice, gentle body, but this elder daughter had most of the wits—though there's a boy in a Worcester regiment they're all very fond and proud of—and she always looked after the others, since the father—who was a Civil servant—died, six years ago. Then two years since, she engaged herself to a young Yeomanry officer—'

'Eh—what?—what do you say?—a Yeomanry officer?' said the Squire, looking round.

'Precisely—a Yeomanry officer. They were engaged and apparently very happy. He was a handsome, upstanding fellow, very popular with women. Then he went out to Egypt with his regiment, and it was intended they should marry when he got his first leave. But presently his letters began to change. Then they only came at long intervals. And at last they stopped. He had complained once of an attack of sunstroke, and she was wretched, thinking he was ill. At last a letter reached her from a brother officer, who seems to have behaved very kindly—with the explanation. Her fiance had got into the clutches—no one exactly knew how—of a Greek family living in Alexandria, and had compromised himself so badly with one of the daughters, that the father, a cunning old Greek merchant, had compelled him to marry her. Threats of exposure, and all the rest! The brother officer hinted at a plot—that the poor fellow had been trapped, and was more sinned against than sinning. However, there it was. He was married to the Greek girl; Miss Bremerton's letters were returned; and the thing was at an end. Our friend says she behaved splendidly. She went on with her work in the War Trade Department—shirked nothing and no one—till suddenly, about six months ago, she had a bad breakdown—'

'What do you mean?' said the Squire abruptly. 'She was ill?'

'A combination of overwork and influenza, I should think; but no doubt the tragedy had a good deal to do with it. She went down to stay for a couple of months with an uncle in Dorsetshire, and got better. Then the family lost some money, through a solicitor's mismanagement—enough anyway to make a great deal of difference. The mother too broke down in health. Miss Bremerton came home at once, and took everything on her own shoulders. You remember, she heard of your secretaryship from that Balliol man you wrote to—who had been a tutor of hers when she was at Somerville? She determined to apply for it. It was more money than she was getting in London, and she had to provide for her mother and to educate her young sister. Plucky woman! All this interested me very much, I confess. I have formed such a high opinion of her! And I thought it would interest you.'

'I don't know what we any of us have to do with it,' grumbled the Squire.

The Rector drew himself up a little, resenting the implied rebuke.

'I hope I don't seem to you to be carrying gossip for gossip's sake,' he said, rather indignantly. 'Nothing was further from my intention. I like and admire Miss Bremerton a great deal too much.'

'Well, I don't know what we can do,' said the Squire testily. 'We can't unmarry the man.'

The Rector pulled up short, and offered a chilly good-bye. As he hurried on towards the village—little knowing the obstacles he would encounter in his path—he said to himself that the Squire's manners were really past endurance. One could hardly imagine that Miss Bremerton would be long able to put up with them.

The Squire meanwhile pursued the rest of his way, wrapped in rather disagreeable reflections. He was not at all grateful to the Rector for telling him the story—quite the reverse. It altered his mental attitude towards his secretary; introduced disturbing ideas, which he had no use for. He had taken for granted that she was one of those single women of the present day whose intellectual interests are enough for them, who have never really felt the call of passion, and can be trusted to look at life sensibly without taking love and marriage into account. To think of Miss Bremerton as having suffered severely from a love-affair—broken her heart, and injured her health over it—was most distracting. If it had happened once—why, of course, it might happen again. She was not immune; in spite of all her gifts, she was susceptible, and it was a horrid nuisance.

He went home all on edge, what with the adventure of the gates, the encounter with the engineer fellow, and now the revelations of the Rector.

As he approached the house, he saw from the old clock in the gable of the northern front that it was two o'clock. He was half-an-hour late for lunch. Luncheon, in fact, must be over. And indeed, as he passed along the library windows, he saw Elizabeth's figure at her desk. It annoyed him that she should have gone back to work so soon after her meal. He had constantly made it plain to her that she was not expected to begin work of an afternoon till four o'clock. She would overdo it: and then she would break down again as she had done before. In his selfishness, his growing dependence on her companionship and her help, he began to dread the mere chance.

How agreeable, and how fruitful, their days of work had been lately! He had been, of course, annoyed sometimes by her preoccupation with the war news of the morning. Actually, this Caporetto business, the Italian disaster, had played the mischief with her for a day or two—and the news from Russia. Any bad news, indeed, seemed to haunt her; her colour faded away; and if he dictated notes to her, they would be occasionally inaccurate. But that was seldom. In general, he felt that he had made great strides during the preceding weeks; that, thanks to her, the book he was attempting was actually coming into shape. She had suggested so much—sometimes by her knowledge, sometimes by her ignorance. And always so modest—so teachable—so docile.

Docile? The word passing through his mind again, as it had in the morning, roused in him mingled laughter and uneasiness. For outside their classical work together, nothing indeed could be less docile than Miss Bremerton. How she had withstood him in the matter of the codicil! He could see her still, as she stood there with her hands behind her, defying him. And that morning also, when she had spoken her mind on the project of the gates.

Well, now, he had to go in and tell her that the deed was done, and the park was closed.

He crept round to a side door, nervous lest she should perceive him from the library, and made Forest get him some lunch. Then he hung about the hall smoking. It was ridiculous—nonsensical—but he admitted to himself that he shrank from facing her.

At last a third cigarette put the requisite courage into him, and he walked slowly to the library. As he entered the room, Elizabeth rose from her chair.

She stood there waiting for his orders, or his report—her quiet eyes upon him.

He told himself not to be a fool, and throwing away his cigarette, he walked up to her, and said in a tone of bravado:

'Well, the barricades are up!'

CHAPTER VIII

The Squire having shot his bolt, looked anxiously for the effect of it.

Elizabeth, apparently, took it calmly. She was standing with one hand on the table behind her, and the autumn sun streaming in through the western windows caught the little golden curls on her temples, and the one or two small adornments that she habitually wore, especially a Greek coin—a gold stater—hanging on a slender chain round her neck. In the Squire's eyes, the stately figure in plain black, with the brilliant head and hands, had in some way gathered into itself the significance of the library. All the background of books, with its pale and yet rich harmony of tone, the glass cases with their bronzes and terra-cottas, the statues, the papers on the table, the few flowers that were never wanting to Elizabeth's corner, the taste with which the furniture had been re-arranged, the general elegance and refinement of the big room in fact, since Elizabeth had reduced it from chaos to order, were now related to her rather than to him. He could not now think of the room without her. She had become in this short time so markedly its presiding spirit. 'Let there be order and beauty!' she had said, instead of dirt and confusion; and the order and beauty were there.

But the presiding spirit was now surveying him, with eyes that seemed to have been watchfully withdrawn, under puckered brows.

'I don't understand,' said Elizabeth. 'You have fastened up the gates?'

'I have,' said the Squire jocularly. 'Mrs. Perley believes the Committee will bring a tank! That would be a sight worth seeing.'

'You really want to stop them from ploughing up that land?'

'I do. I have offered them other land.'

Elizabeth hesitated.

'Don't you believe what the Government say, Mr. Mannering?'

'What do they say?'

'That everything depends upon whether we shall have food enough to hold out? That we can't win the war unless we can grow more food ourselves?'

'That's the Government's affair.' The Squire sat down at his own table and began to look out a pen.

'Well now, Miss Bremerton, I don't think we need spend any more time over this tiresome business. I've already lost the morning. Suppose we get on with the work we were doing yesterday?'

He turned an amicable countenance towards her. She on her side moved a little towards a window near her table, and looked out of it, as though reflecting. After a minute or two he asked himself with a vague anxiety what was wrong with her. Her manner was certainly unusual.

Suddenly she turned, and came half across the room towards him.

'May I speak to you, please, Mr. Mannering?'

'By all means. Is there anything amiss?'

'I think we agreed on a month's notice, on either side. I should be glad if you would kindly accept my notice as from to-day.'

The Squire rose violently, and thrust back his chair.

'So that's what you have been cogitating in my absence?'

'Not at all,' said Elizabeth mildly. 'I have made a complete list of the passages you asked for.' She pointed to her table.

'Yet all the time you were planning this move—you were making up your mind what to do?' She hesitated.

'I was often afraid it would have to be done,' she said at last.

'And pray may I ask your reasons?' The Squire's tone was sarcastic. 'I should like to know in what I have failed to satisfy you. I suppose you thought I was rude to you this morning?'

'Oh, that didn't matter,' she said hastily. 'The fact is, Mr. Mannering,' she crossed her hands quietly in front of her, 'you put responsibilities on me that I am not prepared to carry. I feel I must give them up.'

'I thought you liked responsibility.'

Elizabeth coloured.

'It—it depends what sort. I begin to see now that my principles—and opinions—are so different from yours that, if we go further, I shall either be disappointing you or—doing what I think wrong.'

'You can't conceive ever giving up your opinion to mine?'

'No!' Elizabeth shook her head with decision. 'No! that I really can't conceive!'

'Upon my word!' said the Squire, fairly taken aback. They confronted each other. Elizabeth began to look disturbed. Her eyelids flickered once or twice.

'I think we ought to be quite serious,' she said hurriedly. 'I don't want you to misunderstand me. If you knew how I valued this opportunity of doing this classical work with you! It is wonderful'—her voice wavered a little, or the Squire fancied it—'what you have taught me even in this short time. I am proud to have been your secretary—and your pupil. If it were only that'— she paused—'but you have also been so kind as to—to take me into your confidence—to let me do things for you, outside of what you engaged me for. I see plainly that—if I go on with this—I shall become your secretary—your agent in fact—for a great many things besides Greek.'

Then she made an impetuous step forward.

'Mr. Mannering!—the atmosphere of this house chokes me!'

The Squire dropped back into his chair, watching her with eyes in which he tried—not very successfully—to keep dignity alive.

'Your reasons?'

'I am with the country!' she said, not without signs of agitation; 'and you seem to me to care nothing about the country!'

Disputation was never unwelcome to the Squire. He riposted.

'Of course, we mean entirely different things by the word.'

She threw back her head slightly, with a gesture of scorn.

'We might argue that, if it were peace-time. But this is war! Your country—my country—has the German grip at her throat. A few months—and we are saved—or broken!—the country that gave us birth—all we have—all we are!' Her words came short and thick, and she had turned very white. 'And in this house there is never, in your presence, a word of the war!—of the men who are dying by land and sea—dying, that you and I may sit here in peace—that you may talk to me about Greek poetry, and put spokes in the wheels of those who are trying to feed us—and defend us—and beat off Germany. Nothing for the wounded!—nothing for the hospitals! And you won't let Pamela do anything! Not a farthing for the Red Cross! You made me write a letter last week refusing a subscription. And then, when they only ask you to let your land grow food—that the German pirates and murderers mayn't starve us into a horrible submission—then you bar your gates—you make endless trouble, when the country wants every hour of every man's time—you, in your position, give the lead to every shirker and coward! No! I can't bear it any more! I must go. I have had happy times here—I love the work—I am very glad to earn the money, for my people want it. But I must go. My heart—my conscience won't let me stay!'

She turned from him, with an unconscious gesture which seemed to the Squire to be somewhat mingled with that of the great Victory towering behind her, and went quickly back to her table, where she began with trembling hands to put her papers together.

The Squire tried to laugh it off.

'And all this,' he said with a sneer, 'because I tied up a few gates!'

She made no reply. He was conscious of mingled dismay and fury.

'You will stay your month?' he inquired at last, coldly. 'You don't propose, I imagine, to leave me at a moment's notice?'

She was bending over her table, and did not look up.

'Oh yes, I will stay my month.'

He sat speechless, watching her. She very quickly finished what she was doing, and taking up her note-book, and some half-written letters, she left the room.

'A pretty state of things!' said the Squire, and thrusting his long hands into his pockets he began to pace the library, in the kind of temper that may be imagined—given the man and the circumstances.

The difference, however, between this occasion and others lay in the fact that the penalties of temper had grown so unjustly heavy. The Squire felt himself hideously aggrieved. Abominable!—that he should be hindered in his just rights and opinions by this indirect pressure from a woman, whom he couldn't wrestle with and floor, as he would a man, because of her sex. That was always the way with women. No real equality—no give and take—in spite of all the suffrage talk. Their weakness was their tyranny. Weakness indeed! They were much stronger than men. God help England when they got the vote! The Greeks said it—Euripides said it. But, of course, the Greeks have said everything! Hecuba to Agamemnon, for instance, when she is planning the murder of the Thracian King:

'Leave it to me!—and my Trojan women!'

And Agamemnon's scoffing reply—poor idiot!—'How can women get the better of men?'

And Hecuba's ghastly low-voiced 'In a crowd we are terrible!'—δεινον το πληθος—as she and her women turn upon the Thracian, put out his eyes, and tear his children limb from limb.

But one woman might be quite enough to upset a quiet man's way of living! The moral pressure of it was so iniquitous! Your convictions or your life! It was the language of a footpad.

To pull down the hurdles, and tamely let in Chicksands and his minions—how odious! To part with Elizabeth Bremerton and to be reduced again to the old chaos and helplessness—how still more odious! As to the war—so like a woman to suppose that any war was ever fought with unanimity by any country! Look at the Crimea!—the Boer War!—the Napoleonic Wars themselves, if it came to that! Why was Fox a patriot, and he a traitor? Let her answer that!

And all the time, Elizabeth's light touch upon his will was like the curb on a stubborn horse. Once as he passed her table angry curiosity took him to look at some finished work that was lying there. Perfection! Intelligence, accuracy, the clearest of scripts! All his hints taken—and bettered in the taking. Beside it lay some slovenly manuscripts of Levasseur's. He could see the corners of Miss Bremerton's mouth go up as she looked it through. Well, now he was to be left to Levasseur's tender mercies—after all he had taught her! And the accounts, and the estate, and these infernal rations, that no human being could understand!

The Squire's self-pity rose upon him like a flood. Just at the worst, he heard a knock at the library door. Before he could say 'Come in,' it was hurriedly opened, and his two married daughters confronted him—Pamela, too, behind them.

'Father!' cried Mrs. Gaddesden, 'you must please let us come and speak to you!'

What on earth was wrong with them? Alice—for whom her father had more contempt than affection—looked merely frightened; but Margaret's eyes were angry, and Pamela's reproachful. The Squire braced himself to endurance.

'What do you want with me?'

'Father!—we never thought you meant it seriously! And now Forest says all the gates are closed, and that the village is up in arms. The labourers declare that if the County plough is turned back to-morrow, they'll break them down themselves. And when we're all likely to be starving in six months!'

'You really can't expect working-folk to stand quietly by and see such a thing!' said Margaret in her intensest voice. 'Do, father, let me send Forest at once to tell the gardeners to open all the gates.'

The Squire defied her to do any such thing. What was all the silly fuss about? The County people could open the gates in half-an-hour if they wanted. It was a demonstration—a protest—a case to go to the Courts on. He had principles—if no one else had. And if they weren't other people's principles, what did it matter? He was ready to stand by them, to go to prison for them. He folded his arms magnificently.

Pamela laughed excitedly, and shook her head.

'Oh, no, father, you won't be a hero—only a laughing-stock! That's what Desmond minds so much. They won't send you to prison. Some tiresome old Judge will give you a talking-to in Court, and you won't be able to answer him back. And then they'll fine you—and we shall be a little more boycotted than we were before! That's all that'll happen!'

'"Boycotted"?—what do you mean?' said the Squire haughtily.

'Oh, father, can't you feel it?' cried Pamela.

'As if one man could pit himself against a nation!' said Mrs. Strang, in that manner of controlled emotion which the Squire detested. He rarely felt emotion, but when he did, he let it go.

Peremptorily he turned them all out, giving strict orders that nothing he had done should be interfered with. Then he attempted to go on with some work of his own, but he could not bring his mind to bear. Finally he seized his hat and went out into the park to see if the populace were really rising. It was a cold October evening, with a waxing moon, and a wind that was rapidly bringing the dead leaves to earth. Not a soul was to be seen! Only once the Squire thought he heard the sound of distant guns; and two aeroplanes crossed rapidly overhead sailing into the western sky. Everywhere the war!—the cursed, cursed obsession of it!

For the first time there was a breach in the Squire's defences, which for three years he had kept up almost intact. He had put literature, and art, and the joys of the connoisseur between himself and the measureless human ill around him. It had spoilt his personal life, had interfered with his travels, his diggings, his friendships with foreign scholars. Well, then, as far as he could he would take no account of it, would shut it out, and rail at the men and the forces that made it. He barely looked at the newspapers; he never touched a book dealing with the war. It seemed to him a triumph of mind and intelligence when he succeeded in shutting out the hurly-burly altogether. Only, when in the name of the war his private freedom and property were interfered with, he had flamed out into hysterical revolt. Old aristocratic instincts came to the aid of passionate will, and, perhaps, of an uneasy conscience.

And now in the man's vain but not ignoble soul there stirred a first passing terror of what the war might do with him, if he were forced to feel it—to let it in. He saw it as a veiled Presence at the Door—and struggled with it blindly.

He was just turning back to the house, when he saw a figure approaching in the distance which he recognized. It was that of a man, once a farmer of his, and a decent fellow—oh, that he confessed!—with whom he had had a long quarrel over a miserable sum of money, claimed by the tenant when he left his farm, and disputed by the landlord.

The dispute had gone on for two years. The Squire's law-costs had long since swallowed up the original money in dispute.

Then Miss Bremerton, to whom the Squire had dictated some letters in connection with the squabble, had quietly made a suggestion—had asked leave to write a letter on approval. For sheer boredom with the whole business, the Squire had approved and sent the letter.

Then, this very morning, a reply from the farmer. Grateful astonishment! 'Of course I am ready to meet you, sir—I always have been. I will get my solicitor to put what you proposed in your letter of this morning into shape immediately, and will leave it signed at your door to-night. I trust this trouble is now over. It has been a great grief to me.'

And now there was the man bringing the letter. One worry done with! How many more the same patient hand might have dealt with, if its exacting owner hadn't thrown up her work—so preposterously!

The Squire gave an angry sigh, slipped out of the visitor's way through a shrubbery, and returned to his library. Fires had begun, and the glow of the burning logs shone through the room. The return to this home of his chief studies and pursuits during many delightful years was always, at any hour of the day or year, a moment of pleasure to the Squire. Here was shelter, here was escape—both from the troubles he had brought upon himself, and from the world tumult outside, the work of crazy politicians and incompetent diplomats. But if there was any season when the long crowded room was more attractive than at any other, it was in these autumn evenings when firelight and twilight mingled, and the natural 'homing' instinct of the Northerner, accustomed through long ages to spend long winters mostly indoors, stirred in his blood.

His books, too, spoke to him; and the beautiful dim forms of bronzes and terra-cottas, with all their suggestions of high poetry and consummate art, breathing from the youth of the world. He understood—passionately—the jealous and exclusive temper of the artist. It was his own temper—though he was no practising artist—and accounted largely for his actions. What are politics—or social reform—or religion—or morals—compared to art? The true artist, it has been pleaded again and again, has no country. He follows Beauty wherever she pitches her tent—'an hourly neighbour.' Woe to the interests that conflict with this interest! He simply drives them out of doors, and turns the key upon them!

This, in fact, was the Squire's defence of himself, whenever he troubled to defend himself. As to the pettinesses of a domineering and irritable temper, cherished through long years, and flying out on the smallest occasions—the Squire conveniently forgot them, in those rare moments of self-vision which were all the gods allowed him. Of course he was master in his own house and estate—why not? Of course he fought those who would interfere with him, war or no war—why not?

He sat down to his table, very sorry for himself, and hotly indignant with an unreasonable woman. The absence of her figure from the table on the further side of the room worked upon his nerves. She had promised at least to stay her month. These were working hours. What was she doing? She could hardly be packing already!

He tried to give his attention to the notes he had been working at the day before. Presently he wanted a reference—a line from the Philoctetes. 'The Lemnian fire'—where on earth was the passage? He lifted his head instinctively. If only she had been there—it was monstrous that she wasn't there!—he would just have thrown the question across the room, and got an answer. Her verbal memory was astonishing—much better than his.

He must, of course, get up and look out the reference for himself. And the same with others. In an hour's time he had accomplished scarcely anything, and a settled gloom descended upon him. That was the worst of accustoming yourself to crutches and helps. When they were unscrupulously and unjustly taken away, a man was worse off than if he had never had them.

The evening post came in. The Squire looked through it with disgust. He perceived that several letters were answers to some he had allowed his secretary to draft and send in his name—generally in reply to exasperated correspondents who had been kept waiting for months, and trampled on to boot.

Now he supposed she would refuse to have anything to do with this kind of thing! She would keep to the letter of her bargain, for the few weeks that remained. Greek he might expect from her—but not business.

He opened one or two. Yes, there was no doubt she was a clever woman—unpardonably and detestably clever. Affairs which had been mountains for years had suddenly become mole-hills. In this new phase he felt himself more helpless than ever to deal with them. She, on the contrary, might have put everything straight—she might have done anything with him—almost—that she pleased. He would have got rid of his old fool of an agent and put in another, that she approved of, if she had wished.

But no!—she must try and dictate to him in public—on a matter of public action. She must have everything her own way. Opinionated, self-conceited creature!

When tea-time came he rang for Forest, and demanded that a cup of tea should be brought him to the library. But as the butler was leaving the room, he recalled him.

'And tell Miss Bremerton that I shall be glad of her company when she has finished her tea.'

Forest hesitated.

'I think, sir, Miss Bremerton is out.'

Out!—was she? Her own mistress already!

'Send Miss Pamela here at once,' he commanded.

In a minute or two a girl's quick step was heard, and Pamela ran in.

'Yes, father?'

'Where is Miss Bremerton?' The Squire was standing in front of the fire, angrily erect. He had delivered his question in the tone of an ultimatum.

'Why, father, you've forgotten! She arranged with you that she was to go to tea at the Rectory, and I've just got a note from Mrs. Pennington to ask if they may keep her for the evening. They'll send her home.'

'I remember no such arrangement,' said the Squire, in a fury.

'Oh, father—why, I heard her speak to you! And I'm sure she wanted a little break. She's been looking dead-tired lately, and she said she had a headache at lunch.'

'Very well. That'll do,' said the Squire, and Pamela departed, virtuously conscious of having stood by Elizabeth, though she disliked her.

The Squire felt himself generally cornered. No doubt she was now telling her story to the Penningtons, who, of course, would disapprove the gates affair, in any case. The long hours before dinner passed away. The Squire thought them interminable. Dinner was a gloomy and embarrassed function. His daughters were afraid of rousing a fresh whirlwind of temper, if the gates were mentioned; and nothing else was interesting. The meal was short and spare, and the Squire noticed for the first time that while meat was offered to him, the others fed on fish and vegetables. All to put him in the wrong, of course!

After dinner he went back to the library. Work was impossible. He hung over the fire smoking, or turning over the pages of a fresh section of the catalogue which Elizabeth had placed—

complete—on his desk that morning.

It seemed to him that all the powers of mischief had risen against him. The recent investigation of his affairs made by Elizabeth at his express wish, slight and preliminary though it was, had shown him what he had long and obstinately refused to see—that the estate had seriously gone down in value during the preceding five years; that he had a dozen scraps and disputes on his hands, more than enough to rasp the nerves of any ordinary man—and as far as nerves were concerned, he knew very well that he was not an ordinary man; that, in short, he was impoverished and embarrassed; his agent was a scandal and must be dismissed, and his new lawyers, a grasping, incompetent crew. For a moment, indeed, he had had a glimpse of a clear sky. A woman, who seemed to have the same kind of business faculty that many Frenchwomen possess, had laid hands on his skein of troubles, and might have unravelled them. But she had thrown him over. In a little while he would have to let Mannering—for who would buy an estate in such a pickle?—sell his collections, and go and live in a flat in West Kensington. Then he hoped his enemies—Chicksands in particular—would be satisfied.

But these, to do him justice, were not the chief thoughts, not the considerations in his mind that smarted most. Another woman secretary or woman accountant—for, after all, clever women with business training are now as thick as blackberries—might have helped him to put his affairs straight; but she would not have been a Miss Bremerton, with her scholarship, her taste, her love of the beautiful things that he loved. He seemed to see her fair skin flushing with pleasure as they went through a Greek chorus together, or to watch her tenderly handling a bronze, or holding a Tanagra figure to the light.

Of course some stupid creatures might think he was falling in love with her—wanting to marry her. He laughed the charge to scorn. No! but he confessed her comradeship, her friendship, had begun to mean a good deal to him. For twenty years he had lived in loneliness. Now, it seemed, he had found a friend, in these days when the new independence of women opens a thousand fresh possibilities not only to them, but to men also.

Well, well, it was all over! Better make up his mind to it.

He went to the window, as it was nearing ten o'clock, and looked out. It was foggy still, the moon and stars scarcely visible. He hoped they would have at least the sense at the Rectory to provide her with a lantern, for under the trees the road was very dark.

Oh, far in the distance, a twinkling light! Good! The Squire hastily shut the window, and resumed his pacing. Presently he thought he heard the house door open and shut, and a little while after the library clock struck ten.

Now it would be only the natural thing to go and say good-night to his daughters, and, possibly, to inquire after a headache.

The Squire accordingly emerged. In the hall he found his three daughters engaged in lighting their candles at the Chippendale table, where for about a hundred and fifty years the ladies of Mannering had been accustomed to perform that rite.

The master of the house inquired coldly whether Miss Bremerton had returned safely. 'Oh yes,' said his daughter Margaret, 'but she went up to bed at once. She hasn't got rid of her headache.'

Mrs. Strang's stiff manner, and the silence of the others showed the Squire that he was deep in his daughters' black books. Was he also charged with Miss Bremerton's headache? Did any of them guess what had happened? He fancied from the puzzled look in Pamela's eyes as she said good-night to him that she guessed something.

Well, he wasn't going to tell them anything. He went back to the library, and presently Pamela, in her room upstairs, heard first the library bell, then the steps of Forest crossing the hall, and finally a conversation between the Squire and the butler which seemed to last some time.

It was in the very early morning—between four and five—that Elizabeth was wakened, first by vague movements in the house, and then by what seemed to be cautious voices outside. She drew a curtain back and looked out—a misty morning, between darkness and dawn, and trees standing on the grass in dim robes of amethyst and gold. Two men in the middle distance were going away from the house. She craned her neck. Yes—no doubt of it! The Squire and Forest. What could they be about at that hour of the morning? They were going, no doubt, to inspect the barricades! Yet Forest himself had told her that nothing would induce him to take a hand in the 'row.'

It was strange; but she was too weary and depressed to give it much thought. What was she going to do now? The world seemed emptily open before her once more, chill and lonely as the autumn morning.

CHAPTER IX

On the following morning the breakfast at Mannering was a very tame and silent affair. Forest was not in attendance, and the under housemaid, who commonly replaced him when absent, could not explain his non-appearance. He and his wife lived in a cottage beyond the stables, and all that could be said was that he 'had not come in.'

The Squire also was absent. But as his breakfast habits were erratic, owing to the fact that he slept badly and was often up and working at strange seasons of the night, neither of his daughters took any notice. Elizabeth did not feel inclined to say anything of her own observations in the small hours. If the Squire and Forest had been working at the barricade together, they were perhaps sleeping off their exertions. Or the Squire was already on the spot, waiting for the fray? Meanwhile, out of doors, a thick grey mist spread over the park.

So she sat silent like the other two—(Mrs. Gaddesden was of course in bed)—wondering from time to time when and how she should announce her departure.

Pamela meanwhile was thinking of the letter she would have to write to Desmond about the day's proceedings, and was impatient to be off as soon as possible for the scene of action. Once or twice it occurred to her to notice that Miss Bremerton was looking rather pale and depressed. But the fact only made Pamela feel prickly. 'If father does get into a row, what does it really matter to her. She's not responsible!—she's not one of us!'

Immediately after breakfast, Pamela disappeared. She made her way quietly through the park, where the dank mist still clung to the trees from which the leaf was dropping silently, continuously. The grass was all cobwebs. Every now and then the head of a deer would emerge from the dripping fern only to be swallowed up again in the fog.

Could a motor-plough work in a fog?

Presently, she who knew every inch of the ground and every tree upon it, became aware that she was close to the Chetworth gate. Suddenly the rattle of an engine and some men's voices caught her ear. The plough, sure enough! The sound of it was becoming common in the country-side. Then as the mist thinned and drifted she saw the thing plain—the puffing engine, one man driving and another following, while in their wake ran the black glistening furrow, where the grass had been.

And here was the gate. Pamela stood open-mouthed. Where were the elaborate defences and barricades of which rumour had been full the night before? The big gate swung idly on its hinges. And in front of it stood two men placidly smoking, in company with the village policeman. Not a trace of any obstruction—no hurdles, no barbed wire, only a few ends of rope lying in the road.

Then, looking round, she perceived old Perley, with a bag of ferrets in his hand, emerging from the mist, and she ran up to him breathlessly.

'So they've come, Perley! Was it they forced the gate?'

Perley scratched his head with his free hand.

'Well, it's an uncommon queer thing, Miss—but I can't tell yer who opened them gates! I come along here about seven o'clock this mornin', and the fog was so thick yo couldn't see nothin' beyond a yard or two. But when I got up to the gates, there they were open, just as you see 'em now. At first I thought there was summat wrong—that my eyes wasn't what they used to was. But they was all right.'

'And you saw the gates shut last night?'

'Barred up, so as you couldn't move 'em, Miss!—not without a crowbar or two, an' a couple of men. I thowt it was perhaps some village chaps larkin' as had done it. But it ain't none o' them. It beats me!'

Pamela looked at the two men smoking by the gate—representatives, very likely, of the Inspection Sub-Committee. Should she go up and question them? But some inherited instinct deterred her. She was glad the country should have the land and the corn. She had no sympathy with her father. And yet all the same when she actually saw Demos the outsider forcibly in possession of Mannering land, the Mannering spirit kicked a little. She would find out what had happened from some of their own people.

So after watching the County Council plough for a while as it clove its way up and down the park under the struggling sun which was gradually scattering the fog—her young intelligence quite aware all the time of the significance of the sight—she turned back towards the house. And presently, advancing to meet her, she perceived the figure of Elizabeth Bremerton—coming, no doubt, to get picturesque details on the spot for the letter she had promised to write to a certain artillery officer. A quick flame of jealousy ran through the girl's mind.

Miss Bremerton quickened her step.

'So they're open!' she said eagerly, as she and Pamela met. 'And there's nothing broken, or—or lying about!'

She looked in bewilderment at the unlittered road and swinging gate.

'They were open, Perley says, first thing this morning. He came by about seven.'

'Before the plough arrived?'

'Yes.'

They stood still, trying to puzzle it out. Then a sudden laugh crossed Elizabeth's face.

'Perhaps there were no barricades! Perhaps your father was taking us all in!'

'Not at all,' said Pamela drily. 'Perley saw the gates firmly barred with hurdles and barbed wire, and all tied up with rope, when he and his wife left the Lodge late last night.'

Elizabeth suddenly coloured brightly. Why, Pamela could not imagine. Her fair skin made it impossible for a flush to pass unnoticed. But why should she flush?

Elizabeth walked on rapidly, her eyes on the ground. When she raised them it was to look rather steadily at her companion.

'I think perhaps I had better tell you at once—I am very sorry!—but I shall be leaving you in a month. I told your father so last night.'

Pamela looked the astonishment she felt. For the moment she was tongue-tied. Was she glad or sorry? She did not know. But the instinct of good manners came to her aid.

'Can't you stand us?' she said bluntly. 'I expect you can't.'

Elizabeth laughed uncomfortably.

'Why, you've all been so kind to me. But I think perhaps'—she paused, trying to find her words—'I didn't quite understand—when I came—how much I still wanted to be doing things for the war—'

'Why, you might do heaps of things!' cried Pamela. 'You have been doing them. Taking an interest in the farms, I mean—and all that.'

'Well, but—' Elizabeth's brow puckered.

Then she broke into a frank laugh—'After all, that wasn't what I was engaged for, was it?'

'No—but you seemed to like to do it. And it's war-work,' said Pamela, inexorably.

Elizabeth was dismally conscious of her own apparent inconsistencies. It seemed best to be frank.

'The fact is—I think I'd better tell you—I tried yesterday to get your father to give up his plans about the gates. And when he wouldn't, and it seemed likely that there might be legal proceedings and—and a great fuss—in which naturally he would want his secretary to help him—'

'You just felt you couldn't? Well, of course I understand that,' said Pamela fervently. 'But then, you see,' she laughed, 'there isn't going to be a fuss. The plough just walked in, and the fifty acres will be done in no time.'

Elizabeth looked as she felt—worried.

'It's very puzzling. I wonder what happened? But I am afraid there will be other things where your father and I shall disagree—if, that is, he wants me to do so much else for him than the Greek work—'

'But you might say that you wouldn't do anything else but the Greek work?'

'Yes, I might,' said Elizabeth smiling, 'but once I've begun—'

'You couldn't keep to it?—father couldn't keep to it?'

Elizabeth shook her head decidedly. A little smile played about her lips, as much as to say, 'I am a managing woman and you must take me at that. "Il ne faut pas sortir de son caractère."'

Pamela, looking at her, admired her for the first time. And now that there was to be no more question—apparently—of correspondence with Arthur Chicksands, her mood changed impulsively.

'Well, I'm very sorry!' she said—and then, sincerely, 'I don't know how the place will get on.'

'Thank you,' said Elizabeth. Her look twinkled a little. 'But you don't know what I might be after if I stayed!'

Pamela laughed out, and the two walked home, better friends than they had been yet, Elizabeth asking that the news of her resignation of her post might be regarded as confidential for a few days.

When they reached the house, Pamela went into the morning-room to tell her sisters of the tame ending to all their alarms, while Elizabeth hurried to the library. She was due there at half-past ten, and she was only just in time. Would the Squire be there? She remembered that she had to apologize for her absence of the day before.

She felt her pulse thumping a little as she opened the library door. There was undoubtedly something about the Squire—some queer magnetism—born perhaps of his very restlessness and unexpectedness—that made life in his neighbourhood seldom less than interesting. His temper this morning would probably be of the worst. Something, or some one, had defeated all his schemes for a magnificent assertion of the rights of man. His park was in the hands of the invaders. The public plough was impudently at work. And at the same moment his secretary had given warning, and the new catalogue—the darling of his heart—would be thrown on his hands. It would not be surprising to find him rampant. Elizabeth entered almost on tip-toe, prepared to be all that was meek and conciliating, so far as was compatible with her month's notice.

A tall figure rose from the Squire's table and made her a formal bow.

'Good-morning, Miss Bremerton. I expected your assistance yesterday afternoon, but you had, I understand, made an engagement?'

'I asked you—a few days ago,' said Elizabeth, mildly confronting him. 'I am sorry if it inconvenienced you.'

'Oh, all right—all right,' said the Squire hastily. 'I had forgotten all about it. Well, anyway, we have lost a great deal of time.' His voice conveyed reproach. His greenish eyes were fierily bent upon her.

Elizabeth sat down at her table without reply, and chose a pen. The morning's work generally consisted of descriptions of vases and bronzes in the Mannering collection, dictated by the Squire, and illustrated often by a number of references to classical writers, given both in Greek and English. The labour of looking out and verifying the references was considerable, and the Squire's testy temper was never more testy than when it was quarrelling with the difficulties of translation.

'Kindly take down,' he said peremptorily.

Elizabeth began:

'"No. 190. Greek vase, from a tomb excavated at Mitylene in 1902. Fine work of the fifth century B.C. Subject: Penelope's Web. Penelope is seated at the loom. Beside her are the figures of a young man and two females—probably Telemachus and two hand-maidens. The three male figures in the background may represent the suitors. Size, 23 inches high; diameter, 11 inches. Perfect, except for a restoration in one of the handles."

'Have you got that?'

'Yes.'

'Go on please. "This vase is of course an illustration of the well-known passage in the Odyssey, Book 21. 103. I take Mr. Samuel Butler's translation, which is lively and modern and much to be preferred to the heavy archaisms of the other fellows."'

Elizabeth gave a slight cough. The Squire looked at her sharply.

'Oh, you think that's not dignified? Well, have it as you like.'

Elizabeth altered the phrase to 'other translators.' The Squire resumed. '"Antinous, one of the suitors, is speaking: 'We could see her working on her great web all day long, but at night she would unpick the stitches again by torchlight. She fooled us in this way for three years, and we never found her out, but as time wore on, and she was now in her fourth year, one of her maids, who knew what she was doing, told us, and we caught her in the act of undoing her work, so she had to finish it, whether she would or no....' I tell you, we never heard of such a woman; we know all about Tyro, Alcmena, Mycene, and the famous women of old, but they were nothing to your mother—any one of them."—And yet she was only undoing her own work!—she was not forcing a grown man to undo his!' said the Squire, with a sudden rush of voice and speech.

Elizabeth looked up astonished.

'Am I to put that down?'

The Squire threw away the book he was holding. His shining white hair seemed positively to bristle on his head, his long legs twined and untwined themselves.

'Don't pretend, please, that you don't know what part you've been playing in this affair!' he said with sarcasm. 'It took Forest and me three good hours this morning to take down as fine a barricade as ever I saw put up. I'm stiff with it still. British liberties have been thrown to the dogs—γυναικος ούνεκα—all because of a woman! And there you sit, as though nothing had happened! Yet I chanced to see you just now, coming back with Pamela!'

Elizabeth's flush this time dyed her all crimson. She sat, pen in hand, staring at her employer.

'I don't understand what you mean, Mr. Mannering.' At which her conscience whispered to her sharply, 'You guessed it already—in the park!'

The Squire jumped to his feet, and came to stand excitedly in front of her, his hands thrust into the high pockets of his waistcoat.

'I am extremely sorry!' he said, with that grand seigneur politeness he could put on when he chose—'but I am not able to credit that statement. You make it honestly, of course, but that a person of your intelligence, when you saw those gates, failed to put two and two together, well!'—the Squire shook his head, and shrugged his shoulders, became, in fact, one protesting gesture—'if you ask me to believe it,' he continued, witheringly, 'I suppose I must, but—'

'Mr. Mannering!' said Elizabeth earnestly, 'it would really be kind of you to explain.'

Her blush had died away. She had fallen back in her chair, and was meeting his attack with the steady, candid look that betrayed her character. She was now entirely self-possessed—neither nervous nor angry.

The Squire changed his tone. Folding his arms, he leant against a pedestal which supported a bust of a Roman emperor.

'Very well, then—I will explain. I told you yesterday of a step I proposed to take by way of testing how far the invasion of personal freedom had gone in this country. I was perfectly justified in taking it. I was prepared to suffer for my action. I had thought it all out. Then you came in—and by force majeure compelled me to give it all up!'

Elizabeth could not help laughing.

'I never heard any account of an incident which fitted less with the facts!' she said with vivacity.

'It exactly fits them!' the Squire insisted. 'When I told you what I meant to do, instead of sympathy—instead of simple acquiescence, for how the deuce were you responsible!—you threatened to throw up the work I cannot now possibly accomplish without you—'

'Mr. Levasseur?' suggested Elizabeth.

'Levasseur be hanged!' said the Squire, taking an angry pace up and down. 'Don't please interrupt me. I have given you a perfectly free hand, and you have organized the work—your share of it—as you please. Nobody else is the least likely to do it in the same way. When you go, it drops. And when your share drops, mine drops. That's what comes of employing a woman of ability, and trusting to her—as I have trusted to you!'

Was there ever any attack so grotesque, so unfair? Elizabeth was for one moment inclined to be angry—and the next, she was conscious of yieldings and compunctions that were extremely embarrassing.

'You rate my help a great deal too high,' she said after a moment. 'It is you yourself who have taught me how to work in your way. I don't think you will have any real difficulty with another secretary. You are'—she ventured a smile—'you are a born teacher.'

Never was any compliment less successful. The Squire looked sombrely down upon her.

'So you still intend to leave us,' he said slowly, 'after what I have done?'

'What have you done?' said Elizabeth faintly.

'Made myself a laughing-stock to the whole country-side!—and thrown all my principles overboard—to content you—and save my book!' The reply was given with an angry energy that shook her. 'I have humbled myself to the dust to meet your sentimental ideas—and there you sit—as stony and inaccessible as this fellow here!'—he brought his hand down with vehemence on the Roman emperor's shoulder. 'Not a word of gratitude—or concession—or sympathy! I was indeed a fool to take any trouble to please you!'

Elizabeth was silent. They surveyed each other. 'No agitation!' said Elizabeth's inner mind; 'keep cool!'

At last she withdrew her own eyes from the angry tension of his—dropped them to the table where her right hand was mechanically drawing nonsense figures on her blotting-paper.

'Did you really yourself take down that barricade?' she said gently.

'I did! And it was an infernal piece of work!'

'I'm awfully glad!' Her voice was very soft.

'I daresay you are. It suits your principles, and your ideas, of course—not mine! And now, having driven me to it—having publicly discredited and disgraced me—you can still sit there and talk of throwing up your work.'

The growing passion in the irascible gentleman towering above her warned her that it was time to bring the scene to an end.

'I am glad,' she repeated steadily, 'very glad—especially—for Mr. Desmond.'

'Oh, Desmond!' the Squire threw out impatiently, beginning again to walk up and down.

'He would have minded so dreadfully,' she said, still in a lower key. 'It was really him I was thinking of. Of course I had no right to interfere with your affairs—'

The Squire turned, the tyrant in him reviving fast.

'Well, you did interfere—and to some purpose! Now then—yes or no—is your notice withdrawn?'

Elizabeth hesitated.

'I would willingly stay with you,' she said, 'if—'

'If what?'

She looked up with a sudden flash of laughter.

'If we can really get on!'

'Name your terms!' He returned, frowning and excited, to the neighbourhood of the Roman emperor.

'Oh no—I have no terms,' she said hurriedly. 'Only—if you ask me to help you with the land, I should want to obey the Government—and—and do the best for the war.'

'Condition No. 1,' said the Squire grimly, checking it off. 'Go on!'

'And—I should—perhaps—beg you to let Pamela do some V.A.D. work, if she wants to.'

'Pamela is your affair!' said the Squire impatiently. 'If you stay here, you are her chaperon, and, for the present, head of the household.'

'Only just for the present—till Pamela can do it!' put in Elizabeth hastily. 'But she's nineteen—she ought to take a part.'

'Well, don't bother me about that. You are responsible. I wash my hands of her. Anything else?'

It did not do to think of Pamela's feelings, should she ever become aware of how she was being handed over. But the mention of her, on a sudden impulse, had been pure sympathy on Elizabeth's part; a wish to strike on the girl's behalf while the iron was so very hot. She looked up quietly.

'No, indeed there is nothing else—except indeed—that you won't expect me to hide what I feel about the war—and the little we at home can do to help—'

Her voice failed a little. The Squire said nothing. She went on, with a clearing countenance.

'So—if you really wish it—I will stay, Mr. Mannering—and try to help you all I can. It was splendid of you—to give up your plans. I'm sure you won't regret it.'

'I'm not sure at all—but it's done. Now, then, let us understand. You take over my estate correspondence. You'll want a clerk—I'll find one. You can appoint a new agent if you like. You can do what you like, in fact. I was never meant to be a landowner, and I hate the whole business. You can harry the farmers as you please—I shan't interfere.'

'Allow me to point out,' said Elizabeth firmly, 'that at college I was not trained in land-agency—but in Greek!'

'What does that matter? If women can build Dreadnoughts, as they say they can, they can manage estates. Now, then, as to my conditions. Do what you like—but my book and the catalogue come first!' He looked at her with an exacting eye.

'Certainly,' said Elizabeth.

'But I know what you'll do—you'll go and break down! You are not to break down.'

'Certainly!' said Elizabeth.

'But you have once broken down.'

Her start was perceptible, but she answered quietly.

'I was ill a year ago—partly from overwork. But I am normally quite strong.'

The Squire observed her. It was very pleasant to him to see her sitting there, in her trim serge dress, with its broad white collar and cuffs—the sheen of her hair against the dark wall—her shapely hands ready for work upon his table. He felt as if he had with enormous difficulty captured—recaptured—something of exceptional value; like one of those women 'skilled in beautiful arts' whom the Greek slave-raiders used to carry off from a conquered city, and sell for large sums to the wives of wealthy Greek chieftains. Till now he had scarcely thought of her as a woman, but rather as a fine-edged but most serviceable tool which he had had the extraordinary good luck to find. Now, with his mere selfish feeling of relief there mingled something rather warmer and more human. If only she would stay, he would honestly try and make life agreeable to her.

'Well now, that's settled,' he said, drawing a long breath—'Oh—except one thing—you will of course want a larger salary?'

'Not at all,' said Elizabeth decidedly. 'You pay me quite enough.'

'You are not offended with me for asking?' His tone had become astonishingly deferential.

'Not the least. I am a business woman. If I thought myself entitled to more I should say so. But it is extremely doubtful whether I can really be of any use whatever to you.'

'All right,' said the Squire, returning to his own table. 'Now, then, let us go on with No. 190.'

'Is it necessary now to put in—well, quite so much about Penelope?' asked Elizabeth, as she took up her pen.

'What do you think?'

'It seems a little long and dragged in.' Elizabeth looked critically at the paragraph.

'And we have now unravelled the web?—we can do without her? Yes—let her go!' said the Squire, in a tone of excessive complaisance.

When the morning's work was done, and luncheon over, Elizabeth carried off Pamela to her room. When Pamela emerged, she went in search of Forest, interviewed him in the gun-room, and then shutting herself up in the 'den' she wrote to Desmond.

'MY DEAR DEZZY—There are such queer things going on in this queer house! Yesterday Broomie gave warning, and father barricaded the park gates, and was perfectly mad, and determined not to listen to anybody. In the middle of the night he and Forest took the barricade down, and to-day, Broomie is to be not only secretary, but land-agent, and anything else she pleases—queen, in fact, of all she surveys—including me. But I am bound to say she had been very decent to me over it all. She wants me to do some of the housekeeping—and she has actually made father consent to my helping at the hospital every afternoon. Of course I am awfully glad about that. I shall bicycle over.

'But all the same it is very odd, and perhaps you and I had better consider what it may mean. I know from Broomie herself that she gave notice yesterday—and now she is going to stay. And I know from Forest that father called him up when it was quite dark, between three and four in the morning—Mrs. Forest thought the Germans had come when she heard the knocking—and asked him to come with him and undo the gates. Forest told me that he would have had nothing whatever to do with closing them, nor with anything 'agin the Government! He's a staunch old soul, is Forest. So when father told him what he wanted, he didn't know what to make of it. However, they both groped their way through the fog, which was thick on the other side of the park, and set to at the gates. Forest says it was an awful business to get everything cleared away. Father and Gregson had made an uncommonly good job of it. If Gregson had put in work like that on his own hedges and gates, Forest says he mightn't have been kicked out! It took them ages getting the barbed wire cleared away, because they hadn't any proper nippers. Father took off his coat, and worked like a navvy, and Forest hoisted him up to get at the wire along the wall. Forest says he was determined to leave nothing! "And I believe, Miss, the Squire was very glad of the fog—because there couldn't be any one prying around."

'For it seems to be really true that the village has been in a state of ferment, and that they had determined to free the gates and let in the Council plough. Perley was seen talking to a lot of men on the green last night. I met him myself this morning after breakfast near the gates, and he confessed he had been there already—early. I expect he came to reconnoitre and take back the news. Rather calm, for one of father's own men! But that's the new spirit, Dezzy. We're not going to be allowed to have it all our own way any more. Well, thank goodness, I don't mind. At least, there is something in me that minds. I suppose it's one's forbears. But the greater part of me wants a lot of change—and there are often and often times when I wish I'd been born in the working-class and was just struggling upwards with them, and sharing all their hopes and dreams for "after the war." Well, why shouldn't I? I'm going to set Broomie on to some of the cottages in the village—not that she'll want setting on—but after all, it's I who know the people.

'But that's by the way. The point is why did father give in? Evidently because Broomie gave notice, and he couldn't bear the idea of parting with her. Of course Alice—and Margaret too, to some extent—are convinced it all means that father wants to marry her. Only Alice thinks that Miss Bremerton has been intriguing for it since the first week she set foot in the house; while Margaret is certain that she wouldn't marry father if he asked her. She thinks that Miss B. is just the new woman, who wants to do things, and isn't always thinking about getting married. Well, Dezzy, old boy—I don't know what to think. I'll keep my eyes open, and report to you. I don't—altogether—like her. No, I don't—that's flat. I wish, on the whole, she'd taken her departure! And yet I feel rather a toad for saying so. She is splendid in some things—yes, she is! And the Rectory people take the most rose-coloured view of her—it's too late to tell you why, for the postman is just coming.

'Good-bye, Dezzy—dear Dezzy! I know how glad you'll be about the gates. Write to me as often as you can. By the way, Miss Bremerton has got a brother in the war—with General Maude. That ought to make me like her. But why did she leave us to find it out through the Rectory? She never says anything about herself that she can help. Do you think you'll really get to France in January? Ever your loving
    'PAM.'

CHAPTER X

It was a bright January day. Lunch was just over at Mannering, and the luncheon-party had dispersed—attracted to the garden and the park by the lure of the sunshine after dark days of storm and wind. Mrs. Gaddesden alone was left sitting by the fire in the hall. There was a cold wind, and she did not feel equal to facing it. She was one of those women, rare in these days, who, though still young, prefer to be prematurely old; in whom their great-grandmothers, and the 'elegant' lackadaisical ways of a generation that knew nothing of exercise, thick boots and short skirts, seem to become once more incarnate. Though Mannering was not ill-warmed, Alice moved about it in winter wrapped in a picturesque coat of black velvet trimmed with chinchilla, her head wreathed in white lace. From this rather pompous setting her fair hair, small person, and pinched pale face looked out perhaps with greater dignity than they could have achieved unadorned. Her chilliness, her small self-indulgences, including an inordinate love of cakes and all sweet things, were the standing joke of the twins when they discussed the family freely behind the closed doors of the 'Den.' But no one disliked Alice Gaddesden, though it was hard to be actively fond of her. She and her husband were quite good friends; but they were no longer of any real importance to each other. He was a good deal older than she; and was often away from London on 'war work' in the Midlands. On these occasions Alice generally invited herself to Mannering. She thus got rid of housekeeping, which in these days of rations worried her to death. Moreover, food at Mannering was much more plentiful than food in town—especially since the advent of Elizabeth Bremerton.

It was of Elizabeth that Mrs. Gaddesden was thinking as she sat alone in the hall. From her seat she could perceive a shrubbery walk in the garden outside, along which two figures were pacing—Miss Bremerton and the new agent. Beyond, at some distance, she was aware of another group disappearing among the trees of the park—Pamela with Captain Chicksands and Beryl.

This was the first time that any member of the Chicksands family had been a guest at Mannering since the quarrel in the autumn. The Squire had not yet brought himself to shake hands with Sir Henry. But Beryl on the one side, and Pamela on the other—aided and abetted always by Elizabeth Bremerton—had been gradually breaking down the embargo; and when, hearing from Beryl that her brother Arthur was with them for a few days, Pamela had openly proposed in her father's presence to ask them both to luncheon, the Squire had pretended not to hear, but had at any rate raised no objection. And when the brother and sister arrived, he had received them as though nothing had happened. His manners were always brusque and ungracious, except in the case of persons who specially mattered to his own pursuits, such as archæologists and Greek professors. But the Chetworth family were almost as well acquainted with his ways as his own, and his visitors took them philosophically. Arthur Chicksands had kept the table alive at luncheon with soldier stories, and the Squire's sulky or sarcastic silence had passed unnoticed.

Mrs. Gaddesden's mind was very full of the Captain's good looks and distinction. He was now in London, at the War Office, it seemed, for a short time, on a special mission; hence his occasional weekends with his family. When the mission was over—so Beryl told Pamela—he was probably going out to an important appointment in the Intelligence Department at G.H.Q. 'Arthur's a great swell,' said Beryl, 'though as to what he's done, or what people think of him, you have to dig it out of him—if you can!'

Mrs. Gaddesden did not very much like him. His brusque sincerity made people of her sort uncomfortable. But she would have liked very much to know whether there was anything up between him and Pamela. Really, Miss Bremerton's discretion about such things was too tiresome—ridiculous—almost rude! It was no good trying, even, to discuss them with her.

As to the disinheriting of Aubrey, no more had been heard of it. Miss Bremerton had told Aubrey when he was at home for twenty-four hours at Christmas that, as far as she knew, the codicil was still unsigned. But Aubrey didn't seem to care the least whether it was or no. If Beryl wished him to raise the question again with his father, of course he would; otherwise he greatly preferred to leave it alone. And as Beryl had no will or wishes but his, and was, in Alice's opinion, only too absurdly and dependently in love, the sleeping dogs were very much asleep; and the secret of Mannering's future disposal lay hid impenetrably in the Squire's own breast.

At the same time, Mrs. Gaddesden was firmly persuaded that whatever Elizabeth Bremerton wished or advised would ultimately be done.

What an extraordinary position that young woman now held among them! Nearly three months had now elapsed since Mrs. Gaddesden's autumn visit—since Desmond had gone into training at his artillery camp—since a third of the park had been ploughed up, and since Elizabeth Bremerton had thrown up her post only to come back next day as dictator.

Yes—dictator! Mrs. Gaddesden was never tired of thinking about it, and was excitedly conscious that all the neighbourhood, and all their friends and kinsfolk were thinking and speculating with her. At the beginning of November, before she and Margaret Strang went back to town, the Squire had announced to all of them that Miss Bremerton had become his 'business secretary,' as well as his classical assistant. And now, after three months, the meaning of this notice was becoming very clear. The old agent, Mr. Hull, had been dismissed, and moderately—very moderately—pensioned. It was said that Miss Bremerton, on looking into his accounts, saw no reason at all for any special indulgence. For, in addition to everything else, she turned out to be a trained accountant!—and money matters connected with the estate were being probed to the bottom that had never been probed before. Mrs. Gaddesden's own allowance—for the Squire had always obstinately declined to settle any capital on his married daughters—had been, for the first time, paid at the proper date—by Elizabeth Bremerton! At least, if the Squire had signed it, she had written the cheque. And she might perfectly well have signed it. For, as Pamela had long since reported to her sisters, Elizabeth paid all the house and estate accounts over her own signature, and seemed to have much more accurate knowledge than the Squire himself of the state of his bank balance, and his money affairs generally.

Not that she ever paraded these things in the least. But neither did she make any unnecessary mystery about it with the Squire's family. And indeed they were quite evident to any one living in the house. At times she would make little, laughing, apologetic remarks to one of the daughters—'I hope you don't mind!'—the Squire wants me to get things straight.' But in general, her authority by now had become a matter of course.

Her position in the Mannering household, however, was as nothing to her position in the estate and the neighbourhood. That was the amazing thing which had by now begun to set all tongues wagging. Sir Henry Chicksands, meeting Mrs. Gaddesden at the station, had poured himself out to her. 'That extraordinary young woman your father has got hold of, is simply transforming the whole place. The farmers on the whole like her very much. But if they don't like her, they're afraid of her! For Heaven's sake don't let her kill herself with over-work. She'll soon be leading the county.'

Yes. Work indeed! How on earth did she get through it? In the mornings there she was in the library, absorbed in the catalogue, writing to the Squire's dictation, transcribing or translating Greek—his docile and obedient slave. Then in the afternoon—bicycling all over the estate, and from dark onwards, till late at night, busy with correspondence and office work, except just for dinner and an hour afterwards.

The door of the outer hall opened and shut. Elizabeth and a young man—the new agent—entered the inner hall, where Mrs. Gaddesden was sitting, Elizabeth acknowledging her presence with a pleasant nod and smile. But they passed quickly through to the room at the further end of the hall, which was now an estate office where Elizabeth spent the latter part of her day. It was connected both with the main living-rooms of the house, and with a side entrance from the park, by which visitors on estate matters were admitted.

A man was sitting waiting for Miss Bremerton. He was the new tenant of the derelict farm, on the Holme Wood side of the estate, and he had come to report on the progress which had been made in clearing and ploughing the land, and repairing the farm-buildings. He was a youngish man, a sergeant in a Warwickshire regiment, who had been twice wounded in the war, and was now discharged. As the son of an intelligent farmer, he had had a good agricultural training, and it was evident that his enthusiasms and those of the Squire's new 'business-secretary' were running in harness.

The new agent, Captain Dell, also a discharged Territorial, who had lost an arm in the war, watched the scene between the incoming tenant and Elizabeth, with a shrewd pair of eyes, through which there passed occasional gleams of amusement or surprise. He was every day making further acquaintance with the lady who was apparently to be his chief, but he was well aware that he was only at the beginning of his lesson. Astonishing, to see a woman taking this kind of lead!—asking these technical questions—as to land, crops, repairs, food production, and the rest—looking every now and then at the note-book beside her, full of her own notes made on the spot, or again, setting down with a quick hand something that was said to her. And all through he was struck with her tone of quiet authority—without a touch of boasting or 'side,' but also without a touch of any mere feminine deference to the male. She was there in the Squire's place, and she never let it be forgotten. Heavens, women had come on during this war! Through the young man's mind there ran a vague and whirling sense of change.

'Well, Mr. Denman, that all sounds splendid!' said Elizabeth, at last, as she rose from her table.

'The country won't starve, if you can help it! I shall tell the County Committee all about you on Tuesday. You don't want another tractor?'

'Oh, no, thank you! The two at work are enough. I hope you'll be over soon. I should like to show you what we've been after.' The man's tone was one of eager good will.

'Oh yes, I shall be over before long,' said Elizabeth cheerfully. 'It's so tremendously interesting what you're doing. And if you want anything I can help you in, you can always telephone.'

And she pointed smiling to the instrument on the table—the first that had ever been allowed within the walls of Mannering. And that the Squire might not be teased with it, Elizabeth had long since fitted an extra inner door, covered with green baize, to the door of the office.

The new tenant departed, and Elizabeth turned to the agent.

'I really think we've caught a good man there,' she said, with a smile. 'Now will you tell me, please, about those timber proposals? I hope to get a few words with the Squire to-night.'

And leaning back in her chair, she listened intently while Captain Dell, bringing a roll of papers out of his pocket, read her the draft proposals of a well-known firm of timber merchants, for the purchase of some of the Squire's outlying woods of oak and beech. Lights had been brought in, and Elizabeth sat shading her eyes from the lamp before her,—a strong and yet agreeable figure. Was it the consciousness of successful work—of opening horizons, and satisfied ambitions, that had made a physical presence, always attractive, so much more attractive than before—that had given it a magnetism and fire it had never yet possessed? Pamela, who was developing fast, and was acutely conscious of Elizabeth, asked herself the question, or something like it, about once a week. And during a short Christmas visit that Elizabeth had paid her own people, her gentle mother, much puzzled and a little dazzled by her daughter, had necessarily pondered the why and wherefore of a change she felt, but could not analyse. One thing the mother's insight had been clear about. Elizabeth was not in love. On the contrary, the one love-affair of her life seemed to be at last forgotten and put aside. Elizabeth was now in love with efficiency; with a great task given into her hand. As to the Squire, the owner of Mannering, who had provided her with the task, Mrs. Bremerton could not imagine him or envisage him at all. Elizabeth's accounts of him were so reticent and so contradictory.... 'Well, that's very interesting'—said Elizabeth thoughtfully, when Captain Dell laid down his papers—'I wonder what Mr. Mannering will say to it? As you know, I got his express permission for you to make these enquiries. But he hates cutting down a single tree, and this will mean a wide clearance!'

'So it will—but the country wants every stick of it. And as to not cutting, one sees that from the woods—the tragedy of the woods!'—said the young man with emphasis. 'There has been no decent forestry on this estate for half a century. I hope you will be able to persuade him, Miss Bremerton. I expect, indeed, it's Hobson's choice.'

'You mean the timber will be commandeered?'

'Probably. The Government have just come down on some of Lord Radley's woods just beyond our borders—with scarcely a week's warning. No "With your leave" or "By your leave"! The price fixed, Canadians sent down to cut, and a light railway built from the woods to the station to carry the timber, before you could say "Jack Robinson."'

'You think the price these people offer is a fair one?' She pointed to the draft contract.

'Excellent! The Squire won't get nearly as much from the Government.'

'What one might do with some of it for the estate!' said Elizabeth, looking up, her blue eyes dancing in the lamplight.

'Rebuild half the cottages?' said the other, smiling, as he rose. 'A village club-house, a communal kitchen, a small holdings scheme—all the things we've talked about? Oh yes, you could do all that and more. The Squire doesn't know what he possesses.'

'Well, I'll take the papers to him,' said Elizabeth, holding out her hands for them. 'I may perhaps catch him to-night'

A little more business talk, and the agent departed. Then Elizabeth dreamily—still cogitating a hundred things—touched an electric bell. A girl typist, who acted as her clerk, came in from an adjoining room. Elizabeth rapidly dictated a number of letters, stayed for a little friendly gossip with the girl about her father in the Army Service Corps, who had been in hospital at Rouen, and had just finished, when the gong rang for afternoon tea.

When Elizabeth entered, the hall was crowded. It was the principal sitting-room of the house, now that for reasons of economy fires were seldom lit in the drawing-rooms. Before Elizabeth's advent it had been a dingy, uncomfortable place, but she and Pamela had entirely transformed it. As in the estate so in the house, the Squire did not know what he possessed. In all old houses with a continuous life, there are accumulations of furniture and stores, discarded by the generation of one day, and brought back by the fashion of the next. A little routing in attics and forgotten cupboards and chests had produced astonishing results. Chippendale chairs and settees had been brought down from the servants' bedrooms; two fine Dutch cabinets had been discovered amid a mass of lumber in an outhouse; a tall Japanese screen, dating from the end of the eighteenth century, and many pairs of linen curtains embroidered about the same time in branching oriental patterns by the hands of Mannering ladies, had been unearthed, and Pamela— for Elizabeth having started the search had interfered very little with its results—had spent some of her now scanty leisure in making the best of the finds. The hall was now a charming place, scented, moreover, on this January evening by the freesias and narcissus that Elizabeth had managed to rear in the house itself, and Pamela, who had always been ashamed of her own ill-kept and out-at-elbows home, as compared with the perfections of Chetworth, had been showing Arthur and Beryl Chicksands what had been done to renovate the old house since they were last in it—'and all without spending a penny!'—with a girlish pleasure which in the Captain's opinion became her greatly. Pamela needed indeed a good deal of animation to be as handsome as she deserved to be! A very critical observer took note that her stock of it was rapidly rising. It was the same with the letters, too, which for a month or so past, she had condescended to write him, after treating him most uncivilly in the autumn, and never answering a long screed—'and a jolly good one!'—which he had written her from Paris in November.

As Elizabeth came in, Pamela was reading aloud a telegram just received, and Miss Bremerton was greeted with the news—'Desmond's coming to-night, instead of to-morrow! They've given him forty-eight hours' leave, and he goes to France on Thursday.'

'That's very short!' said Elizabeth, as she took her place beside Pamela, who was making tea. 'Does your father know?'

Forest, it appeared, had gone to tell him. Meanwhile Captain Chicksands was watching with a keen eye the relation between Miss Bremerton and Pamela. He saw that the Squire's secretary was scrupulously careful to give Pamela her place as daughter of the house; but Pamela's manner hardly showed any real intimacy between them. And it was easy to see where the real authority lay. As for himself he had lately begun to ask himself seriously how much he was interested in Pamela. For in truth, though he was no coxcomb, he could not help seeing—all the more because of Pamela's variable moods towards him—that she was at least incipiently interested in him. If so, was it fair to her that they should correspond?—and that he should come to Mannering whenever he was asked and military duty allowed, now that the Squire's embargo was at least partially removed?

He confessed to himself that he was glad to come, that Pamela attracted him. At the same time there was in him a stern sense that the time was no time for love-making. The German hosts were gathering; the vast breakdown in Russia was freeing more and more of them for the Western assault. He himself was for the moment doing some important intelligence work, in close contact with the High Command. No one outside a very small circle knew better than he what lay in front of England—the fierce death-struggle over a thousand miles of front. And were men and women to be kissing and marrying while these storm-clouds of war—this rain of blood—were gathering overhead?

Involuntarily he moved further from Pamela. His fine face with the rather high cheek-bones, strong mouth, and lined brow, seemed to put softness away. He approached Elizabeth.

'What is the Squire doing about his wood, Miss Bremerton? The Government's desperately in want of ash!'

He spoke almost as one official might speak to another—comrade to comrade. What he had heard about her doings from his father had filled his soldier's mind with an eager admiration for her. That was how women should bear themselves in this war—as the practical helpers of men.

He fell into the chair beside her, and Elizabeth was soon deep in conversation with him, a conversation that any one might overhear who would. It turned partly on the armies abroad—partly on the effort at home. There was warmth—even passion—in it, studiously restrained. But it was the passion of two patriots, conscious through every pulse of their country's strait.

The others listened. Pamela became silent and pale. All the old jealousy and misery of the autumn were alive in her once more. She had looked forward for weeks to this meeting with Arthur Chicksands. And for the first part of his visit she had been happy—before Elizabeth came on the scene. Why should Elizabeth have all the homage and the attention? She, too, was doing her best! She was drudging every day as a V.A.D., washing crockery and scrubbing floors; and this was the first afternoon off she had had for weeks. Her limbs were dog-tired. But Arthur Chicksands never talked to her—Pamela—in this tone of freedom and equality—with the whole and not the half of his mind. 'I could hold my own,' she thought bitterly, 'but he never gives me the chance! I suppose he despises girls.'

As the hall clock struck half-past five, however, Elizabeth rose from her seat, gathering up the papers she had brought in from the office, and disappeared.

Arthur Chicksands looked at his watch. Beryl exclaimed:

'Oh, no, Arthur, not yet! Let's wait for Desmond!'

Pamela said perfunctorily—'No, please don't go! He'll be here directly.'

But as they gathered round the fire, expecting the young gunner, she hardly opened her lips again. Arthur Chicksands was quite conscious that he had wounded her. She appeared to him, as she sat there in the firelight, in all the first fairness and freshness of her youth, as an embodied temptation. Again he said to himself that other men might love and marry on the threshold of battle; he could not bring himself to think it justifiable—whether for the woman or the man. In a few weeks' time he would be back in France and in the very thick, perhaps, of the final struggle—of its preparatory stages, at any rate. Could one make love to a beautiful creature like that at such a moment, and then leave her, with a whole mind?—the mind and the nerve that were the country's due?

All the same he had never been so aware of her before. And simultaneously his mind was invaded by the mute, haunting certainty that her life was reaching out towards his, and that he was repelling and hurting her.

Suddenly—into the midst of them, while Mrs. Gaddesden was talking endlessly in her small plaintive voice about rations and queues—there dropped the sound of a car passing the windows, and a boy's clear voice.

'Desmond!' cried Pamela, with almost a sob of relief, and like one escaping from a nightmare she sprang up and ran to greet her brother.

Meanwhile Elizabeth had found the Squire waiting for her, and, as she saw at once, in a state of tension.

'What was that you were saying to me about timber last week?' he demanded imperiously as she entered, without giving her time to speak. 'I hear this intolerable Government are behaving like madmen, cutting down everything they can lay hands on. They shan't have my trees—I would burn them first!'

Elizabeth paused in some dismay.

'You remember—' she began.

'Remember what?' It was long since she had heard so snappish a tone.

'That you authorized me—'

'Oh, I daresay, I gave myself away—I'm always doing so. I don't mean half I say. You're too full of business—you take me up too quick. What are those papers you've got there?'

Elizabeth's red cheeks showed her taken aback. It was the first time for weeks that her employer had turned upon her so. She had grown so accustomed to managing him, to taming the irritable temper that no one else but she could cope with, and, unconsciously, so proud of her success, that she was not prepared for this attack. She met it meekly.

'I have a proposal here to submit to you, from —— & Co.' (she named a firm of timber-merchants famous throughout the Midlands). 'There is nothing in it—Captain Dell is certain—that would injure the estate. You have such masses of timber! And, if you don't sell, you may find it commandeered. You know what's happened to Lord Radley?'

The Squire sulkily demanded to be informed. Elizabeth told the story, standing at his desk, like a clerk making a report. It seemed to enrage her auditor.

'This accursed war!' he broke out, when she had finished—'it makes slaves and idiots of us all. It must—it shall end!' And marching tempestuously up and down, he went off into one of the pessimist and pacifist harangues to which she was more or less accustomed. Who would rid the country of a Government that could neither make peace nor make war?—that foresaw nothing—that was making life unbearable at home, by a network of senseless restrictions, while it wasted millions abroad, and in the military camps! The Labour Party were the only people with a grain of sense. They at least would try to make peace. Only, when they had made it, to be governed by them would be even worse than to be governed by Lloyd George. There was no possible life anywhere for decent quiet people. And as for the ravaging and ruin of the woods that was going on all over England—

'The submarine return is worse this week,' said Elizabeth in a low voice.

She had gone to her own table and was sitting there till the hurricane should pass over. There was in her a fresh and chafing sense of the obstacles laid in her path—the path of the scientific and successful organizer—by the Squire's perversities. It was not as though he were a pacifist by conviction, religious or other. She had seen him rout and trample on not a few genuine professors of the faith. His whole opposition to the war rested on the limitations and discomforts inflicted on his own life. It reminded her of certain fragments of dialogue she had overheard in the winter, where she had chanced to find herself alone in a railway carriage full of a group of disaffected workmen returning from a strike meeting at Leicester. 'If there are many like these, is the country worth saving?' she was saying to herself all the time, in a dumb passion.

Yet, after all, those men had done months and years of labour for the country. Saying 'I will not go!' they had yet gone. Without a spark of high feeling or conscious self-sacrifice to ease their toil, they had yet, week by week, made the guns and the shells which had saved the armies of England. When this temporary outbreak was over they would go back and make them again. And they were tired men—sallow-faced, and bowed before their time.

But what had this whimsical, accomplished man before her ever done for his country that he should rail like this? It was difficult after a tiring day to keep scorn and dissent concealed. They probably showed in her expression, for the Squire turned upon her as she made her remark about the submarines, examining her with a pair of keen eyes.

'Oh, I know very well what you and that fellow Chicksands think about persons like me who endeavour to see things as they are!'—he smote a chair before him—'and not as you and our war-party wish them to be. Well, well—now then to business. Who wants to cut my woods—and what do they offer for them?'

Elizabeth put the papers in front of him. He turned them over.

'H'm—they want the Cross Wood—one of the most beautiful woods in England. I have spent days there when I was young drawing the trees. And who's the idiot'—he pointed to some marginal notes—'who is always carping and girding? "Good forestry" would have done this and not done that. "Mismanagement"—"neglect"! Upon my word, who made this man a judge over me?'

And flushed with wrath, the Squire looked angrily at his secretary. 'Heavens!'—thought Elizabeth—'why didn't I edit the papers before I showed them?' But aloud she said with her good-tempered smile—

'I am afraid I took all those remarks as applying to Mr. Hull. He was responsible for the woods, wasn't he? He told me he was.'

'Nothing of the kind! In the end the owner is responsible. This fellow is attacking me!'

Elizabeth said nothing. She could only wait in hope to see how the large sums mentioned in the contract might work.

'"Maximum price"! What's this?—"Had Mr. Mannering been willing to enter into negotiations with us last year,"'—the Squire began to read a letter accompanying the draft contract—'"when we approached him, we should probably have been able to offer him a better price. But under the scale of prices now fixed by the Government—"'

The owner of Mannering bounded out of his seat.

'And you actually mean to say that I may not only be forced to sell my woods—but whether I am forced or not, I can only sell them at the Government price? Intolerable!—absolutely intolerable! Every day that Englishmen put up with these tyrannies is a disgrace to the country!'

'The country must have artillery waggons and aeroplanes,' said Elizabeth, softly. 'Where are we to get the wood? There are not ships enough to bring it overseas?'

'And suppose I grant you that—why am I not to get my fair price—like anybody else? Just tell me that!'

'Why, everybody's "controlled"!' cried Elizabeth.

'Pshaw! I am sorry to be uncivil'—a sarcastic bow in her direction—'but I really must point out that you talk nonsense. Look at the money in the banks—look at the shops and the advertisements—look at the money that people pay for pictures, and old books, and autographs. Somebody's making profits—that's clear. But a wretched landowner—with a few woods to sell—it is easy to victimize him!'

'It comes to a large sum,' said Elizabeth, looking down. At last she was conscious of a real exasperation with the Squire. For four months now she had been wrestling with him—for his own good and the country's, and everything had always to be begun again. Suddenly her spirits drooped.

The Squire observed her furtively out of the corners of his eyes. Then he turned to the last page of the contract, with its final figures. His eyebrows went up.

'The man's a fool!' he said vehemently. 'I know the value of my own timber a great deal better than he. They're not worth a third of what they put them at.'

'Even at the Government price?' Elizabeth ventured slyly. 'He'll be very glad to give it!'

'Then it's blackmailing the country,' said the Squire obstinately. 'I loathe the war, but I'm not a profiteer.'

Elizabeth was silent. If the Squire persisted in rejecting this deal, which he had himself invited in another mood, half her dreams for the future, the dreams of a woman just beginning to feel the intoxication of power, or, to put it better, the creative passion of the reformer, were undone. She had already saved the Squire much money. When all reasonable provision had been made for investment, replanting, and the rest, this sale would still leave enough to transform the estate and scores of human lives upon it. Her will chafed hotly under the curb imposed upon it by the caprices of a master for whom—save only as a Greek scholar—she had little respect. After a while, as the Squire was still turning over the contract with occasional grunts and mutterings, she asked—

'Will you please tell me what I am to reply?'

Her voice was cold and measured.

The Squire threw up his white head.

'What hurry is there?' he said testily.

'Oh, none—if you wish it delayed. Only—' she hesitated—'Captain Dell tells me the Government inspectors are already in the neighbourhood. He expects them here before long.'

'And if I make a stand—if I oppose you—well—it'll be the gates over again?' She shrugged her shoulders.

'We must try to find the money some other way. It is badly wanted. I thought—'

'You thought I had authorized this—and you've given all your work for nothing? You think I'm an impossible person?'

Suddenly she found him sitting beside her. Perforce she looked him in the face.

'Don't give notice again!' he said, almost with passion.

'It's not so easy now,' she said, with a rather uncertain voice.

'Because you've done so much for me?—because you've slaved and put your heart into it? That's true. Well now, look here. We'll put that beastly thing away to-night—perhaps I shall be in a better temper in a few days.'

There was a note in his voice he seemed unable to keep out of it. Elizabeth looking up caught the fire light on the sketch of Desmond. Had the Squire's eyes been on it too? Impossible to say—for he had already turned away.

'Oh, yes,—put it away!' she said hurriedly.

'And I'll go over the woods with you on—Friday,' said the Squire after a pause. 'Oh, I don't deny that the money is tempting. I'm not such a pauper as I once was, thanks to you. I seem to have some money in the bank—astonishing situation! And—there's a jolly good sale at Christie's coming on.'

He looked at her half-shamefaced, half-ready to resent it if she laughed at him.

Her eyes laughed.

'I thought you'd forgotten that. I saw you mark the catalogue.'

'Beech and oak between two and three hundred years old—in exchange for Greek gems, between two and three thousand. Well—I'll consider it. Now then, are you feeling better?'

And to her amazement he approached her with an outstretched hand. Elizabeth mechanically placed her own in it.

'I know what you want,' he said impetuously. 'You've got a head full of dreams. They're not my dreams—but you've a right to them—so long as you're kind to mine.'

'I try to be,' she said with a rather tremulous lip.

At that moment the library door opened. Neither perceived it. Desmond came in softly, lest his father should be at work. A carved oak screen round the door hid his entrance, and as he emerged into the light his eyes caught the two distant figures standing hand in hand.

Instinctively he stepped back a few paces and noisily opened the door. The Squire walked away.

'Why, Desmond!' said his father, as the boy emerged into the light, 'your train's punctual for once. Thank you, Miss Bremerton—that'll do. Kindly write to those people and say that I am considering the matter. I needn't keep you any longer....'

That night a demon came to Elizabeth and offered her a Faust-like bargain. Ambition—noble ambition on the one side—an 'elderly lunatic' on the other. And she began to consider it!

CHAPTER XI

Everybody in Mannering had gone to bed but Desmond and Pamela. It was not certain indeed that the Squire had gone to bed, but as there was a staircase beside one of the doors of the library leading direct to his room, it was not likely that he would cross the hall again. The twins felt themselves alone.

'I daresay there'll be a raid to-night,' said Desmond, 'it's so bright and still. Put down that lamp a moment, Pamela.'

She obeyed, and he threw away his cigarette, went to one of the windows, and drew up the blinds.

'Listen!' he said, holding up his hand. Pamela came to his side, and they both heard through the stillness that sound of distant guns which no English ear had heard—till now—since the Civil War.

'And there are the searchlights!'

For over London, some forty miles away behind a low range of hills, faint fingers of light were searching the sky.

'At this very moment, perhaps,'—said the boy between his teeth—'those demons are blowing women and children to pieces—over there!'

Pamela shivered and laid her cheek against his shoulder. But both he and she were aware of that strange numbness which in the fourth year of the war has been creeping over all the belligerent nations, so that horror has lost its first edge, and the minds, whether of soldiers in the field, or of civilians at home, have become hardened to facts or ideas which would once have stirred in them wild ferments of rage and terror.

'Shall we win, this year, Desmond?' said Pamela, as they stood gazing out into the park, where, above a light silvery mist a young moon was riding in a clear blue. Not a branch stirred in the great leafless trees; only an owl's plaintive cry seemed to keep in rhythm with that sinister murmur on the horizon.

'Win?—this year?' said the boy, with a shrug. 'Don't reckon on it, Pam. Those Russian fools have dished it all for months!'

'But the Americans will make up?'

Desmond assented eagerly. And in the minds of the English boy and girl there rose a kind of vague vision of an endless procession of great ships, on a boundless ocean, carrying men, and men, and more men—guns, and aeroplanes, and shining piles of shells—bringing the New World to the help of the Old.

Desmond turned to his sister.

'Look here, Pam, this time next week I shall be in the line. Well, I daresay I shan't be at the actual front for a week or two—but it won't be long. We shall want every battery we've got. Now—suppose I don't come back?'

'Desmond!'

'For goodness' sake, don't be silly, old girl. We've got to look at it, you know. The death-rate of men of my age' (men!—Desmond, a man!) 'has gone up to about four times what it was before the war. I saw that in one of the papers this morning. I've only got a precious small chance. And if I don't come back, I want to know what you're going to do with yourself.'

'I don't care what happens to me if you don't come back!' said the girl passionately. She was leaning with folded arms against the side of the window, the moonlight, or something else, blanching the face and her fair hair.

Desmond looked at her with a troubled expression. For two or three years past he had felt a special responsibility towards this twin-sister of his. Who was there to look after her but he? He saw that his father never gave her a serious thought, and as to Aubrey—well, he too seemed to have no room in his mind for Pam—poor old Pam!

'How are you getting on with Broomie?' he asked suddenly.

'I don't like her!' said Pamela fiercely. 'I shall never like her!'

'Well, that's awkward,'—said the boy slowly, 'because—'

'Because what?'

'Because I believe she means to marry father!'

Pamela laughed angrily.

'Ah, you've found that out too!'

Desmond pulled down the blind again, and they went back to the fire, sitting on the floor beside it, with their arms round each other, as they had been used to do as children. And then in a low voice, lest any ears in the sleeping house should be, after all, on the alert, he told her what he had seen in the library. He was rather ashamed of telling her; only there was this queer sense of last words—of responsibility—for his sister, which excused it.

Pamela listened despondently.

'Perhaps they're engaged already! Well,—I can tell you this—if father does marry her, she'll rule him, and me—if I give her the chance—and everybody on the place, with a rod of iron.'

Desmond at first remonstrated. He had been taken aback by the sudden vision in the library; and Pamela's letters for some time past had tended to alter his first liking for 'Broomie' into a feeling more distrustful and uncertain. But, after all, Broomie's record must be remembered. 'She wouldn't sign that codicil thing—she made father climb down about the gates—and Sir Henry says she's begun to pull the estate together like anything, and if father will only let her alone for a year or two she'll make him a rich man.'

'Oh, I know,' said Pamela gloomily, 'she's paid most of the bills already. When I go into Fallerton now—everybody—all the tradesmen are as sweet as sugar.'

'Well, that's something to the good, isn't it? Don't be unfair!'

'I'm not unfair!' cried Pamela. 'Don't you see how she just swallows up everybody's attention—how nobody else matters when she's there! How, can you expect me to like that—if she were an archangel—which she isn't!'

'But has she done anything nasty—anything to bother you?'

'Well, of course, I'm just a cypher when she's there. I'm afraid I oughtn't to mind—but I do!'

And Pamela, with her hands round her knees, stared into the fire in bitterness of spirit. She couldn't explain, even to Desmond, that the inward eye all the time was tormented by two kindred visions—Arthur in the hall that afternoon, talking war work with Elizabeth with such warm and eager deference, and Arthur on Holme Hill, stretched at Elizabeth's feet, and bandying classical chaff with her. And there was a third, still more poignant, of a future in which Elizabeth would be always there, the centre of the picture, mistress of the house, the clever and charming woman, beside whom girls in their teens had no chance.

She was startled out of these reflections by a remark from Desmond.

'You know, Pam, you ought to get married soon.'

The boy spoke shyly—but gravely and decidedly. Pam thought with a sudden anguish—'He would never have said that, unless—'

She laid her head on his shoulder, clinging to him.

'I shan't get married, old boy.'

'Oh, that's nonsense! Look here, Pam—you mustn't mind my poking my nose into things where I've no business. You see, it's because—Well, I've sometimes thought—punch my head, if you like!—that you had a fancy for Arthur Chicksands.'

Pamela laughed.

'Well, as he hasn't got any fancy for me, you needn't take that into your dear old head!'

'Why, he was always very fond of you, Pam.'

'Oh, yes, he liked ragging me when I was a child. I'm not good enough for him now.'

'What do you mean—not good enough?'

'Not clever enough, you silly old boy. He'll marry somebody much older than me.'

Desmond ruminated.

'He seemed to be getting on with Broomie this afternoon?'

'Magnificently. He always does. She's his sort. She writes to him.'

'Oh, does she?' The boy's voice was dry and hostile. He began to understand, or thought he did. Miss Bremerton was not only plotting to marry his father—had perhaps been plotting for it from the beginning—but was besides playing an unfair game with Pam—spoiling Pam's chances—cutting in where she wasn't wanted—grabbing, in fact. Anger was mounting in him. Why should his father be mopped up like this?—and Pamela made unhappy?

'I'd jolly well like to stop it all!' he said, under his breath.

'Stop what? You dear, foolish old man! You can't stop it, Dezzy.'

'Well, if she'll only make him happy—!'

'Oh, she'll be quite decent to him,' said Pamela, with a shrug, 'but she'll despise him!'

'What the deuce do you mean, Pam?'

Whereupon, quite conscious that she was obeying an evil and feverish impulse, but unable to control it, Pamela went into a long and passionate justification of what she had said. A number of small incidents—trifling acts and sayings of Elizabeth's—misinterpreted and twisted by the girl's jealous pain, were poured into Desmond's ears.

'All the servants know that she treats father like a baby. She and Forest manage him in little things—in the house—just as she runs the estate. For instance, she does just what she likes with the fruit and the flowers—'

'Why, you ought to do all that, Pam!'

'I tried when I came home from school. Father wouldn't let me do a thing. But she does just what she pleases. You can hear her and Forest laughing over it. Oh, it's all right, of course. She sends things to hospitals every week.'

'That was what you used to want.'

'I do want it—but—'

'You ought to have the doing of it?'

'Oh, I don't know. I'm away all day. But she might at least pretend to refer to him—or me—sometimes. It's the same in everything. She twists father round her little finger; and you can see all the time what she thinks—that there never was such a bad landlord, or such a miserable, feckless crew as the rest of us, before she came to put us straight!'

Desmond listened—partly resisting—but finally carried away. By the time their talk was over he felt that he too hated Elizabeth Bremerton, and that it was horrid to have to leave Pamela with her.

When they said good-night Pamela threw herself on her bed face downwards, more wretched than she had ever been—wretched because Desmond was going, and might be killed, wretched, too, because her conscience told her that she had spoilt his last evening, and made him exceedingly unhappy, by a lot of exaggerated complaints. She was degenerating—she knew it. 'I am a little beast, compared to what I was when I left school,' she confessed to herself with tears, and did not know how to get rid of this fiery plague that was eating at her heart. She seemed to look back to a time—only yesterday!—when poetry and high ideals, friendships and religion filled her mind; and now nothing—nothing!—was of any importance, but the look, the voice, the touch of a man.

The next day, Desmond's last day at home, for he was due in London by the evening, was gloomy and embarrassed for all concerned. Elizabeth, pre-occupied and shrinking from her own thoughts, could not imagine what had happened. She had put off all her engagements for the day, that she might help in any last arrangements that might have to be made for Desmond.

But Desmond declined to be helped, not rudely, but with a decision, which took Elizabeth aback.

'Mayn't I look out some books for you? I have found some more pocket classics,' she had said to him with a smile, remembering his application to her in the autumn.

'No, thank you. I shall have no time.' And with that, a prompt retreat to Pamela and the Den. Elizabeth, indeed, who was all eagerness to serve him, found herself rebuffed at every turn.

Nor were matters any better with Pamela, who had cried off her hospital work in order to pack for Desmond. Elizabeth, seeing her come downstairs with an armful of khaki shirts to be marked, offered assistance—almost timidly. But Pamela's 'Thank you, but I'd rather not trouble you—I can do it quite well'—was so frosty that Elizabeth could only retire—bewildered—to the library, where she and the Squire gave a morning's work to the catalogue, and never said a word of farm or timber.

But the Squire worked irritably, finding fault with a number of small matters, and often wandering away into the house to see what Desmond was doing. During these intervals Elizabeth would sit, pen in hand, staring absently into the dripping garden and the park beaten by a cold rain. The future began to seem to her big with events and perplexity.

Then with the evening came the boy's leave-taking; full of affection towards his father and sister, and markedly chilly in the case of Elizabeth. When the station taxi had driven off, Elizabeth—with that cold touch of the boy's fingers still tingling on her hand—turned from the front door to see Pamela disappearing to the schoolroom, and the Squire fidgeting with an evening paper which the taxi had brought him from the station.

Elizabeth suddenly noticed the shaking of the paper, over which only the crest of white hair showed. Too bad of Pamela to have gone off without a word to her father! Was it sympathy with the Squire, or resentment on her own account, that made Elizabeth go up to him?—though at a respectful distance.

'Shall we finish the bit of translation we began this morning, if you're not busy?' she said gently. It was very rarely now that she was able to do any classical work after the mornings.

The Squire threw down the newspaper, and strode on before her to the library without a word. Elizabeth followed. Rain and darkness had been shut out. The wood fire glowed on the hearth, and its ruddy light was on the face of the Nikê, and its solemn outstretched wings. All the apparatus of their common work was ready, the work that both loved. Elizabeth felt a sudden, passionate drawing towards this man twenty years older than herself, which seemed to correspond to the new and smarting sense of alienation from the twins and their raw, unjust youth. What had been the reason for their behaviour to her that day?—what had she done? She was conscious of long weeks of effort, in Pamela's case,—trying to please and win her; and of a constant tender interest in Desmond, which had never missed an opportunity of doing or suggesting something he might like—all for this! She must have offended them she supposed in some way; how, she could not imagine. But her mood was sore; and, self-controlled as she was, her pulse raced.

Here, however, she was welcome, she was needed; she could distract and soothe a bitterness of soul best measured by the Squire's most unusual taciturnity. No railing at the Government or the war, not a fling even at the 'd——d pedant, Chicksands!' or 'The Bubbly-jocks,' as he liked to call the members of the County War Committee. Elizabeth put a text of Aristophanes—the Pax—into his hands, and drew her table near to him, waiting his pleasure. There was a lamp behind him which fell on her broad, white brow, her waiting eyes and hand, and all the friendly intelligence of her face. The Squire began haltingly, lost his place, almost threw the book away; but she cheered him on, admired this phrase, delicately amended that, till the latent passion had gripped him, and he was soon in full swing, revelling in all the jests and topicalities of the play, where the strikers and pacifists, the profiteers, the soldiers and munition workers of two thousand odd years ago, fight and toil, prate and wrangle and scheme, as eager and as alive as their descendants of to-day. Soon his high, tempestuous laugh rang out; Elizabeth's gentler mirth answering. Sometimes there was a dispute about a word or a rendering; she would put up her own view, with obstinacy, so that he might have the pleasure of knocking it down. And all through there was the growing sense of comradeship, of mutual understanding, which, in their classical work at least, had been always present for Elizabeth, since her first acquaintance with her strange employer.

When she rose, reluctantly, at the sound of the dressing-bell, the Squire paced up and down while she put her books and papers away. Then as she was going, he turned abruptly—

'I told Forest to order the Times—will you see he does it?'

'Certainly.'

'I loathe all newspapers,' he said sombrely. 'If we must go to the devil, I don't want to know too much about it. But still—'

She waited a moment, but as nothing more came she was leaving the room, when he added—

'And don't forget the timber business to-morrow afternoon. Tell Dell to meet us in Cross Wood.'

When she had gone, the Squire still continued pacing, absorbed in meeting the attack of new and strange ideas. He had always been a man with a singularly small reflective gift. Self-examination—introspection of any sort—were odious to him. He lived on stimulus from outside, attracted or repelled, amused or interested, bored or angry, as the succession of events or impressions might dictate. To collect beautiful things was a passion with him, and he was proud of the natural taste and instinct, which generally led him right. But for 'aesthetics'—the philosophy of art—he had nothing but contempt. The volatile, restless mind escaped at once from the concentration asked of it; and fell back on what the Buddhist calls 'Maia,' the gay and changing appearances of things, which were all he wanted. And it was because the war had interfered with this pleasant and perpetual challenge to the senses of the outer world, because it forced a man back on general ideas that he did not want to consider—God, Country, Citizenship—that the Squire had hated the war.

But this woman who had become an inmate of his house, while she ministered to all the tastes that the Squire had built up as a screen between himself and either the tragic facts of contemporary life, or any troublesome philosophizing about them, was yet gradually, imperceptibly, drawing the screen aside. Her humanity was developing the feeble shoots of sympathy and conscience in himself. What she felt, he was beginning to feel; and when she hated anything he must at least uncomfortably consider why.

But all this she did and achieved through her mere fitness and delightfulness as a companion. He had never imagined that life would bring him anybody—least of all a woman—who would both give him so much, and save him so much. Selfish, exacting, irritable—he knew very well that he was all three. But it had not prevented this capable, kind, clever creature from devoting herself to him, from doing her utmost, not only to save his estate and his income, but to make his life once more agreeable to him, in spite of the war and all the rancour and resentments it had stirred up in him.

How patient she had been with these last! He was actually beginning to be ashamed of some of them. And now to-night—what made her come and give him the extra pleasure of her company these two hours? Sympathy, he supposed, about Desmond.

Well, he was grateful; and for the first time his heart reached out for pity—almost humbled itself—accepted the human lot. If Desmond were killed, he would never choose to go on living. Did she know that? Was it because she guessed at the feelings he had always done his best to hide that she had been so good to him that evening?

What as to that love-story of hers—her family?—her brother in Mesopotamia? He began to feel a hundred curiosities about her, and a strong wish to make life easy for her, as she had been making it easy for him. But she was excessively proud and scrupulous—that he had long since found out. No use offering to double her salary, now that she had saved him all this money! His first advance in that direction had merely offended her. The Squire thought vaguely of the brother—no doubt a young lieutenant. Could interest be made for him?—with some of the bigwigs. Then his—very intermittent—sense of humour asserted itself. He to make interest with anybody—for anybody—in connection with the war! He, who had broken with every soldier-friend he ever had, because of his opinions about the war!—and was anathema throughout the country for the same reason. Like all members of old families in this country he had a number of aristocratic and wealthy kinsfolk, the result of Mannering marriages in the past. But he had never cared for any of them, except to a mild degree for his sister, Lady Cassiobury, who was ten years older than himself, and still paid long visits to Mannering, which bored him hugely. On the last occasion, he was quite aware that he had behaved badly, and was now in her black-books.

No—there was nothing to be done, except to let this wonderful woman have her own way! If she wanted to cut down the woods, let her!—if she wanted to amuse herself by rebuilding the village, and could find the money out of the estate, let her!—it would occupy her, attach her to the place, and do him no harm.

Yes, attach her to the place; bind her! hold her!—that was what he wanted. Otherwise, how hideously uncertain it all was! She might go at any time. Her mother might be ill—old ladies have a way of being ill. Her brother might be wounded—or killed. Either of those events would carry her off—out of his ken. But if she were engaged deeply enough in the estate affairs she would surely come back. He knew her!—she hated to leave things unfinished. He was eager now to heap all kinds of responsibilities upon her. He would be meek and pliable; he would put no sort of obstacles in her way. She would have no excuse for giving him notice again. He would put up with all her silly Jingoism—if only she would stay!

But at this point the Squire suddenly pulled up short in his pacing and excitedly asked himself the question, which half the people about him were already beginning to ask.

'Why shouldn't I marry her?'

He stood transfixed—the colour rising in his thin cheeks.

Hitherto the notion, if it had ever knocked at the outer door of the brain, had been chased away with mockery. And he had no sooner admitted it now than he drove it out again. He was simply afraid of it—in terror lest any suspicion of it should reach Elizabeth. Her loyalty, her single-mindedness, her freedom from the smallest taint of intrigue—he would have answered for them with all he possessed. If, for a moment, she chose to think that he had misinterpreted her kindness, her services in any vile and vulgar way, why, he might lose her on the instant! Let him walk warily—do nothing at least to destroy the friend in her, before he grasped at anything more.

Besides, how could she put up with him? 'I am the dried husk of a man!' thought the Squire, with vehemence. 'I couldn't learn her ways now, nor she mine. No; let us be as we are—only more so!'

But he was shaken through and through; first by that vanishing of his boy into the furnace of the war, which had brought him at last within the grip of the common grief, the common fear, and now by this strange thought which had invaded him.

After dinner, Elizabeth, who was rather pale, but as cheerful and self-possessed as usual, put Mrs. Gaddesden's knitting to rights at least three times, and held the wool for that lady to wind till her arm ached. Then Mrs. Gaddesden retired to bed; the Squire, who with only occasional mutterings and mumblings had been deep in Elizabeth's copy of the Times, which she had at last ventured to produce in public, went off to the library, and Elizabeth and Pamela were left in the hall alone.

Elizabeth lingered over the fire; while Pamela wondered impatiently why she did not go to her office work as she generally did about nine o'clock. Pamela's mood was more thorny than ever. Had she not seen a letter in Elizabeth's handwriting lying that very afternoon on the hall-table for post—addressed to Captain Chicksands, D.S.O., War Office, Whitehall? Common sense told her that it probably contained nothing but an answer to some questions Arthur had put to the Squire's 'business secretary' as to the amount of ash in the Squire's woods—Arthur's Intelligence appointment having something to do with the Air Board. But the mere fact that Elizabeth should be writing to him stirred intolerable resentment in the girl's passionate heart. She knew very well that it was foolish, unreasonable, but could no more help it than a love-smitten maiden of old Sicily. It was her hour of possession, and she was struggling with it blindly.

And Elizabeth, the shrewd and clever Elizabeth, saw nothing, and knew nothing. If she had ever for a passing moment suspected the possibility of 'an affair' between Arthur Chicksands and Pamela, she had ceased to think of it. The eager projects with which her own thoughts were teeming, had driven out the ordinary preoccupations of womankind. Derelict farms, the food-production of the county, timber, village reconstruction, war-work of various kinds, what time was there left?—what room?—in a mind wrestling with a hundred new experiences, for the guessing of a girl's riddle?

Yet all the same she remained her just and kindly self. She was troubled—much troubled—by the twins' behaviour. She must somehow get to the bottom of it.

So that when only she and Pamela were left in the hall she went up to the girl, not without agitation.

'Pamela—won't you tell me?—have I done anything to offend you and Desmond?'

She spoke very quietly, but her tone showed her wounded. Pamela started and looked up.

'I don't know what you mean,' she said coldly. 'Did you think we had been rude to you?'

It was the first hostile word they had ever exchanged.

Elizabeth grew pale.

'I didn't say anything about your being rude. I asked you if you were cross with me.'

'Oh—cross!' said Pamela, suddenly conscious of a suffocating excitement. 'What's the good of being cross? It's you who are mistress here.'

Elizabeth fell back a step in dismay.

'I do think you ought to explain,' she said after a moment. 'If I had done anything you didn't like—anything you thought unkind, I should be very very sorry.'

Pamela rose from her seat. Elizabeth's tone seemed to her pure hypocrisy. All the bitter, poisonous stuff she had poured out to Desmond the night before was let loose again. Stammering and panting, she broke into the vaguest and falsest accusations.

She was ignored—she was a nobody in her own home—everybody knew it and talked of it. She wasn't jealous—oh no!—she was simply miserable! 'Oh, I daresay you can no more help it than I can. You, of course, are twenty times more use here than I am. I don't dispute that. But I am the daughter of the house after all, and it is a little hard to be so shelved—so absolutely put in the background!—as I am—'

'Don't I consult you whenever I can? haven't I done my best to—' interrupted Elizabeth, only to be interrupted in her turn.

—'to persuade father to let me do things? Yes, that's just it!—you persuade father, you manage everything. It's just that that's intolerable!'

And flushed with passion, extraordinarily handsome, Pamela stood tremulously silent, her eyes fixed on Elizabeth. Elizabeth, too, was silent for a moment. Then she said with steady emphasis:

'Of course there can only be one end to this. I can't possibly stay here.'

'Oh, very well, go!' cried Pamela. 'Go, and tell father that I've made you. But if you do, neither you nor he will see me again for a good while.'

'What do you mean?'

'What I say. If you suppose that I'm going to stay on here to bear the brunt of father's temper after he knows that I've made you throw up, you're entirely mistaken.'

'Then what do you propose?'

'I don't know what I propose,' said Pamela, shaking from head to foot, 'but if you say a word to father about it I shall simply disappear. I shall be able to earn my own living somehow.'

The two confronted each other.

'And you really think I can go on after this as if nothing had happened?' said Elizabeth, in a low voice.

Pangs of remorse were seizing on Pamela, but she stifled them.

'There's a way out!' she said presently, her colour coming and going. 'I'll go and stay with Margaret in town for a bit. Why should there be any fuss? She's asked me often to help with her war-workroom and the canteen. Father won't mind. He doesn't care in the least what I do! And nobody will think it a bit odd—if you and I don't talk.'

Elizabeth turned away. The touch of scorn in her bearing was not lost on Pamela.

'And if I refuse to stay on, without saying or doing anything—to put myself right—you threaten to run away?'

'I do—I mean it,' said Pamela firmly. She had not only hardened again under the sting of that contempt she detected in Elizabeth, but there was rising up in her a sudden and rapturous vision of London:—Arthur at the War Office—herself on open ground—no longer interfered with and over-shadowed. He would come to see her—take her out, perhaps, sometimes to an exhibition, or for a walk. The suggestion of going to Margaret had been made on the spur of the moment without after-thought. She was now wedded to it, divining in it a hundred possibilities.

At the same moment she became more cautious, and more ashamed of herself. It would be better to apologize. But before she could speak Elizabeth said:

'Does Desmond agree with what you have been saying?'

Pamela staring at her adversary was a little frightened. She rushed into a falsehood.

'Desmond knows nothing about it! I don't want him dragged in.'

Elizabeth's eyes, with their bitter, wounded look; seemed to search the girl's inmost mind. Then she moved away.

'We had better go to bed. We shall both want to think it over. Good-night.'

And from the darkness of the hall, where fire and lamp were dying, Pamela half spell-bound, watched the tall figure of Elizabeth slowly mounting the broad staircase at the further end, the candle-light flickering on her bright hair, and on a bunch of snowdrops in her breast.

Then, for an hour, while the house sank into silence, Pamela sat crouched and shivering by the only log left in the grate. 'A little while ago,' she was thinking miserably, 'I had good feelings and ideas—I never hated anybody. I never told lies. I suppose—I shall get worse and worse.'

And when she had gone wearily to bed, it was to cry herself to sleep.

The following morning, an urgent telegram from her younger sister recalled Elizabeth Bremerton to London, where her mother's invalid condition had suddenly taken a disastrous turn for the worse.

CHAPTER XII

'Hullo, Aubrey! what brings you here?' And with the words Arthur Chicksands, just emerging from the War Office, stopped to greet a brother officer, who was just entering it.

'Nothing much. I shan't be long. Can you wait a bit?'

'Right you are. I've got to leave a note at the Ministry of Munitions, but I'll be back in a few minutes.'

Arthur Chicksands went his way to Whitehall Gardens, while Major Mannering disappeared into the inner regions of that vast building where dwell the men on whom hang the fortunes of an Empire. Arthur walking fast up Whitehall was very little aware of the scene about him. His mind was occupied with the details of the interview in which he had just been engaged. His promotion had lately been rapid, and his work of extraordinary interest. He had been travelling a great deal, backwards and forwards between London and Versailles, charged with several special enquiries in which he had shown both steadiness and flair. Things were known to him that he could not share even with a friend so old and 'safe' as Aubrey Mannering. The grip of the coming crisis was upon him, and he seemed 'to carry the world in his breast'

'Next year—next February—where shall we all be?' The question was automatically suggested to him by the sight of the green buds of the lilac trees In front of Whitehall Terrace.

'Oh, my dear Susan!—do look at those trees!'

Chicksands, startled from his own meditations, looked up to see two old ladies gazing with an eager interest at a couple of plane trees, which had just shed a profusion of bark and stood white and almost naked in the grey London air. They were dear old ladies from some distant country-side, with bonnets and fronts, and reticules, as though they had just walked out of Cranford, and after gazing with close attention at the plane trees near them they turned and looked at all the other plane trees in Whitehall, which presented an equally plucked and peeled appearance.

Then the one addressed as Susan laughed out—a happy, chuckling laugh.

'Oh, I see! My dear Ellen, how clever people are now! They're camouflaged—that's what it is—can't you see?—all the way down, because of the raids!'

The admiring fervour of the voice was too much for Chicksands. He hurried past them, head down, and ran up the steps of the Ministry of Munitions. From that point of vantage he turned, shaken with amusement, to see the pair advancing slowly towards Westminster, their old-fashioned skirts floating round them, still pointing eagerly at the barkless trees. Had they come from some piny region where the plane is not? Anyway the tension of the day was less.

He repeated the tale to Aubrey Mannering a few minutes later, when they had turned together into Birdcage Walk. But Aubrey scarcely gave it the ghost of a smile. As to his old friend's enquiries about his own work and plans, he answered them quite readily, but shortly, without any expansion; with the manner, indeed, of one for whom talk about himself had no sort of attraction. And as they passed along the front of the barracks, where a few men were drilling, Chicksands, struck by his companion's silence, turned a sudden look upon him. Mannering's eyes were absently and yet intently fixed on the small squads of drilling men. And it was sharply borne in on Chicksands that he was walking beside the mere image or phantom of a man, a man whose mind was far away—'voyaging through strange seas of thought alone.' Mannering's eyes were wide open; but they made the weird impression on the spectator of a double seeing—of some object of vision beyond and behind the actual scene of the barracks and the recruits, and that an object producing terror or pain. Chicksands made a remark and it was not answered.

It was not the first time that Arthur had observed this trance-like state in the man who was to be his brother-in-law, and had been his 'chum' from childhood. Others had noticed it, and he had reason to think that Beryl was often distressed by it. He had never himself seen any signs of strangeness or depression in Aubrey before the Easter of 1915, when they met in Paris, for the first time after the battle of Neuve Chapelle, in which Mannering had lost his dearest friend, one Freddy Vivian, of the Worcesters. During the winter they had met fairly often in the neighbourhood of Ypres, and Aubrey was then the same eager, impulsive fellow that Chicksands had known at Eton and Cambridge, bubbling over with the exploits of his battalion, and adored by his own men. In April, in a raid near Festubert, Mannering was badly wounded. But the change in him was already evident when they were in Paris together. Chicksands could only suppose it represented the mental and nervous depression caused by Vivian's death, and would pass away. On the contrary, it had proved to be something permanent.

Yet it had never interfered with his efficiency as a soldier, nor his record for a dare-devil courage. There were many tales current of his exploits on the Somme, in which again and again he had singed the beard of Death, with an absolute recklessness of his own personal life, combined with the most anxious care for that of his men. Since the battle of Messines he had been the head of a remarkable Officers' School at Aldershot, mainly organized by himself. But now, it seemed, he was moving heaven and earth to get back to France and the front. Chicksands did not think he would achieve it. He was invaluable where he was, and his superiors, to Mannering's indignation, were inclined to regard him as a man who was physically fit rather for home service than the front.

When they reached the Buckingham Palace end of the Walk, Mannering paused.

'Where are you lunching?'

'At Brooks', with my father.'

'Oh, then I'll walk there with you.'

They struck across the park, and talk fell on a recent small set-back which had happened to a regiment with which they were both well acquainted.

Chicksands shrugged his shoulders.

'I've heard some details at the War Office. Just ten minutes' rot! The Colonel stopped it with his revolver. Most of them splendid fellows. Two young subs gave way under a terrific shelling and their men with them. And in ten minutes they were all rushing forward again, straight through the barrage—and the two lieutenants were killed.'

'My God!—lucky fellows!' cried Mannering, under his breath, with a passion and suddenness that struck astonishment into his companion.

'Well, yes,' said Arthur, 'in a sense—but—nothing would have happened to them. They had wiped it out.'

Mannering shook his head. Then with a great and evident effort he changed the conversation. 'You know Pamela's in town?'

'Yes, with Margaret Strang. I'm going to dine there to-night. How's the new agent getting on?' Aubrey smiled.

'Which?—the man—or the lady?'

'Miss Bremerton, of course. I got a most interesting letter from her a fortnight ago. Do you know that she herself has discovered nearly a thousand ash in the Squire's woods, after that old idiot Hull had told her she wouldn't find half-a-dozen? A thousand ash is not to be sneezed at in these days! I happen to know that the Air Board wrote the Squire a very civil letter.'

'"All along of Eliza!"' mused Mannering. 'She's been away from Mannering just lately. Her invalid mother became very seriously ill about three weeks ago, and she had to go home for a time. My father, of course, has been fussing and fuming to get her back.'

'Poor Squire! But how could Pamela be spared too?'

Mannering hesitated.

'Well, the fact is she and my father seem to have had a good old-fashioned row. She tried to fill Miss Bremerton's place, and of course it didn't answer. She's too young, and my father too exacting. Then when it broke down, and he took things out of her hands again, comparing her, of course, enormously to her disadvantage with Miss Bremerton, Pamela lost her temper and said foolish things of Miss Bremerton. Whereupon fury on my father's part—and sudden departure on Pamela's. She actually bicycled off to the railway station, sent a telegram for her things, and came up to Margaret. Alice Gaddesden is looking after father. But of course he and she don't get on a bit.'

The Captain looked much concerned.

'It's a pity Pamela takes that line—don't you think? I really don't see the conspirator in Miss Bremerton. I hoped when I saw her first she would make just all the difference to Pamela.'

'Yes, it's puzzling. I ran down to see my father, who was in a rabid state of mind, not knowing what to do with all the schemes and business this clever woman started—perfectly lost without her.'

'Ah, that's the worst of your Indispensable!' laughed Chicksands.

Mannering threw him a quick, scrutinizing look. Various items of information picked up at Mannering, mostly from his sister Alice, had made him wonder whether some jealousy of a more vital and intimate kind than appeared might not be at the root of Pamela's behaviour. He was not observant at this period of his life, except of things relating to his engagement to Beryl, his work, or those inner pre-occupations which held him. But it had once or twice crossed his mind that Pamela might be interested in Arthur; and there had been certain hints from Beryl, who was, however, he was certain, scarcely better informed than he was. Pamela was a most secretive and independent young woman. He doubted whether even Desmond, whom she adored, knew much about her.

Well, supposing she was jealous—jealous of her father's secretary, and on account of Arthur, was there the smallest cause for it? He understood that Arthur and Miss Bremerton had met occasionally, and he had himself heard Chicksands express the warmest admiration for her as the right sort of new woman, 'as straight as you make 'em'—and with 'a brain like a man'—which, from one who was always rather a critical spectator than a courtier of women, was high praise. But as for any spark of sex in it—Mannering laughed at the notion. No. If that really was Pamela's delusion, something must be done to rid his little sister of it if possible. He would talk to Beryl.

But—as always when any new responsibility presented itself to him—a deep inner weariness rebelled. In small things as in great, he was mentally like a man walking and working with a broken limb.

Arthur Chicksands stood some time that evening waiting on the doorstep of Mrs. Strang's small house, in one of the old streets of Westminster. 'No servants, I suppose,' he said to himself with resignation. But it was bitterly cold, and he was relieved to hear at last the sound of a voice and a girl's laugh inside. Pamela opened the door to him, pulling down the sleeves of a thin black dress over her shapely arms.

'Oh, come in. Margaret's cooking the dinner, and I've laid the table. Bernard's just bringing up some coals, and then we're ready.'

Mr. Bernard Strang, a distinguished Home Office official, appeared at that moment in his shirt-sleeves at the head of the kitchen stairs, bearing a scuttle of coal in each hand.

'Gracious! Give me one of them!' said the Captain, hurrying to the rescue.

But Mr. Strang, putting down the right-hand scuttle, to take breath, warned him off.

'Thank you, Chicksands—but no brass hats need apply! Many thanks—but you're too smart!' He pointed, panting, to the red tabs and to the bit of variegated ribbon on Chicksands' broad chest. 'Go and help Pamela bring in the dinner.'

The Captain obeyed with alacrity.

'All the servants left on Monday,' said Pamela. 'We had a charwoman this morning, but she's gone to-night, because there's a new moon.'

'What—raids?'

Pamela nodded as she gave him the soup, with instructions to carry it carefully and put it by the fire. She seemed to be in her gayest mood, and Chicksands' eyes followed her perpetually as she went backwards and forwards on her household tasks. Presently Mrs. Strang appeared, crimson from the fire, bearing the fishpie and vegetables that were to provide the rationed meal.

'To think,' said Mr. Strang, when they were at last at table, 'that there was a time when we were proud of our "little dinners," and that I never made myself unpleasant unless Margaret spent more than five pounds on the food alone. Shall I ever eat a good dinner again?'

He looked wistfully at the bare table.

'Will you ever want to?' said Arthur, quietly.

A momentary silence fell upon the little party. Bernard Strang had lost two brothers in the war, and Chicksands had no sooner spoken than he reproached himself for a tactless brute. But, suddenly, the bells of the Abbey rang: out above their heads, playing with every stroke on the nerves of the listeners. For the voice of England was in them, speaking to that under-consciousness which the war has developed in us all.

'Any news?' said Strang, looking at Arthur.

'No. The Eastern business gets a little worse every day.'

'And the "Offensive"?'

'Let them! Our men want nothing better.'

On which the dinner resolved itself into a device for making the Captain talk. The War Office crisis, the men gathered in conclave at Versailles, and that perpetual friction between the politician and the soldier, which every war, big or little, brings to the front, and which will only end when war ends—those were the topics of it, with other talk such as women like to listen to of men about individual men, shrewd, careless, critical, strangely damning here, strangely indulgent there, constant only in one quality—that it is the talk of men and even if one heard it behind a curtain and strained through distance, could never by any chance be mistaken for the talk of women.

At intervals Pamela got up to change the plates and the dishes, quieting with a peremptory gesture the two males, who would spring to their feet. 'Haven't I done parlour-work for six months?—no amateurs, please!' And again, even while he talked on, Arthur's eyes would stray after the young full figure, the white neck and throat, the head with the soft hair folded close around it in wavy bands that followed all its lines—as it might have been the head of one of those terra-cottas that her father had stolen from the Greek tombs in his youth.

But unfortunately, after dinner, in a corner of the dark drawing-room, he must needs try and play the schoolmaster a little, for her good of course; and then all went to pieces.

'I hear you ran away!'

The voice that threw out this sudden challenge was half ironical, half affectionate; the grey eyes under their strong black brows looked at her with amusement.

Pamela flushed at once.

'Aubrey told you, I suppose? What was the good of staying? I couldn't do anything right. I was only making things worse.'

'I can hardly believe that! Couldn't you just have kept Miss Bremerton's work going till she came back?'

'I tried,' said Pamela stiffly, 'and it didn't do.'

'Perhaps she attempts too much. But she seemed to me to be very sensible and human. And—did you hear about the ash trees?'

'No,' said Pamela shortly, her foot nervously beating the ground. 'It doesn't matter. Of course I know she's the cleverest person going. But I can't get on with her—that's all! I'm going to take up nursing—properly. I'm making enquiries about the London Hospital. I want to be a real Army nurse.'

'Will your father consent?'

'Fathers can't stop their daughters from doing things—as they used to do!' said Pamela, with her chin in the air.

She had moved away from him; her soft gaiety had disappeared; he felt her all thorns. Yet some perversity made him try to argue with her. The war—pray the Lord!—might be over before her training as an Army nurse was half done. Meanwhile, her V.A.D. work at Mannering was just what was wanted at the moment from girls of her age—hadn't she seen the appeals for V.A.D.'s? And also, if by anything she did at home—or set others free for doing—she could help Captain Dell and Miss Bremerton to pull the estate round, and get the maximum amount of food out of it, she would be serving the country in the best way possible.

'The last ounce of food, mind!—that's what it depends on,' he said, smiling at her, 'which can stick it longest—they or we. You belong to the land—ought you desert it?'

Pamela sat unmoved. She knew nothing about the land. Her father had the new agent—and Miss Bremerton.

'Your sister there,' said Chicksands, nodding towards the front drawing-room, where Strang and his wife were sitting Darby and Joan over the fire discussing rations and food prices, 'thinks Miss Bremerton already overdone.'

'I never saw the least sign of it!'

'But think!—your father never slackens his Greek work—and there is all the rest.'

'I suppose if it's too much for her she'll give it up,' said Pamela in her most obstinate voice.

But even then a normally tactful man still held on.

Never was anything more maladroit. It was the stupidity of a clever fellow, deluding himself with the notion that having refused the rôle of lover, he could at least play that of guardian and adviser; whose conscience, moreover, was so absolutely clear on the subject of Elizabeth Bremerton that he did not even begin to suspect what was rankling In the girl's morbid sense.

The relation between them accordingly went from bad to worse; and when Pamela rose and sharply put an end to their private conversation, the evening would have practically ended in a quarrel but for some final saving instinct on Chicksands' part, which made him mention Desmond as he bade her good-night.

'I could tell you where he is,' he said gravely. 'Only I mustn't. I had a note from him yesterday—the dear old boy! He wrote in the highest spirits. His colonel was "ripping," and his men, of course, the best in the whole battery.'

'If you get any news—ever—before we do,' said Pamela, suddenly choking, 'you'll tell us at once?'

'Trust me. He's never out of my mind.'

On that her good-night was less cold than it would have been five minutes before. But he walked home through the moonlit streets both puzzled and distressed—till he reached his club in Pall Mall, where the news coming through on the tape quickly drove everything out of his soldier's mind but the war.

Mrs. Gaddesden was sitting as usual in the hall at Mannering. A mild February was nearly out. It would be the first of March on the morrow.

Every moment she expected to hear the Fallerton taxi draw up at the front door—bringing Elizabeth Bremerton back to Mannering. She had been away more than a month. Mrs.

Gaddesden went back in thought to the morning when it had been announced to the Squire by his pale and anxious secretary that she had had bad news of her invalid mother, and must go home at once. The Squire—his daughter could not deny it—had behaved abominably. But of all of his fume and fret, his unreasonable complaints and selfish attempts to make her fix the very day and hour of her return, Elizabeth had taken no notice. Go she would, at once; and she would make no promises as to the exact date of her return. But on the morning before she went she had worked superhumanly to put things in order, whether for her typist, or Captain Dell, or Pamela, who must at least take over the housekeeping. The relations between her and Miss Bremerton that morning had struck Mrs. Gaddesden as odd—certainly not cordial. But there was nothing to complain of in Pamela's conduct. She would do her best, she said, and sat listening while Elizabeth gave her instructions about food cards, and servants, and the rest.

Then, when the taxi had driven away with the Dictator, what temper on the Squire's part! Mrs. Gaddesden had very nearly gone home to London—but for the fact of raids, and the fact that two of her most necessary servants had joined the W.A.A.C.'s. Pamela, on the other hand, had gone singing about the house. And really the child had done her best. But how could any one expect her to manage her father and the house, especially on the scraps of time left her by her V.A.D. work? The Squire had been like a fractious child over the compulsory rations. Nobody was less of a glutton—he pecked like a bird; but the proper food to peck at must be always there, or his temper was unbearable. Pamela made various blunders; the household knew hunger for the first time; and the servants began to give warning. Captain Dell could do nothing with his employer, and the timber business was hung up.

Then came Pamela's outbreak after a tirade from the Squire bitterly contrasting his lost secretary's performances, in every particular, with those of his daughter. The child had disappeared, and a message from the station was all that remained of her. Well, who could wonder? Mrs. Gaddesden reflected, with some complacency, that even she had spoken her mind to her father that night, conveniently forgetting some annoying retorts of his about herself, and the custom she had developed of sitting for hours over the fire pretending to knit, but really doing nothing. After her enormous exertions in the cause of the war—she was accustomed to say—of the year before, she was in need of a rest. She was certainly taking it. Since Pamela left, indeed, she had been obliged to do the housekeeping, and considered it very hard work. She had never yet been able to calculate the food coupons correctly.

So she, like all the rest, was looking eagerly for Elizabeth.

Yes!—that was the cracked horn of the village taxi. Mrs. Gaddesden poked the fire with energy and rang for Forest. But his quick ears had heard the signal before hers, and he was already hurrying through the hall to the front door.

And there was the library door opening, so her father too had been on the watch. Voices in the vestibule, and as the outer door of the hall opened, the Squire appeared at the further end. Alice Gaddesden had an odd feeling that something important—decisive—was going to happen.

Yet nothing could have been more unassuming than Elizabeth's entry. It was evident, indeed, that Forest was overjoyed to see her. He shouldered her modest boxes and bags with a will, and a housemaid, all smiles, came running half way downstairs to take some of his burden from him. Elizabeth followed the butler and took Mrs. Gaddesden's hand.

'My train was late. I hope you've not waited tea?'

'Why, of course we have,' said the Squire's voice. 'Forest!—tea at once.'

Elizabeth, not having perceived his approach in the dimness of the February twilight, turned with a start to greet the Squire. He looked, to her eyes, lankier and thinner and queerer than ever. But it was a distinguished queerness. Elizabeth had forgotten that the brow and eyes were so fine, and the hair so glistening white. The large nose and small captious chin passed unnoticed. She was astonished at her own throb of pleasure in seeing her employer again.

His pleasure was boisterously evident, though presently he showed it in his usual way by attacking her. But first Mrs. Gaddesden made the proper enquiries after Elizabeth's invalid mother.

Elizabeth, looking extremely tired as she sat by the fire, in the chair which the Squire—most unwonted attention!—had drawn up for her, said that her mother was better, and volunteered nothing further. The Squire, meanwhile, had observed her looks, and was chafing inwardly against invalid relations who made unjust claims upon their kith and kin and monstrously insisted on being nursed by them. But he had the sense to hold his tongue, and even to profess a decent sympathy.

Then, without any further preamble, he plunged into his own affairs.

'Everything's gone to rack and ruin since you left,' he said vehemently. 'Of course you knew it would!'

Elizabeth's eyebrows lifted. The look, half tolerant, half amused, with which she greeted sallies of this kind was one of her attractions for the Squire.

'What's Captain Dell been doing?' she inquired.

'Marking time!' was the testy reply. 'He's been no good by himself—I knew he wouldn't be—no more use than old Hull.'

Elizabeth's expression showed her sceptical.

'And the timber?'

'Just where you left it. The rascally fellows want all sorts of conditions. You may accept them if you like—I won't. But I told them we'd meet them in the woods to-morrow—you, and Dell and I. And Chicksands, who likes poking his nose into everything, is coming too.'

'Sir Henry?' asked Elizabeth in astonishment.

'Well, I thought you might like the old boy's opinion, so I rang him up on that horrid thing you've put into the office. I don't care about his opinion in the least!'

A treat arranged for her return! Elizabeth felt as if she were being offered Sir Henry's head on a charger.

'That will be a great help!' she said with rather artificial enthusiasm, at which the Squire only shrugged his shoulders. 'Has Sir Henry been over here—'

'While you've been away? Nothing of the sort. He's not crossed the threshold since I turned him out six months ago. But he's coming all the same—as mild as milk.'

'Very good of him!' said Elizabeth with spirit.

'That's as you choose to look at it. And as to everything else—'

'The catalogue?'

'Gone to the crows!' said the Squire gloomily. 'Levasseur took some references to look out last week, and made twenty mistakes in as many lines. He's off!'

Elizabeth removed her hat and pressed her hands to her eyes, half laughing, half aghast. Never had anything been more welcome to the Squire than the sheen of her hair in the semi-darkness. Mrs. Gaddesden had once annoyed him by calling it red.

'And the farms?'

'Oh, that I leave you to find out. I shovelled all the letters on to your table, just as Pamela left them.'

'Pamela!' said Elizabeth, looking up. 'But where is she?'

The Squire held his peace. Mrs. Gaddesden drily observed that she was staying with Mrs. Strang in town. A bright colour spread in Elizabeth's cheeks and she fell silent, staring into the fire.

'Hadn't you better take your things off?' said Mrs. Gaddesden.

Elizabeth rose. As she passed the Squire, he said gruffly:

'Of course you're not ready for any Greek before dinner?'

She smiled. 'But of course I am. I'll be down directly.'

In a few more minutes she was standing alone in her room. The housemaid, of her own accord, had lit a fire, and had gathered some snowdrops for the dressing table. Elizabeth's bags had been already unpacked, and all her small possessions had been arranged just as she liked them.

'They spoil me,' she thought, half pleased, half shrinking. 'But why am I here? Why have I come back? And what do I mean to do?'

CHAPTER XIII

These questions—'Why did I come back?—What am I going to do?' were still ringing through Elizabeth's mind when, on the evening of her return, she entered the library to find the Squire eagerly waiting for her.

But the spectacle presented by the room quickly drove out other matters. She stood aghast at the disorder which three weeks of the Squire's management had brought about. Books on the floor and piled on the chairs—a dusty confusion of papers everywhere—drawers open and untidy—her reign of law seemed to have been wiped out.

'Oh, what a dreadful muddle!'

The Squire looked about him—abashed.

'Yes, it's awful—it's all that fellow Levasseur. I ought to have turned him out sooner. He's the most helpless, incompetent idiot. But it won't take you very long to get straight? I'll do anything you tell me.'

He watched her face appealingly, like a boy in a scrape. Elizabeth shook her head.

'It'll take me a full day. But never mind; we need not begin to-night.'

'No, we won't begin to-night!' said the Squire emphatically. 'There!—I've found a chair for you. Is that fire as you like it?'

What astonishing amiability! The attack of nerves which had assailed Elizabeth upstairs began to disappear. She took the chair the Squire offered her, cleared a small table, and produced from the despatch-box she had brought into the room with her a writing-block and a fountain-pen.

'Do you want to dictate anything?'

'Not at all!' said the Squire. 'I've got nothing ready for dictating. The work I have done during your absence I shall probably tear up.'

'But I thought—'

'Well, I daresay—but can't a man change his mind? Greek be hanged!' thundered the impatient voice. 'I want some conversation with you—if you will allow me?'

The last words slipped awkwardly into another note. It was as though a man should exchange the trombone for the flute. Elizabeth held her peace; but her pulse was beginning to quicken.

'The fact is,' said the Squire, 'I have been thinking over a good many things—in the last hour.' Then he turned upon her abruptly. 'What was that you were saying to Alice in the hall just now, about moving your mother into better rooms?'

Elizabeth's parted lips showed her surprise.

'We do want better rooms for her,' she said hesitatingly, after a moment. 'My sister Joan, who is at home just now, is looking out. But they are not easy to find.'

'Don't look out!' said the Squire impetuously. 'I have a better plan to propose to you. In these horrible days people must co-operate and combine. I know many instances of families sharing a house—and servants. Beastly, I admit, in the case of a small house. One runs up against people—and then one hates them. I do! But in the case of a large house it is different. Now, what do you say to this? Bring your mother here!'

'Bring—my mother—here?' repeated Elizabeth stupidly. 'I don't understand.'

'It's very simple.' The Squire stood over her, his thumbs in his waistcoat pockets, his eyes all vivacity. 'This is a big house—an old barn, if you like, but big enough. Your mother might have the whole of the east wing—which looks south—if she pleased; and neither she nor I need ever come in each other's way, any more than people who have flats in the same building. I heard you say she had a nurse. Well, there would be the nurse—and another servant perhaps. And the housekeeping could be in common. Now do consider it. Be reasonable! Don't mock at it, because it isn't your own plan,' said the Squire severely, perceiving the smile, which she could not repress, spreading over Elizabeth's countenance.

'It's awfully good of you!' she began warmly—'but—'

'But what?'

Then Elizabeth's smile vanished, and instead he saw a dimness in the clear blue eyes.

'My poor little mother is too ill—much too ill—' she said in a low voice. 'She may live a good while yet; but her mind is no longer clear.'

The Squire was checked. This possible aspect of the case had not occurred to him. But he was not to be defeated.

'If you can move her from one house to another, surely you could move her here—in an invalid motor? It would only take an hour and a half.'

Elizabeth shook her head quietly, but decidedly.

'Thank you, but I am afraid it is impossible. She couldn't take the journey, and—no, indeed, it is out of the question!'

'Will you ask your doctor?' said the Squire obstinately.

'I know what he would say. Please don't think of it, Mr. Mannering. It's very, very good of you.'

'It's not the least good,' said the Squire roughly. 'It's sheer, naked self-interest. If you're not at ease about your mother, you'll be throwing up your work here again some day, for good, and that'll be death and damnation!'

He turned frowning away, and threw himself into a chair by the fire.

So the murder was out. Elizabeth must needs laugh. But this clumsy way of showing her that she was indispensable not only touched her feeling, but roused up the swarm of perplexities which had buzzed around her ever since her summons to her mother's bedside on the morning after her scene with Pamela. And again she asked herself, 'Why did I come back? And what am I going to do?'

She looked in doubt at the fuming gentleman by the fire, and suddenly conscience bade her be frank.

'I would like to stay here, Mr. Mannering, and go on with my work. I have told you so before. I will stay—as long as I can. But I mustn't burn my boats. I mustn't stay indefinitely. I have come to see that would not be fair—'

'To whom?' cried the Squire, raising himself—'to whom?'

'To Pamela,' said Elizabeth firmly.

'Pamela!' The Squire leapt from his seat. 'What on earth has Pamela got to do with it!'

'A very great deal. She is the natural head of your house, and it would be very difficult for me to go on living here—after—perhaps—I have just put a few things straight for you, and catalogued the pots—without getting in her way, and infringing her rights!'

Elizabeth was sitting very erect and bright-eyed. It seemed to her that some subliminal self for which she was hardly responsible had suddenly got the better of a hair-splitting casuistical self, which had lately been in command of her, and that the subliminal self had spoken words of truth and soberness.

But instead of storming, the Squire laughed contemptuously.

'Pamela's rights? Well, I'll discuss them when she remembers her duties! I remonstrated with her one morning when the servants were all giving warning—and there was nothing to eat—and she had made a hideous mess of some instructions of mine about a letter to the County Council—and I pointed out to her that none of these things would have happened if you had been here.'

'Oh, poor Pamela!' exclaimed Elizabeth—'but still more, poor me!'

'"Poor me"?' said the Squire. 'What does that mean?'

'You see, I have a weakness for being liked!' said Elizabeth after a moment. 'And how can Pamela like anybody that is being thrown at her head like that?' She looked at her companion reproachfully. But the Squire was not to be put down.

'Besides,' he continued, without noticing her interruption, 'Pamela writes to me this morning that she wants my consent to her training as an Army nurse.'

'Oh no,' cried Elizabeth—'not yet. She is too young!'

Her face showed her distress. So she was really driving this poor child, whom she would so easily have loved had it been allowed her, out of her home! No doubt Pamela had seized on the pretext of her 'row' with her father to carry out her threat to Elizabeth of 'running away,' and before Elizabeth's return to Mannering, so that neither the Squire nor any one else should guess at the real reason. But how could Elizabeth acquiesce?

Yet if she revealed the story of Pamela's attack upon her to the Squire, what would happen? Only a widening of the breach between him and his daughter. Elizabeth, of course, might depart, but Pamela would be none the more likely to return to face her father's wrath. And again for the hundredth time Elizabeth said to herself, in mingled pain and exasperation—'What did she mean?—and what have I ever done that she should behave so?'

Then she raised her eyes. Something impelled her—as it were a strong telepathic influence. The Squire was gazing at her. His expression was extraordinarily animated. It seemed to her that words were already on his lips, and that at all costs she must stop them there.

But fortune favoured her. There was a knock at the library door. The Squire irritably said, 'Come in!' and Forest announced, 'Captain Dell.' The Squire, with some muttered remark, walked across to his own table.

The agent entered with a beaming countenance. All that he knew was that the only competent person in a rather crazy household had returned to it, and that business was now likely to go forward. He had brought some important letters, and he laid them nominally before his employer, but really before Elizabeth. He and she talked; the Squire smoked and listened, morosely aloof. Yet by the end of the agent's visit a grudging but definite consent had been given to the great timber deal; and Elizabeth hurried off as Captain Dell departed—thankful for the distant sound of the first bell for dinner.

Sitting up in bed that night, with her hands behind her head, while a westerly wind blew about the house, Elizabeth again did her best to examine both her conscience and her situation.

The summons which had taken her home had been a peremptory one. Her mother, who had been ill for a good many months, had suddenly suffered some brain injury, which had reduced her to a childish helplessness. She did not recognize Elizabeth, and though she was very soon out of physical danger, the mental disaster remained. A good nurse was now more to her than the daughter to whom she had been devoted. A good nurse was in charge, and Elizabeth had persuaded an elderly cousin, living on a small annuity, to come and share her mother's rooms. Now what was more necessary than ever was—money! Elizabeth's salary was indispensable.

Was she to allow fine feelings about Pamela to drive her out of her post and her earnings—to the jeopardy not only of her mother's comfort, but of the good—the national—work open to her at Mannering?

But there was a much more agitating question behind. She had only trifled with it till now. But on the night of her return it pressed. And as a reasonable woman, thirty years of age, she proceeded to look it in the face.

When Captain Dell so opportunely—or inconveniently—knocked at the library door, Mr. Mannering was on the point of asking his secretary to marry him. Of that Elizabeth was sure.

She had just escaped, but the siege would be renewed. How was she going to meet it?

Why shouldn't she marry the Squire? She was poor, but she had qualities much more valuable to the Squire than money. She could rescue him from debt, put his estate on a paying footing, restore Mannering, rebuild the village, and all the time keep him happy by her sympathy with and understanding of his classical studies and hobbies.

And thereby she would be doing not only a private but a public service. The Mannering estate and its owner had been an offence to the patriotism of a whole neighbourhood. Elizabeth could and would put an end to that. She had already done much to modify it. In her Greek scholarship, and her ready wits, she possessed all the spells that were wanted for the taming of the Squire.

As to the Squire himself? She examined the matter dispassionately. He was fifty-two—sound in wind and limb—a gentleman in spite of all his oddities and tempers—and one of the best Greek scholars of his day. She could make her own terms. 'I would take his name—give him my time, my brains, my friendship—in time, no doubt, my affection.' He would not ask for more. The modern woman, no longer young, an intellectual, with a man's work to do, can make of marriage what she pleases. The possibilities of the relations between men and women in the future are many, and the psychology of them unexplored. Elizabeth was beginning to think her own case out, when, suddenly, she felt the tears running over her cheeks.

She was back in past days. Mannering had vanished. Oh—for love!—for youth!—for the broken faith and the wounded trust!—for the first fresh wine of life that, once dashed from the lips, the gods offer no more! She found herself sobbing helplessly, not for her actual lost lover, who had passed out of her life, but for those beautiful ghosts at whose skirts she seemed to be clutching—youth itself, love itself.

Had she done with them for good and all? That was what marrying the Squire meant.

A business marriage—on her side, for an income, a home, a career; on his, for a companion, a secretary, an agent. Well, she said to herself as she calmed down, that she could face; but supposing, after all, that the Squire was putting more into the scales than she? A sudden fear grew strong in her—fear lest this man should have more heart, more romance in him than she had imagined possible—that while she was thinking of a business partnership, the Squire was expecting, was about to offer, something quite different.

The thought scared and repelled her. If that were indeed the case, she would bid Mannering a long and final farewell.

But no!—she reassured herself; she recalled the Squire's passionate absorption in his archæological pursuits; how his dependence upon her, his gratitude to her, his surprising fits of docility, were all due to the fact that she helped him to pursue them—that his mind sharpened itself against hers—that her hand and brain were the slaves of his restless intelligence.

That was all—that must, that should be all. She thought vigorously of the intellectual comradeships of history—beginning with Michael Angelo and Vittoria Colonna. They were not certainly quite on all fours with her own situation—but give modern life and the new woman time!

Suppose, then, these anxieties set at rest, and that immediately, within twenty-four hours, or a week, the Squire were to ask her to marry him and were ready to understand the matter as she did—what else stood in the way?

Then, slowly, in the darkness of the room, there rose before her the young figures of the twins, with their arms round each other's necks, as she had often seen them—Desmond and Pamela. And they looked at her with hostile eyes!

'Cuckoo!—intriguer!—we don't want you!—we won't accept you!'

But after all, as Elizabeth reflected not without a natural exasperation, she was not—consciously—a cuckoo; she was not an intriguer; there was nothing of the Becky Sharp about her at all; it would have been so very much simpler if there had been! To swallow the Squire and Mannering at one gulp, to turn out the twins, to put Mrs. Gaddesden—who, as Elizabeth had already discovered, was constantly making rather greedy demands upon her father—on rations according to her behaviour, to bring in her own poor mother and all her needy relations—to reign supreme, in fact, over Mannering and the county—nothing would be easier.

The only thing that stood in the way was that the Squire's secretary happened to be a nice woman—and not an adventuress. Elizabeth's sense of humour showed her the kind of lurid drama that Pamela no doubt was concocting about her—perhaps with the help of Beryl—the two little innocents! Elizabeth recalled the intriguing French 'companion' in War and Peace who inveigles the old Squire. And as for the mean and mercenary stepmothers of fiction, they can be collected by the score. That, no doubt, was how Pamela thought of her. So that, after her involuntary tears, Elizabeth ended in a laughter that was half angry, half affectionate.

Poor children! She was not going to turn them out of their home. She had written to Pamela during her absence with her mother, asking again for an explanation of the wild and whirling things that Pamela had said to her that night in the hall, and in return not a single frank or penitent word!—only a few perfunctory enquiries after Mrs. Bremerton, and half a page about an air-raid. It left Elizabeth sorer and more puzzled than before.

Desmond too! She had written to him also from London a long chat about all the things he cared about at Mannering—the animals, Pamela's pony, the old keeper, the few pheasants still left in the woods, and what Perley said of the promise of a fair partridge season. And the boy had replied immediately. Desmond's Eton manners were rarely caught napping; but the polite little note—stiff and frosty—might have been written to a complete stranger.

What was in their minds? How could she put it right? Well, anyhow, Desmond could not at that moment be wasting time or thought on home worries, or her own supposed misdemeanours. Where was the radiant boy now? In some artillery camp, she supposed, behind the lines, waiting for his ordeal of blood and fire. Waiting with the whole Army—the whole Empire—for that leap of the German monster which must be met and parried and struck down before England could breathe again. And as she thought of him, her woman's soul, winged by its passion of patriotism, seemed to pass out into the night across the sea, till it stood beside the English hosts.

'Forces and Powers of the Universe, be with them!—strengthen the strong, uphold the weak, comfort the dying!—for in them lies the hope of the world.'

Her life hung on the prayer. The irresponsive quiet of the night over the Mannering woods and park, with nothing but the wind for voice, seemed to her unbearable. And it only answered to the apathy within doors. Why, the Squire had scarcely mentioned the war since her return! Neither he nor Mrs. Gaddesden had asked her for an evening paper, though there had been a bad London raid the night before. She had seen a letter 'on active service,' and addressed, she thought, in Desmond's handwriting, lying on the library table; and it seemed to her there was a French ordnance map near it. But in answer to her enquiries about the boy, the Squire had vouchsafed only a few irritable words, 'Well—he's not killed yet! The devil's business over there seems to be working up to a greater hell than ever!' Nothing more.

Well, she would see to that! Mannering should feel the war, if she were to live in it. She straightened her shoulders, her will stiffening to its task.

Yes, and while that dear boy was out there, in that grim fighting line, no action of hers, if she could help it, should cause him a moment's anger or trouble. Her resolution was taken. If the Squire did mean to ask her to marry him she would try and stop him in mid-career. If she couldn't stop him, well, then, she would give him his choice—either to keep her, as secretary and friend, and hold his peace, or to lose her. She felt certain of her power to contain the Squire's 'offensive,' if it were really threatened.

But, on the other hand, she was not going to give up her post because the twins had taken some unjust prejudice against her! Nothing of the kind. She had those ash trees to look after! She was tolerably sure that a thorough search would comb out a good many more for the Air Board from the Squire's woods than had yet been discovered. The Fallerton hospital wanted more accommodation. There was an empty house belonging to the Squire, which she had already begun, before her absence, with his grudging permission, to get ready for the purpose. That had to be finished. The war workroom in the village, which she had started, must have another Superintendent, the first having turned out a useless chatterbox. Elizabeth had her successor already in mind. There were three or four applications waiting for the two other neglected farms. Captain Dell was hurrying on the repairs; but there was more money wanted—she must get it out of the Squire. Then as to labour—German prisoners?—or women?

Her brain began to teem with a score of projects. But after lying awake another hour, she pulled herself up. 'This won't do. I must have six hours' sleep.' And she resolutely set herself to repeat one of the nursery poems of her childhood, till, wooed by its silly monotony, sleep came.

It was a bright March day in the Mannering woods, where the Squire, Elizabeth, and Captain Dell were hanging about waiting for Sir Henry Chicksands. The astonishing warmth and sunshine of the month had brought out a shimmer of spring everywhere, reddened the great heads of the oaks, and set the sycamore buds shining like jewels in the pale blue. There was an endless chatter and whirr of wood-pigeons in the high tree-tops, and underfoot the anemones and violets were busy pushing their gentle way through the dead leaves of autumn. The Squire's beechwoods were famous in the neighbourhood, and he was still proud of them; though for many years past they had gone unnoticed to decay, and were in some places badly diseased.

To Elizabeth, in an artistic mood—the mood which took her in town to see exhibitions of Brabazon or Steer—the woods were fairyland. The high slender oak of the middle wood, the spreading oak that lived on its borders, the tall columnar beech feathering into the sky, its grey stem shining as though by some magic property in the beautiful forest twilight—the gleams and the shadows, the sounds and scents of the woodland world—she could talk or write about these things as poetically, and as sincerely, as any other educated person when put to it; but on this occasion, it has to be said frankly, she was thinking of nothing but aeroplanes and artillery waggons. And she had by now developed a kind of flair in the woods, which was the astonishment of Captain Dell, himself no mean forester. As far as ash was concerned, she was a hunter on the trail. She could distinguish an ash tree yards ahead through a mixed or tangled wood, and track it unerringly. The thousand ash that she, and the old park-keepers set on by her, had already found for the Government, were nothing to what she meant to find. The Squire's woods, some of which she had not yet explored at all, were as mines to her in which she dug for treasure—for the timber that might save her country.

Captain Dell delighted in her. He had already taught her a great deal, and was now drilling her in the skilled arts of measurement and valuation. The Squire, in stupefaction, watched her at work with pole and tape, measuring, noting, comparing. Had it been any one else he would have been bored and contemptuous. But the novelty of the thing and the curious fact that the lady who looked up his Greek references was also the lady who was measuring the trees, kept him a half-unwilling but still fascinated spectator of her proceedings.

In the midst of them Sir Henry Chicksands appeared, making his way through the thick undergrowth. Elizabeth threw a hasty look at the Squire. This was the first time the two neighbours had met since the quarrel. The Squire had actually written first—and to please her. Very touching, and very embarrassing! She hoped for the best.

Sir Henry Chicksands advanced as though nothing had happened—solid, ruddy, benevolent, and well dressed, as usual.

He bowed with marked deference to Elizabeth, and then offered a hand to the Squire, which was limply accepted.

'Well, Mannering, very glad to see you. Like every one else, you seem to be selling your woods.'

'Under threat of being shot if I don't!' said the Squire grimly.

'What? They're commandeered?'

'The Government spies are all about. I preferred to anticipate them. Well, what about your ploughed-up grass-lands, Chicksands? I hear they are full of wire-worms, and the crops a very poor show.'

'Ah, it was an enemy said that,' laughed Sir Henry, submitting with a good grace to some more remarks of the same kind, and escaping from them as soon as he could.

'I heard of your haul of ash,' he said. 'A man in the Air Board told me. Magnificent!'

'You may thank her.' The Squire indicated his secretary. 'I knew nothing about it.'

'And you're still hunting?' Sir Henry turned to Elizabeth. 'May I join your walk if you're going through the woods?' Captain Dell was introduced. 'You want my opinion on your deal? Well, I'm an old forester, and I'll give it you with pleasure. I used to shoot here, year after year, with the Squire, in our young days—isn't that so, Mannering? I know this bit of country by heart, and I think I could help you to bag a few more ash.'

Elizabeth's blue eyes appealed with all proper deference to the Squire.

'Won't you come?'

He shook his head.

'I'm tired of timber. Do what you like. I'll sit here and read till you come back.'

Sir Henry's shrug was perceptible, but he held his peace, and the three walked away. The Squire, finding a seat on a fallen tree, took a book out of his pocket and pretended to read it.

'Nobody can be as important as Chicksands looks!' he said to himself angrily. Even the smiling manner which ignored their six months' quarrel had annoyed him hugely. It was a piece of condescension—an impertinence. Oh, of course Chicksands was the popular man, the greatest power in the county, looked up to, and listened to by everybody. The Squire knew very well that he himself was ostracized, even hated; that there had been general chuckling in the neighbourhood over his rough handling by the County Committee, and that it would please a good many people to see all his woods commandeered and 'cut clean.'

Six months before, his inborn pugnacity would only have amused itself with the situation. He was a rebel and a litigant by nature. Smooth waters had never attracted him.

Yet now—though he would never have admitted it—he was often conscious of a flagging will and a depressed spirit. The loneliness of his life, due entirely to himself, had, during Elizabeth Bremerton's absence, begun sharply to find him out. He had no true fatherly relation with any of his children. Desmond loved him—why, he didn't know. He didn't believe any of the others cared anything at all about him. Why should they?

The Squire's eyes followed the three distant walkers, Elizabeth, graceful and vigorous, between the other two. And the conviction gripped him that all the pleasure, the liveableness of life—such as still remained possible—depended for him on that central figure. He looked back on his existence before her arrival at Mannering, and on what it had been since. Why, she had transformed it!

How could he cage and keep her?—the clever, gracious creature! For the first time in his life he was desperately, tremulously humble. He placed no dependence at all on his name or his possessions. Elizabeth was not to be bought.

But management—power—for the things she believed in—they might tempt her. He would give them to her with both hands, if only she would settle down beside him, take a freehold of that chair and table in the library, for life!

He looked back gloomily to his clumsy proposal about her mother, and to her remarks about Pamela. It would be indeed intolerable if his children got in his way! The very notion put him in a fever.

If that tiresome fellow, Dell, had not interrupted them the night before, what would have happened?

He had all the consciousness of a man still in the prime of life, in spite of his white hair; for he had married at twenty-one, and had never—since they grew up—seemed to himself very much older than his elder children. He had but a very dim memory of his wife. Sometimes he felt as if, notwithstanding the heat of boyish passion which had led him to marry her, he had never really known her. There were moments when he had an uncomfortable suspicion that for some years before her death she had silently but irrevocably passed judgment upon him, and had withdrawn her inner life from him. Friends of hers had written to him after her death of beautiful traits and qualities in her of which he himself had known nothing. In any case they were not traits and qualities which appealed in the long run to a man of his pursuits and temperament. He was told that Pamela had inherited some of them.

A light rustling sound in the wood. He looked up to see Elizabeth coming back towards him unaccompanied. Captain Dell and Sir Henry seemed to have left her.

A thrill of excitement ran through him. They were alone in the depths of the spring woodland. What better opportunity would he ever have?

CHAPTER XIV

Elizabeth was coming back in that flushed mood when an able man or woman who begins to feel the tide of success or power rising beneath them also begins to remind himself or herself of all the old commonplaces about Fate or Chance. Elizabeth's Greek reading had steeped her in them. 'Count no man happy till his death'; 'Count nothing finished till the end'; tags of this kind were running through her mind, while she smiled a little over the compliments that Sir Henry had been paying her.

He could not express, he said, the relief with which he had heard of her return to Mannering. 'Don't, please, go away again!' Everybody in the county who was at all responsible for its war-work felt the same. Her example, during the winter, had been invaluable, and the skill with which she had brought the Squire into line, and set the Squire's neglected estate on the road to food-production, had been—in Sir Henry's view—nothing short of a miracle.

'Yes, a miracle, my dear lady!' repeated Sir Henry warmly. 'I know the prickliness of our good friend there! I speak to you confidentially, because I realize that you could not possibly have done what you have done unless you had won the Squire's confidence—his complete confidence. Well, that's an achievement, I can tell you—as bad as storming a redoubt. Go on—don't let go! What you are doing here—the kind of work you are doing—is of national importance. God only knows what lies before us in the next few months!'

And therewith a sudden sobering of the ruddy countenance and self-important manner. For a few seconds, from his mind and Elizabeth's there vanished all consciousness of the English woodland scene, and they were looking over a flayed and ravaged country where millions of men stood ranged for battle.

Sir Henry sighed.

'Thank God, Arthur is still at home—doing some splendid work, they tell me, at the War Office, but, of course, pining to be off to France again. I hear from him that Desmond is somewhere near Armentières. Well, good-bye—I tied my horse to the gate, and must get home. Stick to it! Say good-bye to the Squire for me—I shall be over again before long. If there is anything I can do for you—count upon me. But we count upon you!'

Astonishing effusion!—from an elderly gentleman who, at the beginning of things, had regarded her as elderly gentlemen of great local position do regard young women secretaries who are earning their own living. Sir Henry's tone was now the tone of one potentate to another; and, as we have seen, it caused Elizabeth to tame her soul with Greek, as she walked back through the wood to rejoin the Squire.

When she perceived him waiting for her, she wished with some fervour that she were not alone. She had tried to keep Captain Dell with her, but he had pleaded an urgent engagement at a village near the farther end of the wood. And then Sir Henry had deserted her. It was annoying—and unforeseen.

The Squire observed her as she came up—the light, springing step, the bunch of primroses in her belt. He closed the book, of which he had not in truth read a word.

'You have been a long time?'

'But I assure you it was well worth while!' She paused in front of him, a little out of breath, leaning on her measuring-pole. 'We found ten or twelve more ash—some exactly of the size they want.'

'Who are "they"?'

'The Air Board,' said Elizabeth, smiling.

'The fellows that wrote me that letter? I didn't want their thanks.'

Elizabeth took no notice. She resumed—

'And Sir Henry went into the figures of that contract with Captain Dell. He thinks the Captain has done very well, and that the prices are very fair—very good, in fact.'

'All the same, I don't mean to accept their blessed contract.'

'Oh, but I thought it was settled!' cried Elizabeth in distress. She sat down on a dry stump a little way off, and the Squire actually enjoyed the sight of her discomfiture.

'Why on earth should I allow these people, not only to make a hideous mess of my woods, and murder my trees, but to take three years—three years—over the disgusting business, before they get it all done and clear up the mess? One year is the utmost I will allow.'

Elizabeth looked consternation.

'But think of the labour difficulties,' she pleaded. 'The contractor can't get the men. Of course, he wants to cut and move the trees as soon as he can, so as to get his money back.'

'That's his affair,' said the Squire obstinately. 'I want to get my woods in a decent state again, so that I mayn't be for ever reminded that I sold them—betrayed them—for filthy lucre.'

'No!' said Elizabeth firmly, her colour rising, 'for the Army!'

The Squire shrugged his shoulders.

'So they say. Meanwhile the timber-man makes an unholy profit.'

There was silence for a moment, then Elizabeth said,

'Do you really mean to stick to that condition?'

'I should be glad if Dell would see to it.'

'Then'—said Elizabeth slowly—'the contract will drop. I understand they cannot possibly pledge themselves to removal within the time named.'

'Well, there are other timber-merchants.'

'The difficulty of labour is the same for everybody. And Captain Dell thinks no one else would give the price—certainly not the Government. You will remember that some of the money was to be spent immediately.' Her tone was cold and restrained, but he thought it trembled a little.

'I know,' he interrupted, 'on cottages and the hospital. Money oozes away at every pore! I shall be a bare beggar after the war. Have you the contract there? Or did Dell take it?'

Elizabeth drew a roll of blue paper out of her pocket. Her indignation made her speechless. All the endless negotiations, Captain Dell's work, her work—to go for nothing! What was the use of trying to serve—to work with such a man?

The Squire took the roll from her and searched his pockets for a fountain-pen.

'I will make some notes on it now for Dell's guidance. I might forget it to-night.'

Elizabeth said nothing. He turned away, spread out the papers on the smooth trunk of the fallen tree, and began to write.

Elizabeth sat very erect, her mouth proudly set, her eyes wandering into the distance of the wood. What was she to do? The affront to herself was gross—for the Squire had definitely promised her the night before that the bargain should go through. And she felt hotly for the hard-working agent. Should she put up with it? Her meditations of the night recurred to her—and she seemed to herself a very foolish woman!

'There you are!' said the Squire, as he handed the roll back to her.

She looked at it unwillingly. Then her face changed. She stooped over the contract. Below the signature of the firm of timber-merchants stood large and full that of 'Edmund Mannering.'

The Squire smiled.

'Now are you satisfied?'

She returned the contract to its envelope, and both to her pocket. Then she looked at him uncertainly.

'May I ask what that meant?'

Her voice was still strained, and her eyes by no means meek.

'I am sorry,' said the Squire hurriedly. 'I don't know—it was a whim. I wanted to have the pleasure—'

'Of seeing how a person looks under a sudden disappointment?' said Elizabeth, with rather pinched lips.

'Not at all. It was a childish thing—I wanted to see you smile when I gave you the thing back. There—that's the truth. It was you disappointed me!'

Elizabeth's wrath vanished. She hid her face in her hands and laughed. But there was agitation behind the laughter. These were not the normal ways of a reasonable man.

When she looked up, the Squire had moved to a log close beside her. The March sun was pouring down upon them, and there was a robin singing, quite undisturbed by their presence, in a holly-bush near. The Squire's wilful countenance had never seemed to Elizabeth more full of an uncanny and even threatening energy. Involuntarily she withdrew her seat.

'I wish to be allowed to make a very serious proposition to you,' he said eagerly, 'one that I have been considering for weeks.'

Elizabeth—rather weakly—put up a protesting hand.

'I am afraid I must point out to you, Mr. Mannering, that Mrs. Gaddesden will be waiting lunch.'

'If I know Alice, she will not wait lunch! And anyway there are things more important than lunch. May I take it for granted, Miss Bremerton, that you have not been altogether dissatisfied with your life here during this six months?'

Elizabeth looked him gravely in the face. It was clear there was to be no escape.

'How could I have been, Mr. Mannering? You have taught me a great, great deal—and given me wonderful opportunities.'

The Squire nodded, with a look of satisfaction.

'I meant to. Of course Chicksands would say that it was only my own laziness—that I have given you the work I ought to have done myself. My reply would be that it was not my work. If a man happens to be born to a job he is not in the least fitted for, that's the affair of Providence. Providence bungled it when he, she, or it—take which pronoun you like—τυχη, as you and I know, is feminine—made me a landowner. My proper job was to dig up and decipher what is left of the Greeks. And if any one says that the two jobs are not tanti, and the landowning job is more important than the other, I disagree with him entirely, and it would be impossible for him to prove it. But there was a vacuum—that I quite admit—and Nature—or Providence—disliked it. So she sent you along, my dear lady!'—he turned upon her a glowing countenance—'and you fitted it exactly. You laid hands on what has proved to be your job, and Chicksands, I expect, has been telling you how marvellously you're doing it, and begging you not to let this duffer'—the Squire pointed to his leather waistcoat—'get hold of it again. Hasn't he?'

He smiled triumphantly, as Elizabeth's sudden flush showed that his shaft had hit. But he would not let her speak.

'No—please don't interrupt me! Of course Chicksands took that view. Any sensible man would—not that Henry is really a sensible man. Well, now, then—I want to ask you this. Don't these facts point to a rather—remarkable—combination? You assist me in the job that I was born for. I have been fortunate enough to be able to put into your hands the job that you apparently were born for. And you will forgive me for saying that it might have been difficult for you to find it without my aid. Nature—that is—seems to have endowed you not only with a remarkable head for Greek, but also with the capacity for dealing with the kind of people who drive me distracted—agents and timber-merchants, and stuck-up county officials, whom I want to slay. And you combine your job with an idealism—just as I do mine. You say "it's for the country" or "for the army," as you did just now. And I scribble and collect—for art's sake—for beauty's sake—for the honour of human genius—what you like! What then could be more reasonable—more natural'—the Squire drew himself up gravely—'than that you and I should join forces—permanently? That I should serve your ideas—and you should serve mine?'

The Squire broke off, observing her. Elizabeth had listened to this extraordinary speech with growing bewilderment. She had dreaded lest the Squire—in proposing to marry her—should make love to her. But the coolness of the bargain actually suggested to her, the apparent absence from it of any touch of sentiment, took her completely aback. She was asked, in fact, to become his slave—his bailiff and secretary for life—and the price was offered.

Her face spoke for her, before she could express her feeling in words. The Squire, watching her, hurriedly resumed.

'I put it like an idiot! What I meant was this. If I could induce you to marry me—and put up with me—I believe both our lives might be much more interesting and agreeable!'

The intensity of the demand expressed in his pale hazel eyes and frowning brow struck full upon her.

But Elizabeth slowly shook her head.

'I am very grateful to you, Mr. Mannering, but'—a rather ironical smile showed itself—'I think you hardly understand me. We should never get on.'

'Why?'

'Because our temperaments—our characters—are so different.'

'You can't forgive me about the war?'

'Well, that hurts me,' she said, after a moment, 'but I leave that to Mr. Desmond. No! I am thinking of myself and you. What you propose does not attract me at all. Marriage—in my view—wants something—deeper—to build on than you suggest.'

'Inconsistent woman!' cried the inner voice, but Elizabeth silenced it. She was not inconsistent. She would have resented love-making, but feeling—something to gild the chain!—that she had certainly expected. The absence of it humiliated her.

The Squire's countenance fell.

'Deeper?' he said, with a puzzled look. 'I wonder what you mean? I haven't anything "deeper." There isn't anything "deep" about me.'

Was it true? Elizabeth suddenly recalled those midnight steps on the night of Desmond's departure.

'You know,' he resumed, 'for you have worked with me now for six months—you know at least what kind of a man I am. I assure you it's at any rate no worse than that! And if I ever annoyed you too much, why you could always keep me in order—by the mere threat of going away! I could have cut my throat any day with pleasure during those weeks you were absent!'

Again Elizabeth hid her face in her hands and laughed—rather hysterically. There was something in this last appeal that touched her—some note of 'the imperishable child,' which indeed she had always recognized in the Squire's strange personality.

The Squire waited—frowning. When she looked up at last she spoke in her natural friendly voice.

'I don't think, Mr. Mannering, we had better go on talking like this. I can't accept what you offer me—'

'Again I can't think why,' he interrupted vehemently; 'you have given me no sort of explanation. Why must you refuse?'

'Because I don't feel like it,' she said, smiling. 'That's all I need say. Please don't think me ungrateful. You've offered me now a position and a home—and you've given me my head all this time. I shall never forget it. But I'm afraid—'

'That now I've made such an ass of myself you'll have to go?'

She thought a moment.

'I don't know that I need say that—if—if I could be sure—'

'Of what? Name your conditions!'

His face suddenly lightened again. And again a quick compunction struck her.

She looked at him gently.

'It's only—that I couldn't stay here—you will see of course that I couldn't—unless I were quite sure that this was dead and buried between us—that you would forget it entirely—and let me forget it!'

Was it fancy, or did the long Don Quixotish countenance quiver a little?

'Very well. I will never speak of it again. Will that do?' There was a long pause. The Squire's stick attacked a root of primroses closely, prized it out of the damp ground, and left it there. Then he turned to his companion with a changed aspect. 'Well, now, then—we are as we were—and'—with a long half-indignant breath—'remember I have signed that contract!'

He rose from his seat as he spoke.

They walked home together through the great wood, and across the park. They were mostly silent. The Squire's words 'we are as we were' echoed in the ears of both. And yet both were secretly aware that something irrevocable had happened.

Then, suddenly, beating down all the personal trouble and disquiet in Elizabeth's mind, there rushed upon her afresh, as she walked beside the Squire, that which seemed to shame all personal feeling—the renewed consciousness of England's death-grapple with her enemy—the horror of its approaching crisis. How could this strange being at her elbow be still deaf and blind to it!

They parted in the hall.

'Shall I expect you at six?' said the Squire formally. 'I have some geographical notes I should like you to take down.'

She assented. He went to his study, and shut himself in. For a long time he paced up and down, flinging himself finally into a chair in front of Desmond's portrait. There his thoughts took shape.

'Well, my boy, I thought I'd won some trenches—but the counter-attack has swept me out. Where are you? Are you still alive? If not, I shan't be long after you. I'm getting old, my boy—and this world, as the devil has made it, is not meant for me.'

He remained there for some time, his hands on his knees, staring into the bright face of his son.

Elizabeth too went to her room. On her table lay the Times. She took it up and read the telegrams again. Raid and counter-raid all along the front—and in every letter and telegram the shudder of the nearing event, ghastly hints of that incredible battlefield to come, that hideous hurricane of death in which Europe was to see once more her noblest and her youngest perish.

'Oh, why, why am I a woman?' she clasped her hands above her head in a passion of revolt. 'What does one's own life matter? Why waste a thought—an hour upon it!'

In a second she was at her table putting together the notes she had made that morning in the wood. About a hundred and fifty more ash marked in that wood alone!—thanks to Sir Henry. She rang up Captain Dell, and made sure that they would be offered that night direct to the Government timber department—the Squire's ash, for greater haste, having been now expressly exempted from the general contract. Canadians were coming down to fell them at once. They must be housed. One of the vacant farms, not yet let, was to be got ready for them. She made preliminary arrangements by telephone. Then, after a hasty lunch, at which the Squire did not appear, and Mrs. Gaddesden was more than usually languid and selfish, Elizabeth rushed off to the village on her bicycle. The hospital Commandant was waiting for her, with such workpeople as could be found, and the preparation of the empty house for fifty more beds was well begun. Elizabeth was frugal, but resolute, with the Squire's money. She had leave to spend. But she would not abuse her power; and all through her work she was conscious of a queer remorseful gratitude towards the man in whose name she was acting.

Then she bicycled to the School, where a group of girls whom she had captured for the land were waiting to see her. Their uniforms were lying ready on one of the schoolroom tables. She helped the girls to put them on, laughing, chatting, admiring—ready besides with a dozen homely hints on how to keep well—how to fend for themselves, perhaps in a lonely cottage— how to get on with the farmer—above all, how to get on with the farmer's wife. Her sympathy made everything worth while—put colour and pleasure into this new and strange adventure, of women going out to break up and plough and sow the ancient land of our fathers, which the fighting men had handed over to them. Elizabeth decked the task with honour, so that the girls in their khaki stood round her at last glowing, though dumb!—and felt themselves—as she bade them feel—the comrades-in-arms of their sweethearts and their brothers.

Then with the March twilight she was again at Mannering. She changed her bicycling dress, and six o'clock found her at her desk, obediently writing from the Squire's dictation.

He put her through a stiff series of geographical notes, including a number of quotations from Homer and Herodotus, bearing on the spread of Greek culture in the Aegean. During the course of them he broke out once or twice into his characteristic sayings and illustrations, racy or poetic, as usual, and Elizabeth would lift her blue eyes, with the responsive look in them, on which he had begun to think all his real power of work depended. But not a word passed between them on any other subject; and when it was over she rose, said a quiet good-night, and went away. After she had gone, the Squire sat over the fire, brooding and motionless, for most of the evening.

One March afternoon, a few days later, the following letter reached Pamela, who was still with her sister. It was addressed in Desmond Mannering's large and boyish handwriting.

'B.E.F., March.

'MY DEAR PAMELA—I am kicking my heels here at an engineer's store, waiting for an engineer officer who is wanted to plan some new dug-outs for our battery, and as there is no one to talk to inside except the most inarticulate Hielander I ever struck, I shall at last make use of one of your little oddments, my dear, which are mostly too good to use out here—and write you a letter on a brand new pocket-pad, with a brand new stylo.

'I expect you know from Arthur about where we are. It's a pretty nasty bit of the line. The snipers here are the cleverest beasts out. There isn't a night they don't get some of us, though our fellows are as sharp as needles too. I went over a sniping school last week with a jolly fellow who used to hunt lions in Africa. My hat!—we have learnt a thing or two from the Huns since we started. But you have to keep a steady look-out, I can tell you. There was a man here last night in a sniper's post, shooting through a trench loophole, you understand, which had an iron panel. Well, he actually went to sleep with his rifle in his hand, having had a dog's life for two or three nights. But for a mercy, he had pulled down his panel—didn't know he had!—and the next thing he knew was a bullet spattering on it—just where his eye should have been. He was jolly quick in backing out and into a dug-out, and an hour later he got the man.

'But there was an awful thing here last night. An officer was directing one of our snipers— stooping down just behind him, when a Hun got him—right in the eyes. I was down at the dressing-station visiting one of our men who had been knocked over—and I saw him led in. He was quite blind,—and as calm as anything—telling people what to do, and dictating a post card to the padre, who was much more cut up than he was. I can tell you, Pamela, our Army is fine! Well, thank God, I'm in it—and not a year too late. That's what I keep saying to myself. And the great show can't be far off now. I wouldn't miss it for anything, so I don't give the Hun any more chances of knocking me over than I can help.

'You always want to know what things look like, old Pam, so I'll try and tell you. In the first place, it's just a glorious spring day. At the back of the cranky bit of a ruined farm where we have our diggings (by the way, you may always go back at night and find half your bedroom shot away—that happened to me the other night—there was a tunic of mine still hanging on the door, and when you opened the door, nothing but a hole ten feet deep full of rubble—jolly luck, it didn't happen at night-time!) there are actually some lilac trees, and the buds on them are quite big. And somehow or other the birds manage to sing in spite of the hell the Huns have made of things.

'I'm looking out now due east. There's a tangled mass of trenches not far off, where there's been some hot raiding lately. I see an engineer officer with a fatigue party working away at them— he's showing the men how to lay down a new trench with tapes and pegs. Just to my left some men are filling up a crater. Then there's a lorry full of bits of an old corduroy road they're going to lay down somewhere over a marshy place. There are two sausage balloons sitting up aloft, and some aeroplanes coming and going. Our front line is not more than a mile away, and the German line is about a mile and a quarter. Far off to my right I can just see a field with tanks in it. Ah— there goes a shell on the Hun line—another! Can't think why we're tuning up at this time of day. We shall be getting some of their heavy stuff over directly, if we don't look out. It's rot!

'And the sun is shining like blazes on it all. As I came up I saw some of our men resting on the grass by the wayside. They were going up to the trenches—but it was too early—the sun was too high—they don't send them in till dusk. Awfully good fellows they looked! And I passed a company of Bantams, little Welsh chaps, as fit as mustard. Also a poor mad woman, with a basket of cakes and chocolate. She used to live in the village where I'm sitting now—on a few bricks of it, I mean. Then her farm was shelled to bits and her old husband and her daughter killed. And nothing will persuade her to go. Our people have moved her away several times—but she always comes back—and now they let her alone. Our soldiers indeed are awfully good to her, and she looks after the graves in the little cemetery. But when you speak to her, she never seems to understand, and her eyes—well, they haunt one.

'I'm beginning to get quite used to the life—and lately I have been doing some observation work with an F.O.O. (that means Forward Observation Officer), which is awfully exciting. Your business on these occasions is to get as close to the Germans as you can, without being seen, and you take a telephonist with you to send back word to the guns, and, by Jove, we do get close sometimes!

'Well, dear old Pam, there's my engineer coming across the fields, and I must shut up. Mind— if I don't come back to you—you're just to think, as I told you before, that it's all right. Nothing matters—nothing—but seeing this thing through. Any day we may be in the thick of such a fight as I suppose was never seen in the world before. Or any night—hard luck! one may be killed in a beastly little raid that nobody will ever hear of again. But anyway it's all one. It's worth it.

'Your letters don't sound to me as though you were particularly enjoying life. Why don't you ever give me news of Arthur? He writes me awfully jolly letters, and always says something nice about you. Father has written to me three times—decent, I call it,—though he always abuses Lloyd George, and generally puts some Greek in I can't read. I wonder if we were quite right about Broomie? You never say anything about her either. But I got a letter from Beryl the other day, and what Miss B. seems to be doing with Father and the estate is pretty marvellous.

'All the same I don't hear any gossip as to what you and I were afraid of. I wonder if I was a brute to answer her as I did—and after her nice letter to me? Anyway, it's no wonder she doesn't write to me any more. And she did tell me such a lot of news.

'Good-bye. Your writing-pad is really ripping. Likewise pen. Hullo, there go some more shells. I really must get back and see what's up.—Your loving

'DESMOND.'

Meanwhile in the seething world of London, where the war-effort of an Empire was gathered up into one mighty organism, the hush of expectancy grew ever deeper. Only a few weeks or days could now divide us from the German rush on Paris and the coast. Behind the German lines all was movement and vast preparation. Any day England might rise to find the last fight begun.

Yet morning after morning all the news that came was of raids, endless raids, on both sides—a perpetual mosquito fight, buzzing now here, now there, as information was wanted by the different Commands. Many lives were lost day by day, many deeds of battle done. But it all seemed as nothing—less than nothing—to those whose minds were fixed on the clash to come.

Then one evening, early in the second week in March, a telegram reached Aubrey Mannering at Aldershot. He rushed up to town, and went first to the War Office, where Chicksands was at work.

Chicksands sprang up to meet him.

'You've heard? I've just got this. I made his Colonel promise to wire me if—'

He pointed to an open telegram on his table:

"Desmond badly hit in raid last night. Tell his people. Authorities will probably give permission to come. Well looked after."

The two men stared at each other.

'I have wired to my father,' said Mannering, 'and am now going to meet him at King's Cross. Can you go and tell Pamela to get ready—or Margaret? But he'll want Pamela!'

Neither was able to speak for a moment, till Mannering said, 'I'll bring my father to Margaret's, and then I'll go and see after the permits.'

He lingered a moment.

'I—I think it means the worst.'

Chicksands' gesture was one of despair.

Then they hurried away from the War Office together.

CHAPTER XV

It was afternoon at Mannering.

Elizabeth was walking home from the village through the park. Still the same dry east-wind weather—very cold in the wind, very warm in the sun. If the German offensive began while these fine days held, they would have the luck of weather as we had never had it. Think of the drenching rains and winds of the Passchendaele attack! In the popular mind the notion of 'a German God' was taking actual concrete shape. A huge and monstrous form, sitting on a German hill, plotting with the Kaiser, and ordering the weather precisely as the Kaiser wished—it was thus that English superstition, aided by Imperial speeches and telegrams, began to be haunted.

Yet the world was still beautiful—the silvery stems of the trees, the flitting of the birds, the violet carpets underfoot. On the fighting line itself there was probably a new crop of poets, hymning the Spring with Death for listener, as Julian Grenfell and Rupert Brooke had hymned it, in that first year of the war that seems now an eternity behind us.

Moving along a path converging on her own, Elizabeth perceived the Squire. For the first time that morning he had put off their joint session, and she had not seen him all day. Her mind was now always uneasily aware of him—aware, too, of some change in him, for which in some painful way she felt herself responsible. He had grown strangely tame and placable, and it was generally noticed that he looked older. Yet he was more absorbed than ever in the details of Greek research and the labour of his catalogue. Only, of an evening, he read the Times for a couple of hours, generally in complete silence, while Elizabeth and Mrs. Gaddesden talked and knitted.

An extraordinary softness—an extraordinary compassion—was steadily invading Elizabeth's mind in regard to him. Something suggested to her that he had come into life maimed of some essential element of being, possessed by his fellow-men, and that he was now conscious of the lack, as a Greek Faun might be conscious of the difference between his life and that of struggling and suffering men. Nothing, indeed, could less suggest the blithe nature-life which Greek imagination embodied in the Faun, than the bizarre and restless aspect of the Squire. This spare white-haired man, with his tempers and irritations, was far indeed from Greek joyousness. And yet the Greek sense of beauty, half intellectual, half sensuous, had always seemed to her the strongest force in him. Was it now besieged by something else?—was the Faun in him, at last, after these three years, beginning to feel the bitter grip of humanity?

'"Deeper"? I don't know what you mean. There is nothing "deep" in me!' She often recalled that saying of his, and the look of perplexity which had accompanied it.

To herself of late he had been always courteous and indulgent; she had hardly had an uncivil word from him! But it seemed to her that he had also begun to avoid her, and the suspicion hurt her amazingly. If indeed it were true, then leave Mannering she must.

He came up with her at a cross-road, and threw her a look of enquiry.

'You have been to the village?'

'To the hospital. Thirty fresh wounded arrived last night.'

'I have just seen Chicksands,' said the Squire abruptly. 'Arthur tells him the German attack must be launched in a week or two, and may come any day. A million men, probably, thrown against us.'

'So—the next few months will decide,' said Elizabeth, shuddering.

'My God!—why did we ever go into this war!' cried the man beside her suddenly, in a low, stifled voice. She glanced at him in astonishment. The new excuses, the new tenderness for him in her heart made themselves heard.

'It was for honour,' she breathed—'for freedom!'

'Words—just words. They don't stop bombs!'

But there was nothing truculent in the tone.

'You had a line from Mr. Desmond this morning?'

'Yes—a post card. He was all right.'

Silence dropped between them. They walked on through the beautiful wooded park. Carpets of primroses ran beside them, and masses of wild cherry blossoms were beginning to show amid the beeches. Elizabeth was vaguely conscious of beauty, of warm air, of heavenly sun. But the veil upon the face of all nations was upon her eyes also.

When they reached the house, the Squire said,

'I looked up the passage in the Persae that occurred to me yesterday. Will you come and take it down?'

They went into the library together. On a special table in front of the Squire's desk there stood a magnificent Greek vase of the early fifth century B.C. A king—Persian, from his dress—was sitting in a chair of state, and before him stood a small man apparently delivering a message. Αγγελος was roughly written over his head.

The Squire walked up and down with a text of the Persae in his hand.

'"This vase," he dictated, "may be compared with one signed by Xenophantos, in the Paris collection, the subject of which is the Persian king, hunting. Here we have a Persian king, identified by his dress, apparently receiving a message from his army. We may illustrate it by the passage in the Persae of Æschylus, where Atossa receives from a messenger the account of the battle of Salamis—a passage which contains the famous lines describing the Greek onslaught on the Persian fleet:

'"'Then might you hear a mighty shout arise—

'"'Go, ye sons of Hellas!—free your fathers, free your children and your wives, the temples of your gods, and the tombs of your ancestors. For now is all at stake!...'

'"We may recall also the final summing-up by the αγγελος of the Persian defeat—

'"'Never, on a single day, was there so great a slaying of men.'"'

Elizabeth took down the words, first in Greek and then in English. They rang in her ears, long after she had transcribed them. The Squire moved up and down in silence, absorbed apparently in the play which he went on reading.

Outside the light was failing. It was close on six o'clock, and summer time had not yet begun.

Suddenly the Squire raised his head.

'That, I think, was the telephone?'

Elizabeth rose—

'May I go? It is probably Captain Dell.'

She hurried away to her office-room, where the call-bell was insistently ringing.

'Yes—who is that?'

'A telegram please—for Mr. Mannering—from London.'

'Wait a moment—I will tell Mr. Mannering.'

But as she turned to go back to the library she saw the Squire had followed her, and was standing at the door. He came forward at once and took up the receiver.

Elizabeth watched him with a fast beating pulse. He heard the message, took out a pencil and wrote it down on a piece of paper lying near, put up the receiver, and turned to her.

'It is from Aubrey. "Desmond is severely wounded. Please come at once. Permission will be given to you and Pamela to go to France. I hope to go with you. Will meet you King's Cross 8.40. Aubrey."'

He steadied himself a moment by a hand on Elizabeth's table. She went up to him, and took his other hand, which closed an instant on hers.

'I thought so,' he said, under his breath. 'I knew it.... Telephone, please, to Fallerton for the taxi, while I go and speak to Forest.'

She gave the order and then hastened into the hall where Mrs. Gaddesden was busy trimming a hat. The Squire's eldest daughter sprang up at sight of Elizabeth.

'Oh, what is it? I know it's bad news—it's Desmond!'

Elizabeth repeated the telegram. 'Your father is going off at once. I have telephoned for the car.'

'Oh, but I must go too—of course I must!' said Alice, weeping. 'Where is my maid?'

Elizabeth pointed out gently that, in speaking of the permits for France, Major Mannering had only referred to the Squire and Pamela.

'Oh, but he must have meant me too—of course he must! Where is my maid?' She rang the upstairs' bell violently. 'Oh, father, how awful!'—the Squire had just entered the hall—'of course I'm going with you?'

'What does she mean?' said the Squire impatiently to Elizabeth. 'Tell her I'm going alone.'

'But, father, you must take me!' cried Alice, running forward with clasped hands. 'He is my brother! I must see him again!'

'He asks for Pamela,' said the Squire grimly. 'Aubrey shall wire to you. You'd better stay here—if Miss Bremerton will look after you.'

'I don't want to be looked after—I want to look after Desmond and you,' said Alice, with sobs.

The Squire's eyes travelled over the soft elaboration of her dress and hair—all her perfumed and fashionable person.

'It is impossible,' he said sharply. Then turning to Elizabeth he gave her a few directions about his letters. 'I shall get money in town. I will wire directly we arrive.'

Alice was silenced, and sat half sulky, half sobbing, by the fire, while the preparations for departure went forward. She offered help hysterically once or twice, but it was not needed.

The little car from the village arrived in half an hour. The Squire stood at the hall door waiting for it. He had not spoken since the news arrived except to give the most necessary orders. But as he saw the car nearing the house, he turned to Elizabeth.

'I expect we shall cross to-night. I shall wire you to-morrow.' Then to Forest—

'Do your best to help Miss Bremerton. She is in charge of everything.'

'Aye, sir. You'll give our duty to Mr. Desmond, sir. I trust you'll bring him home.'

The Squire made no reply. He stood motionless till the car arrived, stepped into it, and was gone.

Elizabeth went back into the house, and to Alice Gaddesden, still sobbing by the fire. At sight of Elizabeth she broke out into complaints of her father's unkindness, mixed presently, to Elizabeth's dismay, with jealousy of her father's secretary.

'I don't know why father didn't let me help him with his packing, and it's I who should have been left in charge! I'm his eldest daughter—it is natural that I should be. I can tell you it's very hard—to see somebody—who's not a relation—doing—doing everything for him!—so that he won't let anybody else advise him—or do anything! It is very—very—wounding for us all. Pamela feels it—I know she does—and Desmond too.'

Elizabeth, very white and distressed, knelt down by her and tried to calm her. But the flood of angry self-pity could not be stayed.

'Oh, I daresay you don't mean it, but you have—yes, you have a way of getting everybody's attention. Of course you're awfully clever—much cleverer than I am—or Pamela. But still it—it isn't pleasant. I know Pamela felt it dreadfully—being cut out with people she likes—people she cares about—and who—who might care for her—like Arthur Chicksands. I believe—yes, I do believe—though she never told me—that's why she went to London.'

Elizabeth rose from her knees. For a moment she was struck dumb. And when at last she spoke it was only to repeat the name Mrs. Gaddesden had mentioned in utter bewilderment.

'Captain Chicksands! What can you mean?'

'Why, of course girls can't hold their own with older women when the older women are so charming and clever—and all that'—cried Mrs. Gaddesden, trying desperately to justify herself—'but I've been awfully sorry for Pamela! Very likely it's not your fault—you couldn't know, I daresay!'

'No, indeed, I didn't know!' said Elizabeth, in a low voice, 'and I can't understand now what you mean.'

'Don't you remember the day Arthur Chicksands spent here just before Desmond went? Don't you remember how he talked to you all the afternoon about the woods? Well, I saw Pamela's face as she was sitting behind you.'

Mrs. Gaddesden raised a triumphant though tear-stained countenance. She was avenging not only her father's latest slight, but a long series of grievances—small and great—connected with Elizabeth's position in the house. And the Squire's farewell to her had turned even her grief to gall.

'If Pamela was hurt, I was a most innocent cause!' said Elizabeth at last, indignantly. 'And if you or any one else had given me the smallest hint—'

'How could we?' was the rather sulky reply. 'Pamela, of course, never said a word—to me. But I rather think she did say something to Desmond.'

'Desmond!' cried Elizabeth under her breath. She turned slowly, and went away, leaving Mrs. Gaddesden panting and a little scared at what she had done.

Elizabeth went back to the library, where there was much to put in order. She forced herself to tidy the Squire's table, and to write a business letter or two. But when that was done she dropped her face in her hands, and shed a few very bitter tears.

She seemed to herself to have failed miserably. In truth, her heart clung to all these people. She soon attached herself to those with whom she lived, and was but little critical of them. The warm, maternal temper which went with her shrewd brain seemed to need perpetually objects on which to spend itself. She could have loved the twins dearly had they let her, and day by day, in the absence of the mother, she had been accustomed to nurse, she had even positively enjoyed 'petting' Mrs. Gaddesden, holding her wool for her, seeing to her hot-water bottles, and her breakfast in bed.

Pamela in love with Arthur Chicksands! And she remembered that a faint idea of it had once crossed her mind, only to be entirely dismissed and forgotten.

'But I ought to have seen—I ought to have known! Am I really a vampire?'

And she remembered how she, in her first youth, had suffered from the dominance and the accomplishment of older women; women who gave a girl no chance, who must have all the admiration, and all the opportunities, who would coolly and cruelly snatch a girl's lover from her.

'And that's how I've appeared to Pamela!' thought Elizabeth between laughing and crying. 'Yet all I did was to talk about ash for aeroplanes! Oh, you poor child—you poor child!'

She seemed to feel Pamela's pain in her own heart—she who had had love and lost it.

'Am I just an odious, clever woman?' She sat down and hated herself. All the passing vanity that had been stirred in her by Sir Henry's compliments, all the natural pleasure she had taken in the success of her great adventure as a business woman, in the ease with which she, the Squire's paid secretary, had lately begun to lead the patriotic effort of an English county—how petty, how despicable even, it seemed, in presence of a boy who had given his all!—even beside a girl in love!

And the Squire—'Was I hard to him too?'

The night came down. All the strange or beautiful shapes in the library wavered and flickered under the firelight—the glorious Nikê—the Erôs—the noble sketch of the boy in his cricketing dress....

The following morning came a telegram from Aubrey Mannering to Mrs. Gaddesden. Elizabeth had done her best to propitiate her but she remained cold and thorny, and when the telegram came she was pleased that the news came to her first, and—tragic as it was—that Elizabeth had to ask her for it!

'Terrible wounds. Fear no hope. We shall bring him home as soon as possible.'

But an hour later arrived another—from the Squire to Elizabeth.

'Have a bed got ready in the library. Desmond's wish. Also accommodation near for surgeon and nurses. May be able to cross to-morrow. Will wire.'

But it was nearly two days before the final message arrived—from Pamela to her sister. 'Expect us 7.20 to-night.'

By that time the ground-floor of the west wing had been transformed into a temporary ward with its adjuncts, under the direction of a Fallerton doctor, who had brought Desmond into the world and pulled him through his childish illnesses. Elizabeth had moved most of the statues, transferred the Sargent sketch to the drawing-room, and put all the small archæological litter out of sight. But the Nikê was too big and heavy to be moved, and Elizabeth remembered that Desmond had always admired 'the jolly old thing' with its eager outstretched wings and splendid brow. Doctor Renshaw shook his head over the library as a hospital ward, and ordered a vast amount of meticulous cleaning and disinfection.

'No hope?' he said, frowning. 'How do we know? Anyway there shall be no poison I can help.' But the boy's wish was law.

On the afternoon before the arrival, Elizabeth was seized with restlessness. When there was nothing more to be done in the way of hospital provision (for which a list of everything needed had been sent ahead to Doctor Renshaw)—of flowers, of fair linen—and when, in spite of the spring sun shining in through all the open windows on the bare spotless boards, she could hardly bear the sight and meaning of the transformation which had come over the room, she found herself aimlessly wandering about the big house, filled with a ghostly sense of past and future. What was to be the real meaning of her life at Mannering? She could not have deserted the Squire in the present crisis. She had indeed no false modesty as to what her help would mean, practically, to this household under the shadow of death. At least she could run the cook and the servants, wrestle with the food difficulties, and keep the Squire's most essential business going.

But afterwards? She shivered at the word. Yes, afterwards she would go! And Pamela should reign.

Suddenly, in a back passage, leading from her office to the housekeeper's room, she came upon a boy of fourteen, Forest's hall-boy, really a drudge-of-all-work, on whom essential things depended. He was sitting on a chair beside the luggage lift absorbed in some work, over which his head was bent, while an eager tip of tongue showed through his tightened lips.

'What are you doing, Jim?' Elizabeth paused beside the boy, who had always appeared to her as a simple, docile creature, not very likely to make much way in a jostling world.

'Please, Miss, I'm knitting,' said Jim, raising a flushed face.

'Knitting! Knitting what?'

'Knitting a sock for my big brother. He's in France, Miss. Mother learnt me.'

Elizabeth was silent a moment, watching the clumsy fingers as they struggled with the needles. 'Are you very fond of your brother, Jim?' she asked at last.

'Yes, Miss,' said the boy, stooping a little lower over his work. Then he added, 'There's only him and me—and mother. Father was killed last year.'

'Do you know where he is?'

'No, Miss. But Mr. Desmond told me when he was here he might perhaps see him. And I had a letter from Mr. Desmond ten days ago. He'd come across Bob, and he wrote me a letter.'

And out of his pocket he pulled a grimy envelope, and put it into Elizabeth's hands.

'Do you want me to read it, Jim?'

'Please, Miss.' But she was hardly able to read the letters for the dimness in her eyes. Just a boyish letter—from a boy to a boy. But it had in it, quite unconsciously, the sacred touch that 'makes us men.'

A little later she was in the village, where a woman she knew—one Mary Wilson—was dying, a woman who had been used to come up to do charing work at the Hall, before the last illness of a bed-ridden father kept her at home. Mary was still under fifty, plain, clumsy, and the hardest worker in the village. She lived at the outbreak of war with her father and mother. Her brother had been killed at Passchendaele, and Mary's interest in life had vanished with him. But all through the winter she had nursed her father night and day through a horrible illness. Often, as Elizabeth had now discovered, in the bitterest cold of the winter, she had had no bed but the flagstones of the kitchen. Not a word of complaint—and a few shillings for both of them to live upon!

At last the father died. And the night he died Mary staggered across to the wretched cottage of a couple of old-age pensioners opposite. 'I must rest a bit,' she said, and sitting down in a chair by the fire she fainted. Influenza had been on her for some days, and now pneumonia had set in. The old people would not hear of her being taken back to her deserted cottage. They gave up their own room to her; they did everything for her their feeble strength allowed. But the fierce disease beat down her small remaining strength. Elizabeth, since the story came to her knowledge, had done her best to help. But it was too late.

She went now to kneel at the beside of the dying woman. Mary's weary eyes lifted, and she smiled faintly at the lady who had been kind to her. Then unconsciousness returned, and the village nurse gave it as her opinion that the end was near.

Elizabeth looked round the room. Thank God the cottage did not belong to the Squire! The bedroom was about ten feet by seven, with a sloping thatched roof, supported by beams three centuries old. The one window was about two feet square. The nurse pointed to it.

'The doctor said no pneumonia case could possibly recover in a room like this. And there are dozens of them, Miss, in this village. Oh, Mary is glad to go. She nursed her mother for years, and then her father for years. She never had a day's pleasure, and she was as good as gold.'

Elizabeth held the clammy, misshapen hand, pressing her lips to it when she rose to go, as to the garment of a saint.

Then she walked quickly back through the fading spring day, her heart torn with prayer and remorse—remorse that such a life as Mary Wilson's should have been possible within reach of her own life and she not know it; and passionate praying for a better world, through and after the long anguish of the war.

'Else for what will these boys have given their lives!—what meaning in the suffering and the agony!—or in the world which permits and begets them?'

Then, at last, it was past seven o'clock. The dusk had fallen, and the stars were coming out in a pure pale blue, over the leafless trees. Elizabeth and Alice Gaddesden stood waiting at the open door of the hall. A motor ambulance was meeting the train. They would soon be here now.

Elizabeth turned to Mrs. Gaddesden.

'Won't you give a last look and see if it is all right?'

Alice's weak, pretty face cleared, as she went off to give a final survey to Desmond's room. She admitted that Elizabeth had been 'nice' that day, and all the days before. Perhaps she had been hasty.

Lights among the distant trees! Elizabeth thought of the boy who had gone out from that door, two months before, in the charm and beauty of his young manhood. What wreck was it they were bringing back?

Then the remembrance stabbed her of that curt note from France—of what Mrs. Gaddesden had said. She withdrew into the background. With all the rest to help, she would not be wanted. Yes, she had been too masterful, too prominent.

Two motors appeared, the ambulance motor behind another. They drew up at the side door leading direct through a small lobby to the library, and the Squire, his eldest son, and Captain Chicksands stepped out—then Pamela.

Pamela ran up to her sister. The girl's eyes were red with crying, but she was composed.

'On the whole, he has borne the journey well. Where is Miss Bremerton?'

Elizabeth, hearing her name, emerged from the shadow in which she was standing. To her astonishment Pamela threw an arm round her neck and kissed her.

'Is everything ready?'

'Everything. Will you come and see?'

'Yes. They won't want us here.'

For the lobby was small; and surgeon and nurses were already standing beside the open door of the ambulance, the surgeon giving directions to the stretcher-bearers of the estate who had been waiting.

Pamela looked at the bed, the nurses' table, the bare boards, the flowers. Her face worked pitifully. She turned to Elizabeth, who caught her in her arms.

'Oh, I am glad you have put the picture away!'

One deep sob, and she recovered herself.

'He's not much disfigured,' she murmured, 'only a cut on the forehead. Most of the journey he has been quite cheerful. That was the morphia. But he's tired now. They're coming in.'

But it was the Squire who entered—asking peremptorily for Miss Bremerton.

The well-known voice struck some profound response in Elizabeth. She turned to him. How changed, how haggard, was the aspect!

'Martin—that's the surgeon we've brought with us—wants something from Fallerton at once. Renshaw's here, but he can't be spared for telephoning. Come, please!'

But before she could pass through the door, it was filled by a procession. The stretcher came through, followed by the surgeon and nurses who had come from France. Elizabeth caught a glimpse of a white face and closed eyes. It was as though something royal and sacred entered the hushed room. She could have fallen on her knees, as in a Breton 'pardon' when the Host goes by.

CHAPTER XVI

The bustle of the arrival was over. The doctors had given their orders, the nurses were at their posts for the night, and, under morphia, Desmond was sleeping. In the shaded library there were only hushed voices and movements. By the light of the one lamp, which was screened from the bed, one saw dimly the fantastic shapes in the glass cases which lined the walls—the little Tanagra figures with their sun-hats and flowing dress—bronzes of Apollo or Hermes—a bronze bull—an ibex—a cup wreathed with acanthus. And in the shadow at the far end rose the great Nikê. She seemed to be asking what the white bed and the shrouded figure upon it might mean—protesting that these were not her symbols, or a language that she knew.

Yet at times, as the light varied, she seemed to take another aspect. To Aubrey, sitting beside his brother, the Nikê more than once suggested the recollection of a broken Virgin hanging from a fragment of a ruined church which he remembered on a bit of road near Mametz, at which he had seen passing soldiers look stealthily and long. Her piteous arms, empty of the babe, suggested motherhood to boys fresh from home; and there were moments when this hovering Nikê seemed to breathe a mysterious tenderness like hers—became a proud and splendid angel of consolation—only, indeed, to resume, with some fresh change in the shadows, its pagan indifference, its exultant loneliness.

The Squire sat by the fire, staring into the redness of the logs. Occasionally nurse or doctor would come and whisper to him. He scarcely seemed to hear them. What was the good of talking? He knew that Desmond was doomed—that his boy's noble body was shattered—and the end could only be a question of days—possibly a week. During the first nights of Desmond's sufferings, the Squire had lived through what had seemed an eternity of torment. Now there was no more agony. Morphia could be freely given—and would be given till all was over. The boy's young strength was resisting splendidly, a vitality so superb was hard to beat; but beaten it would be, by the brutality of the bullet which had inflicted an internal injury past repair, against which the energy of the boy's youth might hold out for a few days—not more. That was why he had been allowed to bring his son home—to die. If there had been a ray, a possibility of hope, every resource of science would have been brought to bear on saving him, there in that casualty clearing-station, itself a large hospital, where the Squire had found him.

All the scenes, incidents, persons of the preceding days were flowing in one continuous medley through the Squire's mind—the great spectacle of the back of the Army, with all its endless movement, its crowded roads and marching men, the hovering aeroplanes, the camouflaged guns, the long trains of artillery waggons and motor-lorries, strange faces of Kaffir boys and Chinese, grey lines of German prisoners. And then, the hospital. Nothing very much doing, so he was told. Yet hour after hour the wounded came in, men shattered by bomb and shell and rifle-bullet, in the daily raids that went on throughout the line. And scarcely a moan, scarcely a word of complaint!—men giving up their turn with the surgeon to a comrade—'Never mind me, sir—he's worse nor me!'—or the elder cheering the younger—'Stick it, young'un—this'll get you to Blighty right enough!'—or, in the midst of mortal pain, signing a field postcard for the people at home, or giving a message to a padre for mother or wife. Like some monstrous hand, the grip of the war had finally closed upon the Squire's volatile, recalcitrant soul. It was now crushing the moral and intellectual energy in himself, as it had crushed the physical life of his son. For it was as though he were crouching on some bare space, naked and alone, like a wounded man left behind in a shell-hole by his comrades' advance. He was aware, indeed, of a mysterious current of spiritual force—patriotism, or religion, or both in one—which seemed to be the support of other men. He had seen incredible, superhuman proofs of it in those few hospital days. But it was of no use to him.

There was only one dim glimmer in his mind—towards which at intervals he seemed to be reaching out. A woman's face—a woman's voice—in which there seemed to be some offer of help or comfort. He had seen her—she was somewhere in the house. But there seemed to be insuperable barriers—closed doors, impassable spaces—between himself and her. It was a nightmare, partly the result of fatigue and want of sleep.

When he had first seen his son, Desmond was unconscious, and the end was hourly expected. He remembered telegraphing to a famous surgeon at home to come over; he recalled the faces of the consultants round Desmond's bed, and the bald man with the keen eyes, who had brought him the final verdict:

'Awfully sorry!—but we can do nothing! He may live a little while—and he has been begging and praying us to send him home. Better take him—the authorities will give leave. I'll see to that—it can't do much harm. The morphia will keep down the pain—and the poor lad will die happy.' And then there was much talk of plaster bandages, and some new mechanical appliance to prevent jolting—of the surgeon going home on leave who would take charge of the journey—of the nurses to be sent—and other matters of which he only retained a blurred remembrance.

The journey had been one long and bitter endurance. And now Desmond was here—his son Desmond—lying for a few days in that white bed—under the old roof. And afterwards a fresh grave in Fallerton churchyard—a flood of letters which would be burnt unread—and a world without Desmond.

Meanwhile, in a corner of the hall, Chicksands and Pamela were sitting together—hand in hand. From the moment when he had gone down to Folkestone to meet them, and had seen Pamela's piteous and beautiful face, as she followed the stretcher on which Desmond lay, across the landing-stage of the boat, Chicksands' mind had been suddenly clear. No words, indeed, except about the journey and Desmond had passed between them. But she had seen in his dark eyes a sweetness, a passion of protection and help which had thawed all the ice in her heart, and freed the waters of life. She was ashamed of herself, but only for a little while! For in Desmond's presence all that concerned herself passed clean out of sight and mind. It was not till she saw Elizabeth that remorse lifted its head again; and whatever was delicate and sensitive in the girl's nature revived, like scorched grass after rain.

Since the hurried, miserable meal, in which Elizabeth had watched over them all, Pamela had followed Elizabeth about, humbly trying to help her in the various household tasks. Then when at last Elizabeth had gone off to telephone some final orders to Captain Dell at Fallerton for the morning Pamela and Arthur were left alone.

He came over to where she sat, and drew a chair beside her.

'Poor child!' he said, under his breath—'poor child!'

She lifted her eyes, swimming in tears.

'Isn't it marvellous, how she's thought of everything—done everything?'

Elizabeth had not been in his mind, but he understood the amende offered and was deeply touched.

'Yes, she's a wonderful creature. Let her care for you, Pamela, dear Pamela!'

He lifted her hand to his lips, and put his arm round her. She leant against him, and he gently kissed her cheek. So Love came to them, but in its most tragic dress, veiled and dumb, with haggard eyes of grief.

Then Pamela tried to tell him all that she herself had understood of the gallant deed, the bit of 'observation work' in the course of which Desmond had received his wound. He had gone out with another subaltern, a sergeant, and a telephonist, creeping by night over No Man's Land to a large shell-hole, close upon an old crater where a German outpost of some thirty men had found shelter. They had remained there for forty-eight hours—unrelieved—listening and telephoning. Then having given all necessary information to the artillery Headquarters which had sent them out, they started on the return journey. But they were seen and fired on. Desmond might have escaped but for his determined endeavours to bring in the Sergeant, who was the first of them to fall. A German sniper hidden in a fragment of ruin caught the boy just outside the British line; he fell actually upon the trench.

Desmond had been the leader all through, said Pamela; his Colonel said he was 'the pluckiest, dearest fellow'—he failed 'in nothing you ever asked him for.'

Just such a story as comes home, night after night, and week after week, from the fighting line! Nothing remarkable in it, except, perhaps, the personal quality of the boy who had sacrificed his life. Arthur Chicksands, with three years of the war behind him, felt that he knew it by heart—could have repeated it, almost in his sleep, and each time with a different name.

'The other lieutenant who was with him,' said Pamela, 'told us he was in splendid spirits the day before; and then at night, just before they started, Desmond was very quiet, and they said to each other that whatever happened that night they never expected to see England again; and each promised the other that the one who survived, if either did, would take messages home. Desmond told him he was to tell me, if he was killed—that he'd "had a splendid life"—and lived it "all out." "She's not to think of it as cut short. I've had it all. One lives here a year in a day." And he'd only been seven weeks at the front! He said it was the things he'd seen—not the horrible things—but the glorious things that made him feel like that. Now he did believe there was a God—and I must believe it too.'

The tears ran down her face. Arthur held the quivering hands close in his; and through his soldier's mind, alive with the latest and innermost knowledge of the war, there flashed a terrible pre-vision of the weeks to come, the weeks of the great offensive, the storm of which might break any day—was certain, indeed, to break soon, and would leave behind it, trampled like leaves into a mire of blood, thousands of lives like Desmond's—Britain's best and rarest.

An hour later the hall was deserted, except for Elizabeth, who, after seeing Pamela to bed, came down to write some household letters by the only fire. Presently the surgeon who was sitting up with Desmond appeared, looking worried. His countenance brightened at sight of Elizabeth, with whom he had already had much practical consultation.

'Could you persuade Mr. Mannering to go to bed?'

Elizabeth rose with some hesitation and followed him into the library. The great room, once so familiar, now so strange, the nurses in their white uniforms, moving silently, one standing by the bed, watch in hand—Major Mannering on the farther side, motionless—the smell of antiseptics, the table by the bed with all its paraphernalia of bandages, cups, glasses, medicine bottles—the stillness of brooding death which held it all—seemed to dash from her any last, blind, unreasonable hope that she might have cherished.

The Squire standing by the fire, where he had been opposing a silent but impatient opposition to the attempt of doctor and nurses to make him take some rest, saw Elizabeth enter. His eyes clung to her as she approached him. So she was near him—and he was not cut off from her.

Then the surgeon watched with astonishment the sudden docility of a man who had already seemed to him one of the most unmanageable of persons. What spell had this woman exercised? At any rate, after a few whispered words from her, the Squire bowed his white head and followed her out of the room.

In the hall Elizabeth offered him a candle, and begged him to go to bed. He shook his head, and pointed to a chair by the dying fire.

'That will do. Then I shall hear—'

He threw himself into it. She brought him a rug, for the night was chilly, and he submitted.

Then she was going away, for it was past midnight, but something in his fixed look, his dull suffering, checked her. She took an old stool and sat down near him. Neither spoke, but his eyes gradually turned to hers, and a strange communion arose between them. Though there were no words, he seemed to be saying to her—'My boy!—my boy!'—over and over again—and then—'Stay there!—for God's sake, stay!'

And she stayed. The failing lamp showed her upturned face, with its silent intensity of pity, her hands clasped round her knees, and the brightness of her hair. The long minutes passed. Then suddenly the Squire's eyelids fell, and he slept the sleep of a man physically and mentally undone.

Aubrey Mannering sat by his brother all night. With the first dawn Desmond awoke, and there was an awful interval of pain. But a fresh morphia injection eased it, and Aubrey presently saw a smile—a look of the old Desmond. The nurse washed the boy's hands and face, brought him a cup of tea, took pulse and temperature.

'He's no worse,' she said in a whisper to Aubrey, as she passed him.

Aubrey went up to the bed.

'Aubrey, old chap!' said the boy, and smiled at him. Then—'It's daylight. Can't I look out?'

The nurse and Mannering wheeled his bed to the window, which opened to the ground. A white frost was on the grass, and there was a clear sky through which the sunrise was fast mounting. Along an eastern wood ran a fiery rose of dawn, the fine leaf-work of the beeches showing sharply upon it. There was a thrush singing, and a robin came close to the window, hopped on the ledge, and looked in.

'Ripping!' said Desmond softly. 'There were jolly mornings in France too.' Then his clear brow contracted. Aubrey stooped to him.

'Any news?' said the blanched lips.

'None yet, old man. We shan't get the papers till eight.'

'What's the date?'

'March 18th.'

Desmond gave a long sigh.

'I would have liked to be in it!'

'In the big battle?' Aubrey's lip trembled. 'You have done your bit, old man.'

'But how is it going to end?' said the boy, moving his head restlessly. 'Shall we win?—or they? I shall live as long as ever I can—just to know. I feel quite jolly now—isn't it strange?—and yet I made the doctors tell me—'

He turned a bright look on his brother, and his voice grew stronger. 'I had such a queer dream last night, Aubrey,—about you—and that friend of yours—do you remember?—you used to bring him down—to stay here—when Pam and I were little—Freddy Vivian—'

The boy looking out into the woods and the morning did not see the change—the spasm—in his brother's face. He continued—'We kids liked him awfully. Well, I saw him! I actually did. He stood there—by you. He was talking a lot—I didn't understand—but—'

A sudden movement. Aubrey fell on his knees beside the bed. His deep haggard eyes stared at his brother. There was in them an anguish, an eagerness, scarcely human.

'Desmond!—can't you remember?'

The words were just breathed—panted.

Desmond, whose eyes had closed again, smiled faintly.

'Why, of course I can't remember. He had his hand on your shoulder. I just thought he was cheering you up—about something.'

'Desmond!—it was I that killed him—I could have saved him!'

The boy opened his eyes. His startled look expressed the question he had not strength to put.

Aubrey bent over the bed, speaking hurriedly—under possession. 'It was at Neuve Chapelle. I had gone back for help—he and ten or twelve others who had moved on too fast were waiting in a bit of shelter till I could get some more men from the Colonel. The Germans were coming on thick. And I went back. There was a barrage on—and on the way—I shirked—my nerve went. I sat down for twenty minutes by my watch—I hid—in a shell-hole. Then I went to the Colonel, and he gave me the men. And when we got up to the post, I was just a quarter of an hour too late. Vivian was lying there dead—and the others had been mopped up—prisoners—by a German bombing party. It was I who killed Vivian. No one knows.'

Aubrey's eyes searched those of the boy.

The next moment Mannering was torn with poignant remorse that, under the sudden shock of that name, he should have spoken at last—after three years—to this dying lad. Crime added to crime!

'Don't think of it any more, Desmond,' he said hurriedly, raising himself and laying his hand on his brother's. 'I oughtn't to have told you.'

But Desmond showed no answering agitation.

'I did see him!' he whispered. 'He stood there—' His eyes turned towards the window. He seemed to be trying to remember—but soon gave up the effort. 'Poor old Aubrey!' His feeble hand gave a faint pressure to his brother's. 'Why, it wasn't you, old fellow!—it was your body.'

Aubrey could not reply. He hid his face in his hands. The effort of his own words had shaken him from top to toe. To no human being had he ever breathed what he had just told his young brother. Life seemed broken—disorganized.

Desmond was apparently watching the passage of a flock of white south-westerly clouds across the morning sky. But his brain was working, and he said presently—

'After I was struck, I hated my body. I'd—I'd like to commit my spirit to God—but not my body!'

Then again—very faintly—

'It was only your body, Aubrey—not your soul. Poor old Aubrey!' Then he dozed off again, with intervals of pain.

At eight o'clock Pamela came in—a vision of girlish beauty in spite of watching and tears, in her white dressing-gown, the masses of her hair loosely tied.

She sat down by him, and the nurse allowed her to give him milk and brandy. Paralysis in the lower limbs was increasing, but the brain was clear, and the suffering less.

He smiled at her, after the painful swallowing was over.

'Why!—you're so like mother, Pamela!'

He was thinking of the picture in the 'den.' She raised his hand, and kissed it—determined to be brave, not to break down.

'Where's Broomie?' he whispered.

'She'd like to come and see you, Dezzy. Dezzy, darling!—I was all wrong. She's been so good—good to father—good to all of us.'

The boy's eyes shone.

'I thought so!' he said triumphantly. 'Is she up?'

'Long ago. Shall I tell her? I'll ask Nurse.'

And in a few more minutes Elizabeth was there.

Desmond had been raised a little on his pillows, and flushed at sight of her. Timidly, he moved his hand, and she laid hers on it. Then, stirred by an impulse that seemed outside her will, she stooped over him, and kissed his forehead.

'That was nice!' he murmured, smiling, and lay for a little with his eyes shut. When he opened them again, he said—

'May I call you Elizabeth?'

Elizabeth's tender look and gesture answered. He gazed at her in silence, gathering strength for some effort that was evidently on his mind.

'Father minds awfully,' he said at last, his look clouding. 'And there's no one—to—to cheer him up.'

'He loves you so,' said Elizabeth, with difficulty, 'he always has loved you so.'

The furrow on his brow grew a little deeper.

'But that doesn't matter now—nothing matters but—'

After a minute he resumed, in a rather stronger voice—'Tell me about the woods—and the ash trees. I did laugh over that—old Hull telling you there were none—and you—Why, I could have shown him scores.'

She told him all the story of the woods, holding his hot hand in her cool ones, damping his brow with the eau-de-cologne the nurses gave her, and smiling at him. Her voice soothed him. It was so clear and yet soft, like a song,—not a song of romance or passion, but like the cheerful crooning songs that mothers sing. And her face reminded him even more of his mother than Pamela's. She was not the least like his mother, but there was something in her expression that first youth cannot have—something comforting, profound, sustaining.

He wanted her always to sit there. But his mind wandered from what she was saying after a little, and returned to his father.

'Is father there?' he asked, trying to turn his head, and failing.

'Not yet.'

'Poor father! Elizabeth!' he spoke the name with a boyish shyness.

'Yes!' She stooped over him.

'You won't go away?'

Elizabeth hesitated a moment, and he looked distressed.

'From Mannering, I mean. Do stay, Broomie!'—the name slipped out, and in his weakness he did not notice it—'Pamela knows—that she was horrid!'

'Dear Desmond, I will do everything I can for Pamela.'

'And for father?'

'Yes, indeed—I will be all the help I can,' repeated Elizabeth.

Desmond relapsed into silence and apparent sleep. But Elizabeth's heart smote her. She felt she had not satisfied him.

But before long by the mere natural force of her personality, she seemed to be the leading spirit in the sick-room. Only she could lead or influence the Squire, whose state of sullen despair terrified the household. The nurses and doctors depended on her for all those lesser aids that intelligence and love can bring to hospital service. The servants of the house would have worked all night and all day for her and Mr. Desmond. Yet all this was scarcely seen—it was only felt—'a life, a presence like the air.' Most of us have known the same experience—how, when human beings come to the testing, the values of a house change, and how men and women, who have been in it as those who serve, become naturally and noiselessly its rulers, and those who once ruled, their dependents. It was so at Mannering. A tender, unconscious sovereignty established itself; and both the weak and the strong grouped themselves round it.

Especially did Elizabeth seem to understand the tragic fact that as death drew nearer the boy struggled more painfully to live, that he might know what was happening on the battlefield. He would have the telegrams read to him night and morning. And he would lie brooding over them for long afterwards. The Rector came to see him, and Desmond accepted gratefully his readings and his prayers. But they were scarcely done before he would turn to Elizabeth, and his eager feverish look would send her to the telephone to ask Arthur Chicksands at the War Office if Haig's mid-day telegram was in—or any fresh news.

On the 20th of March, Chicksands, who had been obliged to go back to his work, came down again for the night. Desmond lay waiting for him, and Arthur saw at once that death was much nearer. But the boy had himself insisted on strychnine and morphia before the visit, and talked a great deal.

The military news, however, that Chicksands brought him disappointed him greatly.

'Not yet?'—he said miserably—'not yet?'—breathing his life into the words, when Chicksands read him a letter from a staff officer in the Intelligence Department describing the enormous German preparations for the offensive, but expressing the view—'It may be some days more before they risk it!'

'I shall be gone before they begin!' he said, and lay sombre and frowning on his pillows, till Chicksands had beguiled him by some letters from men in Desmond's own division which he had taken special trouble to collect for him.

And when the boy's mood and look were calmer, Arthur bent over him and gave him, with a voice that must shake, the news of his Military Cross—for 'brilliant leadership and conspicuous courage' in the bit of 'observation work' that had cost him his life.

Desmond listened with utter incredulity and astonishment.

'It's not me!'—he protested faintly—'it's a mistake!'

Chicksands produced the General's letter—the Cross itself. Desmond looked at it with unwilling eyes.

'I call it silly—perfectly silly! Why, there were fellows that deserved it ten times more than I did!'

And he asked that it should be put away, and did not speak of it again.

In all his talk with him that night, the elder officer was tragically struck by the boy's growth in intelligence. Just as death was claiming it, the young mind had broadened and deepened—had become the mind of a man. And in the vigil which he kept during part of that night with Martin, the able young surgeon who had brought Desmond home, and was spending his own hard-earned leave in easing the boy's death, Chicksands found that Martin's impression was the same as his own.

'It's wonderful how he's grown and thought since he's been out there. But do we ever consider—do we ever realize—enough!—what a marvellous thing it is that young men—boys—like Desmond—should be able to live, day after day, face to face with death—consciously and voluntarily—and get quite used to it? Which of us before the war had ever been in real physical danger—danger of violent death?—and that not for a few minutes—but for days, hours, weeks? It seems to make men over again—to create a new type—by the hundred thousand. And to some men it is an extraordinary intoxication—this conscious and deliberate acceptance—defiance!— of death—for a cause—for their country. It sets them free from themselves. It matures them, all in a moment—as though the bud and the flower came together. Oh, of course, there are those it brutalizes—and there are those it stuns. But Desmond was one of the chosen.'

The night passed. The Squire came in after midnight, and took his place by the bed.

Desmond was then restless and suffering, and the nurse in charge whispered to the Squire that the pulse was growing weaker. But the boy opened his eyes on his father, and tried to smile. The Squire sat bowed and bent beside him, and nurses and doctors withdrew from them a little—out of sight and hearing.

'Desmond!' said the Squire in a low voice.

'Yes.'

'Is there anything I could do—to please you?' It was a humble and a piteous prayer. Desmond's eyes travelled over his father's face.

'Only—love me!' he said, with difficulty. The Squire grew very white. Kneeling down he kissed his son—for the first time since Desmond was a child.

Desmond's beautiful mouth smiled a little.

'Thank you,' he said, so feebly that it could scarcely be heard. When the light began to come in he moved impatiently, asking for the newspapers. Elizabeth told him that old Perley had gone to meet them at the morning train at Fallerton, and would be out with them at the earliest possible moment.

But when they came the boy turned almost angrily from them. 'The Shipping Problem— Attacks on British Ports—Raids on the French Front—Bombardment of German Towns— Curfew Regulations'—Pamela's faltering voice read out the headings.

'Oh, what rot!' he said wearily—'what rot!'

After that his strength ebbed visibly through the morning.

Chicksands, who must return to town in the afternoon, sat with him, Pamela and Elizabeth opposite—Alice and Margaret not far away. The two doctors watched their patient, and Martin whispered to Aubrey Mannering, who had come down by a night train, that the struggle for life could not last much longer.

Presently about one o'clock, Aubrey, who had been called out of the room, came back and whispered something to Chicksands, who at once went away. Elizabeth, looking up, saw agitation and expectancy in the Major's look. But he said nothing.

In a few minutes Chicksands reappeared. He went straight to Desmond, and knelt down by him.

'Desmond!' he said in a clear voice, 'the offensive's begun. The Chief in my room at the War Office has just been telephoning me. It began at eight this morning—on a front of fifty miles. Can you hear me?' The boy opened his eyes—straining them on Arthur.

'It's begun!' he said eagerly—'begun! What have they done?'

'The bombardment opened at dawn—about five—the German infantry attacked about eight. It's been going on the whole morning—and down the whole front from Arras to the Scarpe.'

'And we've held?—we've held?'

'So far magnificently. Our outpost troops have been withdrawn to the battle-zone—that's all. The line has held everywhere. The Germans have lost heavily.'

'Outpost troops!' whispered the boy—'why, that's nothing! We always expected—to lose the first line. Good old Army!'

A pause, and then—so faintly breathed as to be scarcely audible, and yet in ecstasy— 'England!—England!'

His joy was wonderful—heart-breaking—while all those around him wept.

He lay murmuring to himself a little while, his hand in Pamela's. Then for a last time he looked at his father, but was now too weak to speak. His eyes, intently fixed on the Squire, kept their marvellous brightness—no one knew how long. Then gently, as though an unseen hand put out a light, the brilliance died away—the lids fell—and with a few breaths Desmond's young life was past.

CHAPTER XVII

It was three weeks after Desmond's death. Pamela was sitting in the 'den' writing a letter to Arthur Chicksands at Versailles. The first onslaught on Amiens was over. The struggle between Bethune and Ypres was in full swing.

'DEAREST—This house is so strange—the world is so strange! Oh, if I hadn't my work to do!—how could one bear it? It seems wrong and hateful even, to let one's mind dwell on the wonderful, wonderful thing, that you love me! The British Army retreating—retreating—after these glorious years—that is what burns into me hour after hour! Thank God Desmond didn't know! And if I feel like this, who am just an ignorant, inexperienced girl, what must it be for you who are working there, at the very centre, the news streaming in on you all the time?—you who know how much there is to fear—but also how much there is to be certain of—to be confident of—that we can't know. Our splendid, splendid men! Every day I watch for the names I know in the death list—and some of them seem to be always there. The boy—the other sub-lieutenant—who was with Desmond when he was wounded, was in the list yesterday. Forest's boy is badly wounded. The old gardener has lost another son. Perley's boy is "missing," and so is the poor Pennington boy. They are heroic—the Penningtons—but whenever I see them I want to cry.... Oh, I can't write this any more. I have been writing letters of sympathy all day.

'Dearest, you would be astonished if you could see me at this moment. I am to-day a full blown group leader. Do you know what that means? I have had a long round among some of our farms to-day—bargaining with the farmers for the land-girls in my group, and looking after their billets. Yesterday I spent half the day in "docking" with six or eight village women to give them a "send off." I don't believe you know what docking means. It is pretty hard work, and at night I have a nightmare—of roots that never come to an end, and won't pull out!

'You were quite right—it is my work. I was born in the country. I know and love it. The farmers are very nice to me. They see I don't try to boss them as the Squire's daughter—that I'm just working as they are. And I can say a good deal to them about the war, because of Desmond. They all knew him and loved him. Some of them tell me stories about his pluck out hunting as a little chap, and though he had been such a short time out in France he had written to two or three of them about their sons in the Brookshires. He had a heavenly disposition—oh, I wish I had!

'At the present moment I am in knee-breeches, gaiters, and tunic, and I have just come in. Six o'clock to five, please sir, with half-an-hour for breakfast and an hour for dinner (I eat it out of a red handkerchief under a hedge). It was wet and nasty, and I am pretty tired. But one does not want to stop—because when one stops one begins to think. And my thoughts, except for that shining centre where you are, are so dark and full of sorrow. I miss Desmond every hour, and some great monstrous demon seems to be clutching at me—at you—at England—everything one loves and would die for—all day long. But don't imagine that I ever doubt for one moment. Not I—

For right is right, since God is God,
And right the day must win;

To doubt would be disloyalty,
To falter would be sin.
I know that's not good poetry. But I just love it—because it's plain and commonplace, and expresses just what ordinary people feel and think.

'Oh, why was I such a fool about Elizabeth! Now that you are at a safe distance—and of course on the understanding that you never, never say a word to me about it—I positively will and must confess that I was jealous of her about you—yes, about you, Arthur—because you talked to her about Greek—and about ash for aeroplanes—and I couldn't talk about them. There's a nice nature for you! Hadn't you better get rid of me while you can? But the thing that torments me is that I can never have it quite out with Desmond. I told him lies, simply. I didn't know they were lies, I suppose; but I was too angry and too unjust to care whether they were or not. On the journey from France I said a few little words to him—just enough, thank Heaven! He was so sweet to her in those last days—and she to him. You know one side of her is the managing woman—and the other (I've only found it out since Desmond's death)—well, she seems to be just asking you to creep under her wings and be mothered! She mothered him, and she has mothered me since he shut his dear eyes for ever. Oh, why won't she mother us all—for good and all!—father first and foremost.

'I told you something about him last time I wrote, but there is a great deal more to tell. The horrible thing is that he seems not to care any more for any of his old hobbies. He sits there in the library day after day, or walks about it for hours and hours, without ever opening a book or looking at a thing. Or else he walks about the woods—sometimes quite late at night. Forest believes he sleeps very little. I told you he never came to Desmond's funeral. All business he hands over to Elizabeth, and what she asks him he generally does. But we all have vague, black fears about him. I know Elizabeth has. Yet she is quite clear she can't stay here much longer. Dear Arthur, I don't know exactly what happened, but I think father asked her to marry him, and she said no. And I am tolerably sure that I counted for a good deal in it—horrid wretch that I am!—that she thought it would make me unhappy.

'Well, I am properly punished. For if or when she goes away—and you and I are married—if there is to be any marrying any more in this awful world!—what will become of my father? He has been a terrifying mystery to me all my life. Now it is not that any longer. I know at least that he worshipped Desmond. But I know also that I mean nothing to him. I don't honestly think it was much my fault—and it can't be helped. And nobody else in the family matters. The only person who does matter is Elizabeth. And I quite see that she can't stay here indefinitely. She told me she promised Desmond she would stay as long as she could. Just at present, of course, she is the mainspring of everything on the estate. And they have actually made her this last week Vice-Chairman of the County War Agricultural Committee. She refused, but they made her. Think of that—a woman—with all those wise men! She asked father's leave. He just looked at her, and I saw the tears come into her eyes.

'As to Beryl and Aubrey, he was here last Sunday, and she spent the day with us. He seems to lean upon her in a new way—and she looks different somehow—happier, I think. He told me, the day after Desmond died, that Dezzy had said something to him that had given him courage—"courage to go on," I think he said. I didn't ask him what he meant, and he didn't tell me. But I am sure he has told Beryl, and either that—or something else—has made her more confident in herself—and about him. They are to be married quite soon. Last week father sent him, without a word, a copy of his will. Aubrey says it is very fair. Mannering goes to him, of course. You know that Elizabeth refused to witness the codicil father wrote last October disinheriting Aubrey, when he was so mad with Sir Henry? It was the first thing that made father take real notice of her. She had only been six weeks here!

'Good-night, my dearest, dearest Arthur! Don't be too much disappointed in me. I shall grow up some day.'

A few days later the Squire came back from Fallerton to find nobody in the house, apparently, but himself. He went through the empty hall and the library, and shut himself up there. He carried an evening paper crumpled in his hand. It contained a detailed report of the breaking of the Portuguese centre near Richebourg St. Vaast on April 10, and the consequent retreat, over some seven miles, since that day of the British line, together with the more recent news of the capture of Armentières and Merville. Sitting down at his own table he read the telegrams again, and then in the stop-press Sir Douglas Haig's Order of the Day—

'There is no other course open to us but to fight it out. Every position must be held to the last man: there must be no retirement. With our backs to the wall, and believing in the justice of our cause, each one of us must fight to the end. The safety of our homes and the freedom of mankind depend alike upon the conduct of each one of us at this critical moment.'

The Squire read and re-read the words. He was sitting close to the tall French window where through some fine spring days Desmond had lain, his half-veiled eyes wandering over the woods and green spaces which had been his childhood's companions. There—submissive for himself, but, for England's sake, and so that his mind might receive as long as possible the impress of her fate, an ardent wrestler with Death through each disputed hour—he had waited; and there, with the word England on his lips, he had died. The Squire could still see the marks made on the polished floor by the rolling backward of the bed at night. And on the wall near there was a brown mark on the wall-paper. He remembered that it had been made by a splash from a bowl of disinfectant, and that he had stared at it one morning in a dumb torment which seemed endless, because Desmond had woke in pain and the morphia was slow to act.

England! His boy was dead—and his country had its back to the wall. And he—what had he done for England, all these years of her struggle? His carelessness, his indifference returned upon him—his mad and selfish refusal, day by day, to give his mind, or his body, or his goods, to the motherland that bore him.

'Is it nothing to you, all ye that pass by?'

No—it had been nothing to him. But Desmond, his boy, had given everything. And the death-struggle was still going on. 'Each one of us must fight on to the end.' Before his eyes there passed the spectacle of the Army, as he had actually seen it—a division, for instance, on the march near the Salient, rank after rank of young faces, the brown cheeks and smiling eyes, the swing of the lithe bodies. And while he sat there in the quiet of the April evening, thousands of boys like Desmond were offering those same lithe bodies to the Kaiser's guns without murmur or revolt because England asked it. Now he knew what it meant—now he knew!

There was a knock at the door, and the sound of something heavy descending. The Squire gave a dull 'Come in.' Forest entered, dragging a large bale behind him. He looked nervously at his master.

'These things have just come from France, sir.'

The Squire started. He walked over in silence to look while Forest opened the case. Desmond's kit, his clothes, his few books, a stained uniform, a writing-case, with a number of other miscellaneous things.

Forest spread them out on the floor, his lips trembling. On several nights before the end Desmond had asked for him, and he had shared the Squire's watch.

'That'll do,' said the Squire presently; 'I'll look over them myself!'

Forest went away. After shutting the door he saw Elizabeth coming along the library passage, and stopped to speak to her.

'The things have just come from France, Miss,' he said in a low voice.

Elizabeth hesitated, and was turning back, when the library door opened and the Squire called her.

'Yes, Mr. Mannering.'

'Will you come here, please, a moment?'

She entered the room, and the Squire closed the door behind her, pointing mutely to the things on the floor.

The tears sprang to her eyes. She knelt down to look at them.

'Do you remember anything about this?' he said, holding out a little book. It was the pocket Anthology she had found for Desmond on the day of his going into camp. As she looked through it she saw a turned-down leaf, and seemed still to hear the boy's voice, as he hung over her shoulder translating the epigram—

'Shame on you, mountains and seas!'

With a swelling throat she told the story. The Squire listened, and when afterwards she offered the book to him again, he put it back into her hand, with some muttered words which she interpreted as bidding her keep it.

She put it away in the drawer of her writing-table, which had been brought back to its old place only that morning. The Squire himself went to his own desk.

'Will you sit there?' He pointed to her chair. 'I want to speak to you.'

Then after a pause he added slowly, 'Will you tell me—what you think I can now do with my time?'

His voice had a curious monotony—unlike its usual tone. But Elizabeth divined a coming crisis. She went very white.

'Dear Mr. Mannering—I don't know what to say—except that the country seems to want everything that each one of us can do.'

'Have you read Haig's Order of the Day?'

'Yes, I have just read it.'

The Squire's eyes, fixed upon her, had a strange intensity.

'You and I have never known—never dreamt—of anything like this.'

'No—never. But England has had her back to the wall before!'

She sat proudly erect, her hands quietly crossed. But he seemed to hear the beating of her heart.

'You mean when Pitt said, "Roll up the map of Europe"? Yes—that too was vital. But the people at home scarcely knew it—and it was not a war of machines.'

'No matter! England will never yield.'

'Till Germany is on her knees?' His long bony face, more lined, more emaciated than ever, seemed to catch a sombre glow from hers.

'Yes—though it last ten years! But the Americans are hurrying.'

'Are all women like you?'

Her mouth trembled into scorn.

'Oh, think of the women whose shoe-strings I am not worthy to unloose!—the nurses, the French peasant-women, the women who have given their husbands—their sons.'

His look showed his agitation.

'So we are to be saved—by boys like Desmond—and women like you?'

'Oh, I am a cypher—a nothing!' There was a passionate humiliation in her voice. 'I should be nursing in France—'

'If it weren't for your mother and your sister?'

She nodded. There was a pause. Then the Squire said, in a different tone,

'But you have not answered my question. I should be obliged if you would answer it. How am I, being I—how is a man of my kind to fill his time—and live his life? If the country is in deadly peril—if the ground is shaking beneath our feet—if we are to go on fighting for years, with "our backs to the wall," even I can't go on cataloguing Greek vases. I acknowledge that now. So much I grant you. But what else am I good for?'

The colour flushed in her fair skin, and her eyes filled again with tears.

'Come and help!' she said simply. 'There is so much to do. And for you—a large landowner—there is everything to do.'

His face darkened.

'Yes, if I had the courage for it. But morally I am a weakling—you know it. Do you remember that I once said to you if Desmond fell, I should go with him—or after him?'

She waited a moment before replying, and then said with energy, 'That would be just desertion!—he would tell you so.'

Their eyes met, and the passion in hers subdued him. It was a strange dialogue, as though between two souls bared and stripped of everything but the realities of feeling.

'Would it be? That might be argued. But anyway I should have done it—the very night Desmond died—but for you!'

'For me?' she said, shading her eyes with a hand that trembled. 'No, Mr. Mannering, you could not have done such a thing!—for your honour's sake—for your children's sake.'

'Neither would have restrained me. I was held to life by one thread—one hope only—'

She was silent.

'—the hope that if I was to put my whole life to school again—to burn what I had adored, and adore what I had burned—the one human being in the world who could teach me such a lesson—who had begun to teach it me—would stand by me—would put her hand in mine—and lead me.'

His voice broke down. Elizabeth, shaken from head to foot, could only hide her face and wait. Even the strength to protest—'Not now!—not yet!' seemed to have gone from her. He went on vehemently:

'Oh, don't imagine that I am making you an ordinary proposal—or that I am going to repeat to you the things I said to you—like a fool—in Cross Wood. Then I offered you a bargain—and I see now that you despised me as a huckster! You were to help my hobby; I was to help yours. That was all I could find to say. I didn't know how to tell you that all the happiness of my life depended on your staying at Mannering. I was unwilling to acknowledge it even to myself. I have been accustomed to put sentiment aside—to try and ignore it. To feel as I did was itself so strange a thing to me, that I struggled to express it as prosaically as possible. Well, then, you were astonished—and repelled. That I saw—I realized it indeed more and more. I saw that I had perhaps done a fatal thing, and I spent much time brooding and thinking. I felt an acute distress, such as I had never felt in my life before—so much so that I began even to avoid you, because I used to say to myself—"She will go away some day—perhaps soon—and I must accustom myself to it." And yet—'

He lifted the hand that shaded his eyes, and gave her a long touching look.

'Yet I felt sometimes that you knew what was happening in me—and were sorry for me. Then came the news of Desmond. Of those days while he lay here—of the days since—I seem to know now hardly anything in detail. One of the officers at the front said to me that on the Somme he often lost all count of time, of the days of the week, of the sequence of things. It seemed to be all one present—one awful and torturing now. So it is with me. Desmond is always here'—he pointed to the vacant space by the window—'and you are always sitting by him. And I know that if you go away—and I am left alone with my poor boy—though I shall never cease to hear the things he said to me—the things he asked me to do—I shall have no strength to do them. I cannot rise and walk—unless you help me.'

Elizabeth could hardly speak. She was in presence of that tremendous thing in human experience—the emergence of a man's inmost self. That the Squire could speak so—could feel so—that the man whose pupil and bond-slave she had been in those early weeks should be making this piteous claim upon her, throwing upon her the weight of his whole future life, of his sorrow, of his reaction against himself, overwhelmed her. It appealed to that instinctive, that boundless tenderness which lies so deep in the true woman.

But her will seemed paralysed. She did not know how to act—she could find no words that pleased her. The Squire saw it, and began to speak again in the same low measured voice, as though he groped his way along, from point to point. He sat with his eyes on the floor, his hands loosely clasped before him.

'I don't, of course, dare to ask you to say—at once—if you will be my wife. I dread to ask it—for I am tolerably certain that you would still say no. But if only now you would say, "I will go on with my work here—I will help a man who is weak where I am strong—I will show him new points of view—give him new reasons for living—"'

Elizabeth could only just check the sobs in her throat. The sad humility of the words pierced her heart.

The Squire raised himself a little, and spoke more firmly.

'Why should there be any change yet awhile? Only stay with us. Use my land—use me and all I possess—for the country—for what Desmond would have helped in—and done. Show me what to do. I shall do it ill. But what matter? Every little helps. "We have our backs to the wall." I have the power to give you power. Teach me.'

Then reaching, he took her hand in his. His voice deepened and strengthened.

'Elizabeth!—be my friend—my children's friend. Bring your poor mother here—and your sister—till Pamela goes. Then tell me—what you decide. You shall give me no pledge—no promise. You shall be absolutely free. But together let us do a bit of work, a bit of service.'

She looked up. The emotion, the sweetness in her face dazzled him.

'Yes,' she said gravely—'I will stay.'

He drew a long breath, and stooping over the hands she had given him, he kissed them.

Then he released her and, rising, walked away. The portrait of Desmond had been brought back, but it stood with its face to the wall. He went to it and turned it. It shone out into the room, under the westering sun. He looked at it a little—while Elizabeth with trembling fingers began to re-arrange her table in the old way.

Then he returned to her, speaking in the dry, slightly peremptory voice she knew well.

'I hear the new buildings at the Holme Hill Farm are nearly ready. Come and look at them to-morrow. And there are some woods over there that would be worth examining. The Air Board is still clamouring for more ash.'

Elizabeth agreed. Her smile was a gleam through the mist.

'And, on the way back, Pamela and I must go and talk to the village—about pigs and potatoes!'

'Do you really know anything about either?' he asked, incredulously.

'Come and hear us!'

There was silence. The Squire threw the window open to the April sunset. The low light was shining through the woods, and on the reddening tops of the beeches. There was a sparkle of leaf here and there, and already a 'livelier emerald' showed in the grass. Suddenly a low booming sound—repeated—and repeated.

'Guns?' said the Squire, listening.

Elizabeth reminded him of the new artillery camp beyond Fallerton.

But the sounds had transformed the April evening. The woods, the grass, the wood-pigeons in the park had disappeared. The thoughts of both the on-lookers had gone across the sea to that hell of smoke and fire, in which their race—in which England!—stood at bay. A few days—or weeks—or months, would decide.

The vastness of the issue, as it came flooding in upon the soul of Elizabeth, seemed to strain her very life—to make suspense unbearable.

An anguish seized her, and unconsciously her lips framed the passionate words of an older patriotism—

'Oh! pray—pray for the peace of Jerusalem! They shall prosper that love thee!'

Printed in Great Britain
by Amazon

29799097R00096